MW01515805

Elizabeth,

Happy Expo!

STEFANIE BARNFATHER

YOU DIDN'T HAVE TO

thirteen short stories about alternate reality what-ifs

BARNFATHER BOOKS
Calgary, Canada

YOU DIDN'T HAVE TO
STEFANIE BARNFATHER

Print edition ISBN: 978-1-7387157-7-0
eBook edition ISBN: 978-1-7387157-8-7

This book is a work of fiction. Names, characters, events, and incidents are products of the author's imagination. Any resemblance to actual persons (except for satirical purposes) is coincidental. The author in no way represents the companies, corporations, brands, or historical figures mentioned in these stories.

In the spirit of respect, reciprocity, and truth, Barnfather Books honours and acknowledges Moh'kinsstis, and the traditional Treaty 7 territory and oral practices of the Blackfoot confederacy: Siksika, Kainai, Piikani, as well as the Îyâxe Nakoda and Tsuut'ina nations. Barnfather Books acknowledges that they operate in the territory that is home to the Métis Nation of Fairfield, Region 3, within the historical Northwest Métis homeland. Finally, they acknowledges all Nations—Indigenous and non—who live, work, and play on this land and who honour and celebrate this territory.

All rights reserved. Copyright © 2023 Barnfather Books.

Designed by Barnfather Books
www.barnfatherbooks.com

No part of this publication may be reproduced, stored in a retrieval system, or transmitted, in any form or by any means, without prior written permission, nor be otherwise circulated in any form of binding or cover other than that in which it is published and without a similar condition being imposed on the subsequent purchaser.

For Fred—

whose belief brought this book to life.

YOU DIDN'T HAVE TO

table of contents

JUST THE END OF THE WORLD

1

THE DREAM

Levy stepped onto his front porch. His screen door swung lazily on its hinges, creaking in the dry, desert wind. He covered his face with his hand to protect his eyes from the glare pulsating out of the crimson sun.

Levy stopped. He hesitated. His hand hovered around his chin.

He choked.

Just like the day before—and every other day—the sun hung above the horizon. Huge. Luminous. Radiating heat. It burned scarlet. It blazed and blistered. The massive helium spectre brooding menacingly within its spacial spectrum was so commonplace that Levy rarely noticed it. Except that day.

Because that day, unlike every other day, the red giant didn't dominate the hazy pink and purple sky. It wasn't exceptional. It wasn't alone.

The comet had arrived.

Levy's heart gave a gravitational *thud!*, then started pounding arrhythmically in his chest. His weakened limbs shook—they barely held him upright. Levy grabbed his screen door, then clung to it like it was a life raft and if he let go, he'd drown.

Levy tried to swallow. His throat crackled in the dry air. His skin felt parched, paper thin. He took a breath, then coughed as wind scorched his lungs. His eyes burned; *they* were the comet, not the meteor that was quickly consuming his view. Levy stood on his porch on shaking legs, staring into the disappearing sky. He couldn't look away.

The orb of fire travelled slowly through the atmosphere, creeping towards the ground with lazy inevitability, taking its time, almost as though it were taunting him. The comet grazed the top of a distant mountain range, loomed over the foothills, spit flames at a winding roadway, and set Hamilton—Levy's town, his home, his world—ablaze.

The comet drew nearer. It grew larger.

The comet came closer. It burned hotter.

The comet picked up speed, spinning faster and faster and—

Levy's neighbourhood saturated with smoke. His nostrils tingled from the acrid scent of doom. His mouth filled with char.

Bopp and Bennett Borisov's hover-trailer exploded as the power tank ignited. Dr. Thatcher's backyard pool boiled and the chlorine-infused water converted instantly to noxious steam. Hale's flower beds burst apart, then settled to the smoldering dirt in piles of grey, oily ash.

Tongues of flame trailed behind the comet's bulk; under its fire, Earth looked like it was drenched in gore. The comet incinerated. It dismembered. It lovingly smothered Levy's life in hellish hot sauce while metaphorically barbecuing his loved ones at 450 degrees Fahrenheit before finishing off the massacre by pairing the perishing population with a playful pyromancer pinot and a pomegranate-and-Primo-pepper pastry.

Fear washed over Levy's mind like a wave. He clung to the doorframe, watching the comet hurtle towards his home. Towards his friends. Towards his family.

A smile pulled at the corner of Levy's mouth.

At least he was right. At least he could die knowing he wasn't crazy. Or insecure. He didn't have unresolved trauma. He wasn't afraid of the unknown. He didn't need distractions from his worries. His life could end with assured finality; he'd done everything he could to warn them.

He was right.

Levy took one last breath—one last choking breath—before the comet hit and his body disintegrated.

Levy woke up.

DR. THATCHER

"So. Levy. What did you want to talk about today?"

Levy glanced at the woman sitting beside his bed. She stared at him from within her mane of vast hair. His toes curled in his canvas loafers under her unblinking gaze, but he tried not to be intimidated. Levy took a breath, then spoke directly to the domineering doctor.

"I had the dream again."

Dr. Thatcher smiled, then shook out her mane. She sucked on the end of her litescrawler. "Reframe."

Levy sighed. "My inner child is worrying again."

"Excellent." Dr. Thatcher tapped her digiboard. Her hair fell in front of her face as her scrawler sent a ray of light across her tablet. "What is your inner child worrying about?"

Levy looked at his toes. He was lying on his back on Dr. Thatcher's therapy bed, though she called it her therapy couch. His shoes were covered in grit from his walk across the street. They rose like small mountains from their place on the end of the bed.

Couch.

Eff it. The thing was a bed.

His shoes sullied Dr. Thatcher's damask coverlet, though he always offered to take them off before lying down—to save her the trouble of scrubbing the bed's surface after he left. Thatch always said she didn't mind, then followed with a quip about manual labour being an effective form of therapy.

Levy glared at his toes. Manual labour? Therapy? Tell that to his brother, whose construction company was still repairing Hamilton's infrastructure after the War. Manual labour was necessary for survival. He wiggled his toes and watched more dust fall on the coverlet.

Levy sighed, then stared at the ceiling. Thatch had painted it red; red like the burning sun. "My inner child is worrying about the dream."

Dr. Thatcher smiled. She always smiled when he said something she thought was stupid. "Levy."

"Yes?"

"It's just a dream. What are you really worried about?"

"I'm worried that a comet is going to hit the planet and kill us."

"Are you?" Dr. Thatcher smiled, then tapped her digiboard. "Or are you worried about something bigger?"

Levy snorted. "Bigger than a comet?"

Dr. Thatcher peered at him between her curtain of hair.

Levy's fingers curled. "I don't know."

"Levy."

"I don't know, Thatch."

"Levy."

"What?" Levy glared at the therapist. "I've had the same dream for months now, Thatch. Months. No matter how much we talk about it, it doesn't stop. It happens every night. The same effing comet. Wouldn't that worry you?"

"Levy."

"Sorry," Levy said. "Thatcher. Dr. Thatcher. I won't call you Thatch."

"Thank you." The end of the scrawler went into Thatch's mouth. "I'm sorry the dream isn't going away. Have you been practicing your fresh perspective patter before bed?"

"Yes."

"Levy."

Levy scowled at his toes. "No."

Dr. Thatcher nodded. "Excellent. Why not?"

Levy mumbled an excellent insult under his breath as his eyes went back to Thatch's flaming ceiling.

"Levy?"

"I don't remember the whole thing!" Levy pushed himself up on his elbows. "Your fresh perspective patter is impossible to memorize, Thatch. I didn't have to learn speeches that long when I advocated for Recovery Aid."

"Levy."

"Sorry!" Levy lay down, staring at Thatch's bookshelf. There were spaces in the stacks; holes where digibooks should have stood. He'd borrowed the books that filled those holes and didn't plan on returning them any time soon. They were sitting, unread, in a pile on his kitchen counter. He grinned, thinking about the heap of borrowed self-help garbage.

Levy pulled his eyes away from the shelf and back to his toes. "My apologies, Dr. Thatcher. I won't call you Thatch again."

"Thank you." Thatch sucked on her litescrawler. She tapped her board with her finger. "Shall we practice the fresh perspective patter together?"

"I would like you to give me useful advice instead of a paragraph you stole from the DMV-XI."

"Leviticus."

Levy closed his eyes. "What?"

"The advice outlined in the DSM manual for cases like yours is helpful, if you allow it to be helpful," Dr. Thatcher said. "Don't you want to heal, Leviticus?"

Levy's toes twitched. "Yes."

"Good." Dr. Thatcher's digiboard clanked against her metal

desk as she discarded the notetaker.

Levy opened his eyes.

Thatch leaned towards him, smiling her evil smile. "Sit up."

Levy rolled on his side, then swung his dusty shoes to Dr. Thatcher's sullied floor.

"Are you ready, Levy?"

"Ready, Thatch."

Dr. Thatcher's smile wavered. "Re-try. Are you ready, Leviticus?"

"Yes, Dr. Thatcher. I am ready. Please. Let us begin."

"Excellent." Dr. Thatcher clasped her hands together, making one large fist. She shook it as she spoke, emphasizing the important words in her therapy soliloquy. "*You* finish *my* sentences. Dreams *are* not..." Her fist hovered impotently over her lap as Levy stayed silent. Dr. Thatcher frowned. "Levy? Dreams *are* not?"

Levy sighed. "Dreams aren't real."

"Excellent." Dr. Thatcher's fist shook syllabically. "Dreams *are*...?"

"My shadow-self trying to make me face my fears."

"Excellent. *You* are afraid *of*...?"

"Failure."

"Failure *means*—"

"I can't protect myself."

"When *you can't* protect yourself—"

"I feel helpless."

"When *you* feel help—"

"My self-esteem lowers."

"*When* your self—"

"When my self-esteem lowers, I feel helpless and like I can't protect myself, so I become concerned about failing, and then I get afraid which makes me worry, so I have the reoccurring dream about the effing comet." Levy flung himself back on the bed. "I adapted the ending."

Dr. Thatcher picked up her board and scribbled on the screen. "Say the proper ending, Leviticus."

"We've been doing this exercise for months. The dreams aren't getting better, they're getting worse. Please, can we try something different—"

"You know that therapy often makes life worse before it gets better. You signed a contract acknowledging that. Say the proper ending."

Levy's fingers clenched. "Hale agrees with me. She used to help me with the patter every night. She knows it doesn't work. Call her. She'll tell you."

"This is your session, Levy. Not your girlfriend's. You're the one with the problem, Levy. Not Hale. Say the proper ending."

"But Dr. Thatcher—"

"You're deflecting, Levy."

"But you—"

"You're projecting, Levy."

"I don't think—"

"You're relying on your habitually extreme view of the world, Levy."

"*You're* relying on—"

"Say the proper ending, Leviticus."

Levy glared at the spaces in the bookshelf. "When my self-esteem lowers, the only thing I can do is self-soothe. I have to tell my inner child that I love him. That he is safe. That I am safe. That my past does not define my present." He rolled his eyes. "Or my non-existent future."

Dr. Thatcher grunted—a lock of hair fluttered in front of her turned down mouth. "Your stubbornness is preventing your progress. Tell me what's really going on."

"What's really going on?" Levy sat up. "I told you what's really going on. I'm deeply afraid that a comet is heading for Earth and it's going to hit us, and we can't stop it." He shook his head, incredulously. "Why don't you believe me? I feel like I'm going crazy."

Dr. Thatcher smiled. "I don't believe a comet is heading for Earth, but I do believe you have deep childhood wounds of abandonment from losing your caregivers in the War when you were too young to save them, which impacts your ability to live a life free from fear. The comet is a symbol for your insecurities. My job is to remind you that you're capable: you can handle anything."

Levy's eyes widened. "You think I'm capable of handling a comet hitting the planet? Killing me and everyone I love? Plunging humanity into extinction? That's what you think? When the end of the world arrives I'll grab a bag of chips, crack open a beer, unfold a hover-chair, then sit back and think about my blessings?"

Dr. Thatcher smiled her matronizing smile. "The world isn't ending, Leviticus. The comet is just a dream."

HALE

"Bopp came by while you were at Thatch's." Hale pushed through Levy's screen door and ambled into the kitchen, carrying grocery bags in her plump arms. "I told him you were getting your head fixed."

"Thanks, babe." Levy sat on his kitchen stool, feeling the familiar swoop in his stomach only Hale's presence could cause. They'd been together for years, but every day with Hale felt like their first date—falling in love on one of the rescue balloons that floated them to safety during the War.

Hale swayed across the room.

Levy's stomach dipped, dived, and swerved. "Can I help? With the groceries?"

"No." Hale smiled at him through the space between the bags. "You'll get in the way. You don't know my system."

Levy's stomach soared. "You could show me your system."

"I have shown you my system." Hale hoisted the grocery bags onto the counter, shoving Levy's pile of digibooks to the side. "I've taken you on a tour of our house twenty times since we bought the place. And every time you help, I find flower seeds in the dish cabinet, forks in the storage drawer, and canned soup in the freezer."

Levy grinned. "You're the fancy chef. Putting soup in the freezer should save you time."

"Freezing cans of soup is not how fancy chefs make gazpacho, cutie." Hale flung open the cold cupboard. "But back to Bopp—he wants you to message him. He had an idea about your comet." She disappeared into the frosty fridge, then her eyes peered over the top of the door. "Comet dream. It's just a dream." Her head poked higher. "You need to learn how to be less convincing, cutie. You've described your dream so many times—and so well—I'm starting to believe it's real. Anyway, you need to message Bopp." She thumbed the communication device that wound around her wrist: an ArmCom; the cruder version of older, more advanced AI converse models. "He said he knows how to stop your nightmares."

Levy turned away from his stomach-swinging girlfriend and looked out his screen door. His brother—and neighbour—usually puttered around inside his hover-trailer in the afternoons, but the floating RV looked empty.

Levy craned his neck, trying to see through Bopp's open living room window: his brother might be putting his kids down for their nap. "I don't think we can trust Bopp's medical advice, babe."

"He didn't say his cure was medical."

Levy leaned further back on his stool. Bopp might be in his kitchen: their two houses mirrored each other. "It doesn't look like he's home. But he left his window open again." Levy clenched his loafered toes. "Dust is going to get in his house."

"Would you listen to me for once?" Hale's eyes peered over the fridge door. "I said message him. *Message* him. Bennett and the kids are home, which is why the window's open—and their soot strainers are running. Bopp wants you to message him. *Message* him."

"Later." Levy hopped to his feet. He pushed aside another kitchen stool so he had room to wrap his arms around his chilly girlfriend.

Hale squirmed, then swatted his chest. "Stop it! The iced peanut bars are going to melt."

"Let them." Levy squeezed Hale tighter. He lowered his lips to her goose-pimpled neck. "I like melted nut cream."

"Ew! Levy!" Hale laughed, then ducked under his arm to dart across the kitchen. "We don't have time for that. I have chores."

"Later."

"Levy." Hale shook her head. Her pixie-cut hairstyle clung to her cheekbones. "The groceries need to be put away, I haven't fixed the screen door, and if I don't finish gardening, you won't get fresh tomatoes in your basil salad."

"I hate basil salad. Your garden can wait." Levy jogged around the counter, opening his arms. "Come here."

"I'm not coming anywhere," Hale said. "And neither are you. You have to message Bopp. There's no time for melted cream." She ignored Levy's attempted embrace to resume her fridge loading. "Bopp might have good insights about your dream. Definitely better than Thatch's."

Levy grinned, dropped his outstretched arms, then sat heavily on his stool and spun around, leaning over the counter for a better look at his lover. "Don't delude yourself, babe. Bopp's life is a mess—he can't fix mine. Pardon my unpopular opinion, but I trust Doctor Patter over Bopp any day. Even though I'm starting to think doctors are useless."

"What did she say today?" Hale's shapely tush wiggled as she placed a bag of chips in the cabinet where he normally stacked the glass baking dishes. Hale looked over her shapely shoulder, then frowned as she slid a six-pack of beer into the fridge. "You okay? Do I need to rough Thatch up? I can ask to borrow her pool floaties, then never return them." She pointed out the screen door to the colonial across the street where Dr. Thatcher lived and ran her practice. "She'll be done with her current client in a minute."

Levy gave another playful spin on his stool. "You know her schedule?"

"No, I'm psychic," Hale said. "I can see the future."

Levy grinned. "Can you read minds, too? That would be great. Thatch thinks the dream is a metaphor."

Hale bent over, sliding the folded grocery bags into a drawer; her tush did the talking. "Your comet dream? A metaphor for what?"

"Abandonment."

Hale laughed. Her tush wiggled. "You're paying this woman? Of course you're afraid of abandonment. We all lost people in the War."

"Well, Thatcher thinks my parents' death is the reason I'm dreaming about the end of the world."

"Obsessing about the end of the world."

"Obsessing about the end of the world." Levy spun lazily on his stool. "She thinks I have unresolved issues. From my past. And—"

"Hold that thought," Hale's tush said. "I *can* read your mind. I know exactly what's going on."

Levy grabbed the countertop, halting his stool spins. "You do? Tell me!"

"Your dream started a while ago, right? Around the time we bought this house?"

"Yeah."

"And moved in together?"

"Yeah."

"The comet isn't a metaphor for unresolved issues. We all have those. The comet is a sign that you're afraid of what's to come." Hale straightened, beaming triumphantly. "Your dream is about the future. Or, you're worried you won't have a future. With me. Or, at all. Cutie. You're worried about your afterlife."

Levy leaned into the counter: Hale's shapely mind might be onto something. "That's not a half-bad idea."

"I know. I'm a gorgeous genius," Hale said, plopping her tush on the second stool. "Which is why you don't need to be afraid—of your future, *or* what happens after you die. Because I'll be in your future, and you bet your cute mind I'm sticking with you after we pass on."

"Is that supposed to make me feel better?" Levy grinned. "What if you pass on first?"

"I'll haunt you." Hale propped her elbows on the counter and her chin on her hands. "You can't escape me."

Levy mimicked his girlfriend's posture. They were eye to eye, nose to nose, trimmed brown hair to spiky black. "You're right. I shouldn't be afraid of my dreams. 'Ghost Hale' is more terrifying than any comet."

Hale's spiky head nodded. "Better believe it." She sat up, then placed her palms on her shapely thighs. "Now that I've fixed your problem, will you stop stressing?'

Levy glanced at his screen door. The sound of creaking hinges resonated in his ears. His mouth went dry, and he tried to swallow, but fear stuck in his throat—so he clenched his toes. "I can't shake the feeling that there really is a comet. It's coming for us, and—" He relaxed his toes, then sighed. "I know this sounds weird, but I think we should prepare. Being sad about my past or pretending our future's going to be okay isn't the answer."

"Prepare how?" Hale smirked. "Do you have a secret spaceship in a storage shed?"

Levy shook his head. "Don't make fun."

"Cutie," Hale said. "The comet isn't real."

Levy's stomach sank.

"I need to fix my flowers." Hale slid off her stool. "Don't forget to message Bopp." She headed for the porch, chuckling, "And don't forget: the comet is just a dream."

BOPP BORISOV

"Here." Bopp held out a wrench. "My power connectors are loose. Hard work will get rid of your comet."

Levy eyed the pre-war tool. "I'm not really a hard work guy."

"I know, you're Mr. Advocate." Bopp wiped his wet hands on his t-shirt: the hover-trailer's reactor liquid complemented the dried egg and baby poop already staining his shirt. Bopp sniffed mournfully as he picked at the yolk—then he frowned at Levy. "Your conviction is your tool."

"I like that." Levy grinned at his brother. "Should I add that to my resume?"

"Did Thatch clear your return to work?"

"Not yet." Levy clenched his hands as his brother leaned over the RV's power tank. "But I'm wearing her down. She'll sign off on my sanity—once she believes me."

"So, you're lying to her? You told her you stopped having the dream?" Bopp banged the tank with his wrench. He straightened, then looked up at the sky. "Or should I be worried? Is a comet really heading our way?"

"I think so." Levy sat on the weathered strip of lawn that ran from Bopp's house to the hovercraft's parking pad. "I'm sure of it."

Bopp looked over his shoulder; the wrench hung limply from his fingers. "Really?"

"Yeah," Levy said. "My feelings in the dream are strong, Bopp. Really strong. When I wake up, I'm certain the end of the world is coming. The more I think about it—the more I talk about it—the stronger my certainty gets."

"Huh." Bopp tossed the wrench onto the grass and bent over, hitching up his mismatched socks. "Your brain is strange, Levo."

"The comet is strange," Levy said. "My brain is great."

"Your brain is bored," Bopp said. "You have too much time to think—too much time to feel. If you can't go back to work, you need to find something to do." He pulled his arms into his t-shirt, then spun it around before poking them out the sleeves: his top had been on backwards. Bopp stared at a pink stain on the front of his tee. "You and Hale should have kids, like me and Bennet. Then you won't have time to think."

"This might surprise you, but reproducing isn't the best way to get rid of anxiety."

"But living in the moment is." Bopp folded onto the grass. He picked at a hole in his trousers. "That's what I wanted to talk to you about. Bennet read a News Alert that said doing a mundane task can help clear the calamity cobwebs."

"Right," Levy said. "Do a mundane task." He looked at the sun. It burned gold as it lowered towards the horizon. "That will definitely stop the comet from destroying the planet."

"It won't stop the comet. It'll stop you from thinking about the comet." Bopp nodded at Levy's front yard. "Hale spends a lot of time in her garden?"

"Yeah."

"Why don't you help her?"

Levy laughed. "I can't garden. The soil in our neighbourhood sucks so hard Hale's green thumb can barely coax life out of it. I'd kill her plants with my—" He looked at his clenched hands. "My brown thumb."

"It's worth a shot," Bopp said. "Better than sitting in your house all day, waiting for your sessions with Thatch." He jerked his stubbled chin towards his open window. "If you can't garden, you can give Bennet and me a hand. We could use an extra brown thumb."

Levy ripped a brown blade of grass out of the brown ground and threw it at his brown brother. "If you want a babysitter, just ask. You don't have to pretend you want to help me just to get me over here."

"I do think distracting yourself is a good idea," Bopp said. "If three kids under the age of six are too much for you—"

"I didn't say your girls were too much."

"—why don't you volunteer somewhere?" Bopp grabbed the wrench. "Or get a hobby. Or, I don't know, organize your sock drawer. Mine is always mixed up."

Levy mumbled under his breath, "Matching socks isn't the solution."

"Fine. Screw the socks. Accept this hard truth: Your dream is meaningless, Levo." Bopp climbed to his feet. "You're having nightmares about the end of the world because you can't accept how great your life is."

"Uh, I'm having nightmares about the end of the world because I'm a misunderstood prophet, bro," Levy said. "My life isn't great."

"Your life *is* great," Bopp said. "Hale's awesome. We survived the War. You have the universe's greatest sibling." He poked Levy in the shoulder with the wrench. "You just need to realize it—realize your life's full potential. If you stop thinking about the comet and pay attention to what's real, you'll feel nothing but gratitude. Your fear will—" He looked up at the polluted sky. "It will float away. On a brown cloud."

Levy stared at the brown ground. "Just... stop thinking about the comet?"

"Yeah," Bopp said. "Stop thinking about the comet."

"Easy as that?"

"Why not?" Bopp shrugged. "Mind over matter. Brain over your dream. You over the meteor. Let it go."

"Did you and Bennett watch *Frigid* with the kids last night?"

"Of course—we love ancient flix—but that's not why I'm saying this. You need to release the comet's hold over you. Dominate your thoughts." Bopp rotated his shoulders. "Shake it off."

"The kids are listening to Saylor Fleet, too?"

"She was a talented singer. Stop bugging me for liking classical music."

"You are the only person I know who still clings to content from a hundred years ago."

"And you are the only person I know who runs to a talk-doc when their nighty-nights get too scary." Bopp shook the wrench in Levy's direction. "You know I'm right. The dreams will disappear with a little willpower."

"Bopp." Levy stood, brushing dead grass off his trousers. "It would take a lot of willpower to make the comet disappear."

Bopp sighed, bent over the RV, then banged on the power tank. "The comet is just a dream, Levy. Get over it. Pay attention to what's real. Live your great life."

Levy looked up at the sky. "But it's about to end."

THE COMET

Levy woke in his bed, covered with sweat. The comet consumed his mind's eye and controlled his heart's pulse. He shook his head to erase it from his vision. He unclenched his hands.

Hale's chest rose and fell as she lay beside him, peacefully sleeping. Levy rolled out of bed and onto his feet, then stumbled out of the bedroom and into his kitchen. He grabbed a bottle of water from the fridge. With a twist of the metal top, he poured the purified liquid into his parched mouth, then headed for the porch. The cool night air would clear his head.

Levy pushed open his screen door.

He stepped onto his front porch. The screen door swung lazily on its hinges, creaking in the dry, desert wind. He covered his face with his hand to protect his eyes from the glare pulsating out of the crimson sun.

Levy stopped, his hand hovering over his face.

He placed his hand on his throat. His cracked throat.

It wasn't nighttime. No, it *was* nighttime, but it wasn't dark. A giant, blazing sun dominated the pink and orange sky. Except it wasn't a sun. It wasn't a sun at all.

It was the comet.

Levy's breath caught on his lips. "Hale." His tongue turned to dust. "Hale."

"Cutie?" Hale's voice wafted out the door. "Why are you up? Dream again?"

"Hale, come here." Levy's weakened legs shook. He grabbed the screen door, clutching onto it for his life—the last moments of his life. The last moments of Hale's life, Thatcher's life, Bopp and his family's life.

Levy tried to swallow. Despite the water he was now desperately chugging, his throat stayed dry. "Hale, come here. I don't think I'm dreaming."

Levy's eyes were comets.

The sound of bare feet slapping against kitchen tile echoed in his empty house, then the screen door screeched on its hinges.

"I really need to fix that." Hale stepped onto the porch, rubbing the back of her shorn neck. "Cutie, I'm worried. What's going on?

Why are you—" She stopped. Her eyes grabbed onto the comet. "Mother fucker."

Levy couldn't look away. The orb of fire drew nearer and larger, closer and hotter.

Hale's hand clawed at his back. "Levy. Levy. What the fuck is this? Is this your dream? Did you bring me into your dream? Why am I in your dream? What the fuck, Levy? How did you—"

Levy grabbed Hale's hand, pulling his girlfriend into his arms.

Hale's eyes absorbed the comet. "We're going to die, Levy."

Levy nodded. "That's what I've been saying."

"Levo!" Bopp streaked across his lawn, carrying a child in his arms.

The child clung to Bopp's neck, stunned into silence. The toddler's eyes were glued on the rapidly approaching meteor. A woman in a nightgown trailed behind Bopp, holding the hands of two little girls wearing identical pajamas. Tears poured down Bennett's cheeks, but the children stayed silent.

Their faces were comets.

"Levo." Bopp flew up the porch steps. "Tell me this isn't real, Levo. This is a nightmare. Tell my kids this isn't real."

Levy's neighbourhood saturated with smoke. His mouth filled with char. "This is real, Bopp."

"Oh, shit." Bopp folded to his knees as Bennett and the girls stopped on the lawn, staring up at Levy's face. Bopp buried his head into his daughter's body and sobbed. "No, Levo. Oh, shit."

Tongues of flame trailed behind the comet's bulk. Earth burned scarlet under its flames.

"Leviticus!" A shriek tore through the neighbourhood. Dr. Thatcher tore across the road and across Levy's lawn. "Do you know what's happening? How could this be happening? This isn't supposed to happen! I don't think I can handle this, Levy! It's a comet! It isn't a symbol, it's a comet! Leviticus, it's a com—"

Levy slapped Thatch's face.

She gasped, then fell onto the porch. Her hair fell around her cheeks; rays of light penetrated her mane.

Levy stared down at his therapist, then up at the comet. He looked at his girlfriend, then took a burning breath. "Hale? Can you grab the hover-chairs from the shed? At least eight, babe. Okay?"

Hale stared at the comet. "Hover-chairs?"

"Hover-chairs, babe. Grab the hover-chairs." He pushed Hale down the steps.

She stumbled across the lawn, then disappeared into their gardening shed.

Levy knelt in front of Bopp. "There's a six-pack in our fridge and bags of chips in the cupboard. Take the kids and get the snacks. Take a moment—Bennett can calm everyone down—then come back, out here."

Bopp blinked up at the comet. "Out here?"

"Out here." Levy turned to Bennett. "Got that?"

She nodded at the comet. "Beer, chips, calm, here."

"Good." Levy stepped aside as Bopp, Bennett, and the girls stumbled through the screen door and into his kitchen.

"Help Hale." Levy grabbed Dr. Thatcher's hand, then yanked her to her feet. He pushed her down the steps. "In the shed."

Levy slowly stepped onto his lawn. All around him, his girlfriend, family, and neighbours made their preparations for the end of the world. Without taking his eyes off the comet, Levy unfolded the hover-chairs as Hale dragged them out of the shed. He settled onto a seat. He thought about his parents. He thought about his family, and his world, and his—

Levy's thoughts swung to Hale.

He thought about their stomach-swooping relationship and her shapely tush. He thought about his beaten-down brother and their talks under hazy skies. He thought about how hard the citizens in his country had fought to escape their past and the efforts they'd made to build a future. He thought about his life. His glorious life.

Levy leaned back in his chair.

Hale, Dr. Thatcher, Bopp and his family settled onto their hover-chairs. Levy cracked open a beer, stuffed a handful of chips in his mouth, then looked up.

The sky was purple. Pink.

Red.

The sky was the comet.

Levy took one more breath—one last, glorious breath—and grabbed Hale's hand. A rush of heat filled his heart—

—and the comet hit.

RESET

2

It was the kind of day you expect terrible things to happen. When Nicole's alarm clock rang it jolted her off her mattress. Her head bumped the headboard, her sheets got tangled in her legs, and her arm thwacked her partner—who was sleeping peacefully, unaware it was morning. Until Nicole's hand smacked her in her freckled face.

It was a day that promised disasters. And fulfilled those promises.

The toaster broke. It had been on the fritz for a while, and Merry—Nicole's partner—had been urging Nicole to pick up a replacement appliance on her way home from the hospital; a Perfect Purchases mega store hunkered beside the city's medic centre. But Nicole forgot. Between filling prescriptions and making sure her pharm techs complied with provincially mandated medicinal standards, Nicole barely had enough energy to drag herself home at the end of the day, let alone slip into a super store to buy an elite brand of bread baker.

Without toast, Nicole's breakfast was ruined. And Merry, who was a vegan, wouldn't touch Nicole's scrambled eggs with her side of sliced tomato.

After breakfast, Nicole realized she'd forgotten to do a load of laundry, so she had to spot clean her least soiled scrubs. And the cat—Merry's ginger cat—had a urinary tract infection flare-up, so he peed wherever he needed to which was, that morning, Merry's makeup case. And the water flow pouring from the calcium-covered showerhead left conditioning glops in Nicole's long brown hair. And she forgot to wheel out the compost bin the night before, even though Merry reminded her about it—again—and the green plastic container was briming with rotting refuse, causing Nicole's neighbours to sneer at her with disapproval whenever she left her townhouse.

So, that day, when Nicole eventually left her townhouse—late, hungry, soggy, and irritable—it wasn't a shock that the weather mirrored her rough start.

An overcast sky covered the city. The trees lining the block thrust their dried branches towards the clouds, casting thin shadows on the brownstone facades of the townhouse block. Brittle autumn leaves whirled around sidewalk grates, snapping when morning commuters crunched through disparate piles, then billowing up in rough whirlwinds when the air caught them in its chilled claws. Pumpkins put on stoops too early curled inwards, unable to retain their plump carvings during the frosty nights and frigid days.

Decorative wheat stalks wound through the iron fence that separated the townhouses from the sidewalk but, instead of adding a touch of fall frivolity to the drab city street, in the murky dawn they looked like tangled strands of hair caught in the teeth of a comb.

Nicole flipped up the collar of her tweed coat to protect her own tangled hair. She squinted her eyes to protect them from the cold, and avoid the glares from her neighbours. But her neighbours didn't care about her overflowing compost bin that day. With a thunderous boom and a laser-bright *crack!* the sky split in two: rain poured from the clouds in sheets.

Nicole lowered her head and kept walking. Because it was the kind of day you expect terrible things to happen.

And they did.

By the time the sun set and Nicole crawled under her covers, all she could do was flip off her bedside lamp and squeeze her eyes shut to deny her current reality.

She'd been fired. Her supervisor said her pessimistic attitude was affecting the vulnerable patients. Since she couldn't slap on a smile when she doled out their medication from behind the pharmaceutical counter—or show up looking clean and present-able—the hospital board declared her attitude a liability. They'd had no choice but to let her go, union be damned.

Perfect Purchases was closed by the time her dismissal meeting resolved: Nicole couldn't replace the toaster.

After braving the rain to save money on a taxi, Nicole pulled her compost bin across the stubby townhouse lawn and through the iron gate that distinguished her property from her neighbours, only to trip over a tree root—sprawling backwards onto the sidewalk and taking the green bin with her. Covered in compost and bemoaning her bad luck, Nicole accepted that it made sense for her most judgmental neighbour—a surly man named Grayson—to step over her mess on his way to his front steps. And she accepted his sneer. And his smug head shake. Because it was a terrible day. And she was terrible.

Nicole also accepted when the cat ran out her front door and into the rain, disappearing inside an untrimmed hedge—probably forever. After all, what creature would want to live with a stinky, irresponsible, unemployed person like her?

Merry didn't. When Nicole stumbled into her foyer—wet and miserable—her girlfriend unleashed. Merry vented all her pent-up relationship disappointments she'd accumulated over the years they'd been together, from their rapidly-diminishing intimacy, and Nicole's constantly distracted state, to the lost cat—sure to be dead!—which meant there was no possible way Merry could stay in Nicole's spiral of doom a second longer. No way! She was gone, with a slam of the door and a kick of the overturned bin.

Nicole lay in her dark, empty bedroom—on her dark, empty bed—and listened to the rain on the dark, empty street. She pictured it pounding against her brick building, turning the maroon and brown stones black. She imagined water running through the rock's ridges—cracked stone and dark liquid, pooling on the sidewalk and reflecting the moon to passersby when the clouds eased enough for its light to wink upon the street below.

With her eyes squeezed shut and her life in shambles, Nicole did what any desperate, self-loathing, terrible person would do: she grabbed her phone.

Her friend apps were their typical jumble of expected shares. Nicole's cousin overseas was finishing the remodel of her walk-in closet: it looked fantastic. Nicole's high school crush had moved into a farming commune that produced sustainable watercress for restaurant salad bars: his sun-pinched face made Nicole's sad heart sigh.

Then there were the less aspirational posts: illness announcements, financial losses, celebrities revealing their humanity. Nicole liked those shares; not because she felt sad for the original posters, or because she wanted to show her support. She liked them because a tiny part of her was comforted to see scores of people whose lives were worse than hers. Much worse.

Much, much worse.

But not for long.

As Nicole scrolled up on her phone screen—and more and more discouraged strangers shared their stories of strife—her comfort turned to guilt for her brief moment of superior glee. Then her guilt turned to shame. Then her shame dampened her other feelings like the cloudy sky dampened the moonlight.

She *was* in a spiral of doom.

Nicole kept scrolling. Stories blurred together. Posts lost their clarity. Videos and pics disappeared in Nicole's cloud of self-pity— and regret.

Until an ad popped up on her screen, pulling Nicole out of her spiral.

It was the kind of ad you expect to see in the middle of the night. An inspirational ad, selling a quick-fix app for losers who ruined their lives. Usually, Nicole scrolled past those ads but, that night—after that day—*she* was a loser who had ruined her life. She desperately needed a quick-fix. So, Nicole watched the ad, then clicked a link to purchase the app.

An app with a logo in the shape of a snake, wound in a circle, eating its tail. The app was called, *Perpetual*.

Perpetual's product was straightforward, and user-friendly. By utilizing modern algorithms and the best AI modelling $2.99 could buy, the app promised people a new life. Unlike other augmented reality tools, Perpetual changed reality: forever. Nicole just had to upload her conscious memories into its databank, then select a point in her timeline before her life fell apart. Perpetual would erase her life after that point and place her "firmly in a position to change the future." She'd get a fresh start. A new beginning. A chance to try again—while retaining the memories of how she messed up in the first place.

Nicole paid the fee, downloaded the app, and set up her account with a quick click on the Terms and Agreements. She held her phone screen in front of her widened eyes so her camera could access her memories, then counted down from ten—as Perpetual's automated coach instructed. With a blink and a *beep!* her timeline appeared on the screen—reel-style—and Nicole selected a day to start over.

September 1st. Two months before. The day the leaves changed colour and the rain began.

The room spun. Nicole dropped her phone. She clung to her bedsheets as though the flimsy fabric would somehow keep her grounded. Thunder boomed and sheet lightning streaked outside her spinning window. Nicole bit her tongue, waiting for Perpetual to complete its time travel cycle.

It didn't take long. In seconds the spinning slowed, the rain disappeared, and clear sunlight shone through Nicole's window, illuminating her lover—and the sleeping cat—beside her on the bed.

"Morning, Nic," Merry said with a yawn. "Want some toast? I picked up a flaxseed loaf at the market."

Nicole lay back on her pillow as Merry padded into their kitchen. This time she would do better. This time life would be different.

"Nic?" Merry stuck her head through the bedroom door. "Can you clean Bumble's litterbox before we eat? He's doing his dirty dance again."

"Mmm." Nicole turned onto her side and shut her eyes, luxuriating in the smell of browning bread and the sound of her partner's voice. "It's on my list."

Nicole didn't notice the silence before Merry padded back into the kitchen. She didn't see the cat awkwardly leap off the bed and onto the floor, bladder full to bursting. She'd fallen asleep, warmed by the certainty her life would improve.

"—and you never—never!—ask how my day has been, or what I need." Merry's scrunched up face screamed as she stood on the front steps in the pouring rain, ignoring the costumed Trick-or-Treaters who avoided the house—and the shrieking occupants—like Nicole was giving out raisins. "I'm sick of this, Nic. Sick of your attitude, and sick of—of everything!"

Greyson sauntered down his steps, holding an umbrella in his clenched fist. He grinned at Merry before picking his way over the compost strewn across the sidewalk. Merry looked at the judgmental neighbour, then back at Nicole with vindication in her glare, as though his disapproval was proof that Nicole *should* be left, and the relationship *should* be discarded, and Nicole *was* a terrible person who deserved to die alone.

The door slammed and Merry left. Forever. Again.

But not for long.

With a resentful sigh—why hadn't Perpetual worked?—Nicole opened her phone and fired up her timeline. She'd try again. There wasn't any harm in trying again.

September 1st blinked on her screen.

Nicole went back to September 1st twelve times. Each amended timeline ended in the same way—a lost job, a missing pet, and Merry storming out into the rain. Nicole didn't understand why her different choices couldn't change the outcome of events. She'd learned to fake a grin with hospital patients and be more attentive to Merry, but despite the vet visits—and trips to the Farmers Market—the cat stayed sick, her partner scowled, and Nicole stumbled home after being let go, turning up her tweed collar to protect her neck from the cold.

But it didn't matter. Nicole was determined to keep trying. The next time she'd get it right. The next time it would work out.

During Nicole's twenty-third attempt at perfection, everything changed.

But not for the better.

As Nicole sat in the hospital cafeteria, going through her schedule for the day—September 6th—her phone rang. She pulled it out of her pocket and held the device to her mouth. "Yeah?"

It was her supervisor, requesting a meeting.

Nicole sat in the lounge where informal chats took place between colleagues, waiting for Cheryl—the hospital admin—to appear. The domineering supervisor strode into the lounge with a look of concern on her normally neutral face.

Cheryl leaned against the coffee counter, staring at Nicole with her arms crossed over her ample chest. "This is awkward."

Nicole crossed her arms, too. When she'd researched how to appear more approachable, a website recommended mimicking other people's physical stance; familiarity made them like her more. "What's awkward?"

Cheryl furrowed her brow, then turned to the lounge's coffee dispenser to auto-brew a beverage. "You know our code of conduct, Nicole."

Nicole furrowed her brow, too, though it wasn't intentional. It was a reaction to Cheryl's odd statement. "Sure."

Cheryl jabbed the coffee button angrily. "Then explain to me what you were doing in the supply warehouse in the middle of the night."

"I wasn't in the warehouse in the middle of the night," Nicole said. "I was asleep in the middle of the night. I'm always asleep in the middle of the night."

"Not last night." Cheryl pulled her phone out of her scrubs' pocket. "Not according to our security footage."

Nicole took a confident step towards her supervisor. "Why do you have security cameras in my bedroom?"

"I've never understood your sense of humour," Cheryl said, walking towards Nicole with her phone extended. "And now I can stop trying. You're fired."

Shocked, Nicole watched the video on Cheryl's screen: a video of someone who looked like her rifling through shelves of bandages, syringes, and pill bottles. "That isn't me."

"Again, I've never understood your humour." Cheryl shoved her phone in her pocket. "Breaking into a hospital—even if it's your hospital—isn't funny. That *is* you on the video. Go home."

Nicole carried her box of personal items down the street. The weak September sunshine warmed the back of her neck, but it didn't heat her body enough to cause the sweat that beaded along her scrubs' neckline. How had this happened? Who was the person in the video? Was it her, sleepwalking? Sleep stealing? Nicole might've needed to change her behaviour, but not that drastically— she'd never done anything illegal.

Nicole lifted her box higher as she neared her home. How was she going to tell Merry about this? She was supposed to be fixing their relationship, not giving Merry more reasons to leave her.

Unless—

Nicole stopped short in front of her townhouse, then sat on her bottom step. She placed the box on the ground—beside a decorative bale of hay that smelled like cinnamon—and frowned up at a tree, at the leaves still valiantly clinging to its limbs.

Nicole didn't have to tell her about this. Merry wasn't going to be home for hours. She could just start the timeline over—on September 1st—and pretend this whole bizarre incident never happened. It had to be a glitch in the app. Perpetual was new, after all, and the developers probably had kinks they were working out. Nicole pulled her phone from the bottom of the box where she'd shoved in it her haste to leave the hospital. She opened the app and— yes! There! On the settings menu the update calendar was displayed, and there was an upgrade scheduled for that afternoon.

Nicole patted her phone fondly, then swiped right to open her timeline. Clicking on September 1st, she closed her eyes as the street spun and her life started over.

"I saw you, Nic! I saw you with that man!" Merry stormed down the townhouse's front steps, clutching the cat to her chest. "Don't deny it. You were in the bar, with your hand on his leg and his hand on your ass. I saw you."

"Merry!" Nicole chased after her partner. This was silly. She hadn't been in a bar with a man. She'd never cheat on Merry.

"Don't gaslight me, Nic." Merry sobbed as she hailed a cab. "I know what people like you do—you convince everyone else that they're the problem when, really, it's you. It's always been you. And I'm done."

"Merry!" Nicole swayed on the sidewalk as Merry leapt into a taxi. She stared—shocked—as the cab drove around a corner, taking her partner and best friend away. Forever.

Again.

Nicole stomped her foot. She threw her hands in the air. She whirled around on her heels—and bumped into Greyson, who was leaning against his recycling bin, smugly flicking a leaf off the lid.

Greyson turned his nose in her direction. "Trouble?"

"You don't care," Nicole said, flopping down on her bottom step. "And I don't want to talk about it."

"While we're not talking about it, can I make a request?" Greyson pushed himself away from the bin, then sauntered over to sneer at her. "Neighbour to neighbour?"

Nicole ignored the snooty snoop and, instead, gazed up the street—willing the taxi to back around corner and bring Merry home.

"Fine," Greyson said. "Don't look at me. Listen. The next time you get fired and run out of money to buy groceries, don't steal garbage from the guy who lives next door."

Nicole turned. "What?"

"I have cameras covering every centimeter of my property." Greyson waved his hand at the lintel above his door, and the ledge underneath his windowpane. "I saw you. Every night this week: going through my bins and stealing leftovers from my dinner."

Nicole leapt to her feet. "What?"

Greyson glided up his stairs. "There are food banks if you're that desperate."

"What?" Nicole took a shaky step after Greyson, until she came to her senses—there was no point talking to the man, who'd judged her the second she and Merry moved in. But why would he invent such a strange story? Especially one that was so easy to disprove?

Nicole watched the cameras blink above and beneath her neighbour's door and window. She could ask to see Greyson's footage.

Or—she could start over.

Nicole shrugged, and took out her phone.

During the fifty-fifth attempt at Nicole's new and better life, things got weird. Really, really weird. Midway through October—after still struggling to support Merry at home, the cat with his health, and the hospital's patients with their lives—Nicole began to stumble. Into herself. Or, into people who looked like herself. People who showed up in places she usually visited, doing things she usually did. But terribly.

While Nicole was at Perfect Purchases purchasing the perfect toaster for the fifty-fifth time, a woman with long brown hair and hips like hers pulled a drip brewer off a high shelf before running out the mega store's sliding doors.

When Nicole was at the vet, getting the cat checked for worms (which were supposed to be the cause of his pee problem) she heard a low voice—*her* low voice!—loudly yelling in the room next door. The familiar voice carried through the thin veterinarian clinic's walls, demanding pain killers for a pet and claiming if she didn't receive them—immediately!—she'd sue!

Then—the weirdest of all—when she was in Greyson's office viewing his tapes after another garbage stealing accusation, Nicole watched a woman with her mother's height and her father's shoulders root through her neighbour's black bin.

"See?" Greyson flipped on his lights, which had been off so they could see Nicole's midnight excursion clearly on his computer. "What do you have to say for yourself?"

"I don't know." Nicole didn't know. She didn't know, at all. "That isn't me, I promise, but I have no idea why the thief and I are identical."

"Because you're the thief," Greyson said. "You are." He pinched the bridge of his nose with his thumb and forefinger. "Never mind. I'm going to make tea. You want chai?"

Nicole nodded absentmindedly as Greyson glided from his office. She flicked off the light, then rewound the footage, ready to watch it for the hundredth time. She couldn't figure out who the mysterious doppelgänger was, roaming her neighbourhood, accidentally causing trouble. At least, she hoped it was accidental. Nicole wasn't prepared to consider an intentional adversary who wished her harm. She had enough to worry about.

Nicole sat on Greyson's wheely chair, staring at the computer on his desk. The footage from the night before played on his screen. The Nicole-twin lumbered up the darkened street, then dove—head first—into Greyson's black bin to rummage through his refuse. Then the Nicole-twin stood, half-eaten sandwich in hand, and lumbered away.

Nicole let the video play out, lost in her thoughts. On the computer the wind blew the last of the leaves off the tree outside Greyson's window. They flew into the air in a clump, brushing against the building's bricks before falling—deflated—to the stone steps. Then the Nicole-twin returned.

The real Nicole sat up. This was new. Greyson hadn't told her the twin reappeared after she stole his sandwich: maybe he didn't know about it? Maybe. Nicole leaned closer to the screen, scanning the figure for signs of a mask, or physical padding under her clothes. She had to be a fake. Then Nicole shot out of Greyson's chair and backed away from the desk.

"I was out of chai, so I made squash spice," Greyson said as he re-entered his office with two steaming mugs clasped in his hands. "They're basically the same, so—" He paused in the doorway. "What are you doing?"

Nicole raised her shaking finger to point at the computer. "Did you know about them?"

Greyson slowly placed the tea on his desk, then leaned over the computer. On the screen, three Nicole-twins—triplets!—stood side by side, surveying the block. "Uhhh—"

"Right?" Nicole said, her back still pressed against Greyson's wall. "That's different, isn't it? It's new."

"Definitely different," Greyson said. "I would've told you if I'd seen this part of the video. And *you* should've told the Home Owners Association you were a quadruplet."

"I'm not a quadruplet," Nicole said. "I'm me. Just me. A singular Nicole, not part of a team."

"Or a squad," Greyson said as a fourth Nicole-twin joined the trio. He peered over his shoulder: his eyes accused Nicole of mischief, most foul. "You really haven't seen these women before?"

"How do we know they're women?" Nicole lowered her finger. "They could be witches. Or demons. Or—"

"Zombies living in the sewers?" Greyson smirked. "I thought you were a pharmacist. Aren't people like you supposed to be smart?"

"I have to go." Nicole ran towards the front door, pausing only to call to Greyson, "I'll let you know once I've figured out what's going on."

She ran down Greyson's front steps, through his gate, along

their sidewalk, through her gate, then up her front steps. Merry was still at work—thank goodness—and the cat was sleeping on her gym bag. Nicole had time. Time to do what, she didn't know, but some time was better than no time, which was better than every time, which was better than—

Nicole bent over to catch her breath. She reached for her phone, then opened Perpetual. The doppelgängers had to be related to the app. They had to be something she could fix. There had to be a way to start over and try again, without the tech glitch creating multiple hers.

An alert hovered over her settings button. Aha! There *was* a glitch. Nicole read the update statement, then felt her lungs constrict like she'd been punched in the stomach. The upgrade merely added stricter privacy laws to the Terms and Agreements; apparently, she wasn't allowed to disclose her use of the app to anyone, at and *in* any time.

Nicole snorted; like she'd tell anyone she'd replayed the last two months fifty-five times. Out of sheer annoyance more than anything, Nicole clicked open Perpetual's user policies. She read through the amendment, then agreed to the Terms. Throwing her phone on her living room table, Nicole sunk onto her sofa. She stared at her ceiling lamp and debated when she should start her next timeline. It was the twelfth of October. Merry always made chili on the twelfth, and Merry's chili was really good, so maybe she should start the next morning when Merry started to digest her chili—

Nicole's phone screen wavered: the battery was dying. Grumbling, she picked up her cell and searched for the phone charger. Normally she left it on the kitchen counter, but Merry always put it in a drawer because she didn't like electronics in her food prep space and—

Nicole paused, half in the kitchen and half in the living room. Perpetual's Terms and Agreements blinked up at her—and there was a clause she hadn't seen before. A clause that stipulated payment for the app. Payment in addition to the $2.99. When Nicole agreed to the Terms and Agreements, she'd consented to let the app collect her data: and allow Perpetual's parent company to use her data how they wanted.

Each version of her life she'd already lived—each Nicole in each timeline that had already happened—was uploaded to a bot. A living bot. A fully autonomous bot. An Intelligent bot that acted according to the app developers wishes. A bot that was supposed to look like a unique human, with a unique personality and attributes that were inspired by 'the host.' Her. The real Nicole.

The real Nicole dropped her phone. She backed away from the device, then found herself on Greyson's step, hammering on his door.

Her snooty neighbour stood in his entryway with his mouth twisted crookedly. "Yeeeeees?"

"I need your help," Nicole said, pushing past Greyson into his home. "You can't tell anyone, though. Not Merry, and not—I dunno—your precious Home Owners Association."

"This better be good," Greyson said. "You've caused enough problems already."

"You work in tech development, right?" Nicole paced back and forth across Greyson's foyer. "You build apps?"

"I dabble in experimental technology, yes."

"Have you ever worked with technology like this?" Nicole thrust her phone in Greyson's face.

His skin took on a green tinge as Greyson read her screen. "Why would you?—Why did you?—Why on earth would you sign up for a service like this?"

Nicole threw her phone across Greyson's living room, then grabbed a crocheted pillow off a spindly-legged chair. She used the dainty pillow to smother her communication device, pressing it into Greyson's shag rug.

"What did you do that made you start your life over fifty-five times?" Greyson wasn't angry—or shocked, or disappointed. He was amused. Mildly amused.

Nicole wasn't amused. She was angry. Very angry. "I didn't do anything! It's just—well, things kept falling apart. I had to repeat my timeline over and over because I kept losing my job, and Merry kept breaking up with me, and her cat kept dying—"

"And it didn't occur to you, after fifty-five repeats, that maybe those things were supposed to happen?" Greyson picked up his pillow and smoothed the knitted surface. "It also didn't occur to you to stop when your Nicole bots took over the planet?"

"I didn't know what they were," Nicole said. "And they're not supposed to be Nicole bots. They're supposed to be regular bots."

"Regular or not, you didn't think there was something wrong with selling your replication to an app?"

"I didn't know they'd replicate," Nicole said, sinking to the rug.

Greyson pinched the bridge of his nose. "You didn't know about the bots? At all?"

"No."

"Why? How? Why?"

"I didn't—" Nicole snatched the pillow from Greyson's arms. She hugged it to her chest. "I didn't read the contract before I downloaded the app."

With a groan, Greyson sank to the floor beside Nicole. "So, because you're the worst human in existence, fifty-five bonus 'yous' are running around?"

"I'm not the worst." Nicole hugged the pillow tighter. "I'm trying to be better."

Greyson gently took back his pillow. He tossed it onto his spindly chair. "You're right. You aren't the worst. It's not your fault Perpetual stole your identity and is using it to steal my garbage. And..." He tilted his head. "Why was there a bot squad scouring my home?"

"They were probably looking at *my* home."

"At your bins—I knew it," Greyson said. "Even bots are bothered by your irresponsibility. You'd think after fifty-five attempts to fix your life you'd get in the habit of putting out your compost—"

"Enough with the bins, Greyson," Nicole said. "You're the only person in my timeline who cares about the bins. The bots must've realized I noticed them—noticed the flaw in the software. They aren't supposed to look like me. Perpetual probably wants to... I dunno, make the problem go away."

"And you're the problem?"

"Yes. I'm the problem," Nicole said. "I'm always the problem."

They sat on Greyson's rug as Nicole's depressing statement sank in, then Greyson nudged Nicole's shoulder. "You aren't the problem. You're just going through a rough patch. It happens to lots of people."

Nicole stared at her phone, upside down in the corner of Greyson's living room. "Lots of people buy an app to redo two months of their lives, only to have their alternate timelines turned into independently functioning robots who engage in small crimes under the direction of a software company that wants hospital syringes?"

"Who knows how popular this app is." Greyson dragged Nicole to her feet. "It might be happening to lots of people."

"Then we have to stop it," Nicole said. "Maybe I got lucky. Maybe the glitch with the multiple Nicoles was the clue we needed—"

"We?"

"—to stop Perpetual, and save other people from... I dunno, being fired. And save vet clinics from frivolous lawsuits. And mega stores from having their kitchen appliances stolen." Nicole squeezed her eyes shut. "Maybe."

"Why should I help you?" Greyson perched on the edge of his spindly chair and crossed his legs. "I don't care about hospital supplies and capitalists' bottom line."

"What do you care about?"

Greyson sneered. "I care about my property. I care about my

neighbours putting out their compost bins every week so tomato skins don't stink up the street."

Nicole opened her eyes. "You don't care about the people who bought Perpetual? Like me?"

"Why would I care about desperate humans who can't accept the reality of their circumstances and, instead, try to manipulate their lives with cheap gimmicks and experimental technology?"

"Is that why you work in experimental technology?"

"I work in experimental technology because I'm good at experimental technology."

Nicole sat on the edge of Greyson's sofa and crossed her legs. "If you're so good at experimental technology, tell me how to get rid of the multiple Nicoles—and if it works, I'll put out my compost bin every week, on time."

The real Nicole's physical mirroring and air-tight offer cracked Greyson's resolve. He uncrossed his legs. "Every week?"

"Every week."

"Even when it rains?"

"Even when it snows."

"Fine," Greyson said. "Getting rid of robots is easy. Getting rid of your insecurities about things beyond your control is a whole other problem."

"If the multiple Nicoles kill me—and you—"

"Me?"

"—maybe, by association—my inability to let go of a doomed relationship, pet, and career won't matter."

"Who said anything about killing?"

"Tell me how to get rid of the robots, and I'll deal with the app," Nicole said. "If I delete it off my account—and cancel my subscription—"

"And accept your girlfriend, job, and cat aren't meant to be?"

Nicole ignored the air that was stuck in her chest. "Yes, that too. If I delete Perpetual, that should fix the bot problem, right?"

"For you." Greyson fiddled with his pillow. "But not for the other desperate humans who're using it."

Nicole groaned. "Being a good person is hard."

"I'll tell you what," Greyson said. "If you put out your compost bin—every week!—I'll file a complaint with the App Developers Association so the glitch gets fixed for other users."

"The ADA won't shut the app down? After this extreme violation of privacy and attempt to build a bot army?"

"That depends on how profitable Perpetual has been this quarter—"

"Greyson!"

"I'll get the ADA to shut the app down."

"Thank you. And tell me how to kill the Nicole bots? Please?" Nicole walked to Greyson's window to peer through the lacy curtains that hung on either side of the glass. "I want to be me again. The only Nicole, no matter how messed up she is."

Greyson joined Nicole at the window. The street was empty— no robot Nicoles that night. "It's easy. You have to talk to them. Once they're engaged in a dialogue, tell them to reset."

"Reset?" Nicole dropped the curtain. "That's it?"

"Artificially Intelligent beings can learn and obey commands, but they're still machines," Greyson said. "Every machine has a failsafe. Every program has to be able to be shut down. The magic word for bots is, 'reset.' Tell them to reset and they'll disappear."

"It's kind of ironic," Nicole said. "That's what I was trying to do."

"Disappear?" Greyson arched his brows as he scanned the street. "So you made fifty-five versions of yourself?"

"For the last time, I didn't know my lived lives were being siphoned into robots," Nicole said. "I wasn't trying to disappear. I was resetting."

"You can't reset," Greyson said. "You can only learn."

That night, after the clouds rolled in, Nicole sat on her front step, waiting for the Nicole squad. Greyson had elected to hide in his home, claiming he was useless until the robots were gone. Given how simple the elimination task was supposed to be, Nicole agreed. She waited in the dark. Alone. Without Merry, who was asleep upstairs. Without the cat, who was mewling in the bathroom. And without a purpose, since she was destined to be alone in every version of her life, forever.

The Garbage Nicole stepped out of the shadows.

The Real Nicole climbed to her feet. "Can I help you?"

Garbage Nicole hesitated before squaring off her shoulders. "I'm putting out the bins."

Nicole grinned. "In the middle of the night?"

"I forget to put them out when I come home," the robot said with a menacing sneer. "I live on this street."

"Me too," Nicole said. "I live here, and I forget to put out the compost." She took a deep breath, hoping Greyson's magic word would work. "And I never reset."

Garbage Nicole shuddered, then its eyes folded backwards into its face. With a *snap!* and a flare of green light, the robot disappeared.

Before she had time to feel relief, the squad of Nicole bots rounded the corner.

Nicole planted her feet, ready for the face-off. Literally. "Can I help you?"

The four Nicole bots halted, confused. Then the leader stepped forward. "We're lost. We just moved into this area and we can't seem to find our house."

"They all look the same, hey?" Nicole laughed with genuine sincerity as she nodded at the brownstone façade that covered every connected property on her block. "Sometimes I forget, too."

"You live here?" The second robot Nicole frowned. "Are you sure?"

"Pretty sure," Nicole said. "Even though I'm going to have to move, soon." She looked up at her darkened window. "Really soon."

"Yes," the first robot Nicole said. "You should move."

"I would," Nicole said, annoyed at the conviction in her replica's voice, "—but it's so hard to find places to reset."

The *pop!* and green flare.

The first Nicole disappeared.

"Hey!" The second flipped her long brown hair over her shoulder. "You can't do that."

"Do what?" Nicole stared into the metallic eyes of her doppelgänger. "Reset?"

Pop! Flash. The second folded in on itself.

The two remaining robots began to yell and spin in circles, clearly waiting for direction from their developer. Nicole replied to the desperate cries of her copies with an assertive, "Reset!"

Snap! Flare. The street emptied, with only neon afterimage left behind.

Greyson stuck his head out his door. "Fifty more to go."

Nicole spent the rest of her fifty-fifth timeline hunting down her replicas and screaming, "Reset!" It took several weeks to find them all—weeks she spent growing closer with Greyson and tying up loose ends with the parts of her life she couldn't support. Nicole and Merry took the cat—Bumble—to the vet to be humanely put down. After his funeral, Nicole held Merry's hand as her partner tearfully broke up with her. Then Nicole gave her resignation to Cheryl, who accepted it after saying she understood because Nicole wasn't the best caregiver—at least, she wouldn't be until she learned to care for herself. Nicole agreed. She wanted to care. About her whole self. Even the parts she didn't like and wanted to reset.

After the last robot was found graffitiing a serpent on a church—and it folded inward into its flare of green—Nicole found herself on

Greyson's couch, sipping apple cider and crocheting a doily for another pillow. "Did you contact the App Developers Association?"

"I did," Greyson said, sipping his cider with his pinky finger raised. "They've reached out to Perpetual's parent company. If the developer doesn't shut the app down immediately, the ADA will file a class action suit. You could make money off this."

"I don't want money," Nicole said. "I'm just happy the bots didn't do anything worse than steal a drip brewer and make out with a random guy in a bar."

"And plot your demise," Greyson said. "If that's what the squad was doing."

"I guess we'll never know what they were up to," Nicole said. "Or what could have happened. It's out of my hands."

"And isn't that better than being responsible for everything?" Greyson sipped his drink. "Living one life—instead of 'fixing' all the errors you caused over the course your timeline—means having to accept what you're capable of managing and what you aren't."

"And what I can change—and what I can't," Nicole said. "Merry and I weren't ever really happy. I hated my job, and I'm not a cat person." She wrinkled her nose. "I can't even keep a plant alive."

"Don't worry about plants," Greyson said. "Focus on putting your bins out without covering the sidewalk in trash. Houseplants can happen after you master your basic life skills. And honour our deal."

"I put them out this week, didn't I?" Nicole grabbed Greyson's empty mug off his table, then headed for his kitchen. "And I don't want to become a responsible person because I made a deal with you." She paused by Greyson's office, then smiled at her un-expected friend. "I want to do it for me."

Greyson stared through his curtains, out his window at the autumn street. Nicole grinned, turned—then stopped. A light blinking on Greyson's computer caught her eye. A light she hadn't noticed before. A light in the shape of a snake, wound in a circle, eating its tail.

"Greyson?" Nicole called to the living room. "Which experimental technology company do you work for again?"

YOU'VE BEEN SERVED

3

There's a knock on my door.

Straightening my tie, I shrug into my dinner jacket and stand by the entryway, ready to greet my date. The hired help opens the door, and a dainty foot—clad in lurid greed stilettos—steps onto my tiled floor. A petite hand, gloved in reptilian skin, reaches out to take the arm offered by the Help. The male I employed to take care of my extensive household duties escorts my guest into my home. He passes me the magnificent creature attached to the green shoe and scaled glove—Selene.

"Hugo, you cad." Selene clutches my arm as she kisses my cheek. Her spicy scent floats around her supple body. She pulls off her gloves, one finger at a time, then hands them to the Help without a glance in his direction. "I had to take four taxis to get here. You never told me you lived so far outside the city."

I place my hand on the small of Selene's back as I guide her away from the entryway and towards the salon. My date sighs with pleasure as she takes in the richness of my ten-story mansion—then she pushes her breasts into my bicep.

Bemused, I lean over to murmur in her ear, "We all have secrets."

Selene laughs, low in her throat, and squeezes my forearm. "I knew you were going to be fun." She gazes up at me; her eyes are as green as her stilettos. "What other secrets have you kept?"

I guide Selene into the salon, then step aside with a flourish.

The salon is my favourite room in the mansion: it showcases my collections, which surround a linen-draped dining table under a coral chandelier. The wall opposite is hung with 19th century paintings, so rare they're each worth several billion. To my right is a floor-to-ceiling shelf, stacked with printed texts by self-published authors who sold less than fifty books over their lifetime. The wall to my left is covered in photographs, images of my adventurous exploits; like the time I killed a pod of whales in my 800 FT yacht, and when I sunk a low-population island with my homemade nuclear explosives. But behind me is my masterpiece: a mirror. Its frame is wrapped with Giant Panda fur, and it has Black Rhino horns holding the joints together instead of embarrassing metal nails. When I look at my fair hair and fit body in that mirror I feel alive.

I feel free.

Selene gasps as she steps into the salon. Her petite hand brushes her full lips. "Hugo! I don't know what to say!"

Grinning, I guide my date farther into the room. "You could start with 'thank you.'"

Selene whirls around. Placing her hands on my shoulders, she presses her lips into my ear. "That's what you'll say to me. Later."

With a grin, Selene steps out of my arms. She twirls on her toes, laughing as she takes in the splendor of the salon. "It's beautiful, Hugo. I knew when we met in the hotel lobby you were a male with taste." Her fingers stroke the fabric draping my dining table. "So much taste."

I pull back her chair. She caresses my cheek, then sits, tucking her legs under her seat. I hold my hand against the back of her neck—a control move I learned on Readit—then I stride around the table to take my place at the head.

Selene strokes the table setting; bamboo plates imported from overseas, lines of utensils made from porous cave rocks, and AI crystal glassware that plays music harvested from dead composers. "How did you get these?" Selene licks her lips. "With the new sanctions, I thought global importing was illegal."

"Hey, now." I grin. "Let me keep my secrets."

"I can keep secrets." Selene's bare foot rubs my ankle. "Tell me your secrets." Her toes slide up my calf, slither along my thigh and—

"M. Hugo?" The Help hovers in the salon's doorway. "Dinner is ready."

Selene withdraws her foot from my crotch. I breathe deeply to release the tension coursing through my groin, then nod at my male. "You may begin Service."

The Help snaps his fingers. A line of serving staff carry heaping trays of food into the salon; endangered snails, rare turnips, and sauces from conflict-ravaged continents. As the staff places each dish on the table—too many dishes, more than we could ever consume—Selene's eyes glow brighter. Her nipples harden behind her flimsy blouse.

"This must have cost you a fortune." Selene leans over the first course, inhaling sensuously. "How did you arrange this, Hugo?"

"Connections can be useful." I spear a snail with my cave-rock fork. "If you make the right ones."

Selene's throaty laugh sends a shiver up my spine. "I'd be jealous if you hadn't done all this for me. But does this dinner of yours have to be eaten hot, or can it wait?" She unclasps the single pin holding her blouse together. "I'd like an appetizer before the main course."

I don't realize I'm out of my chair until Selene's thigh is hitched over my hip and her tongue winds inside my—

"M. Hugo?"

Selene slides to the ground. She glides to her seat, adjusting her clothing.

I glare at the Help and zip up my pants. "What now?"

"Another guest has arrived. Would you like me to show them in?"

With a roar, I pick up my chair and fling it at the Help. He ducks and the chair crashes against the bookshelf, breaking in two and sending manuscripts tumbling to the floor. I cross the room, grab the Help's collar, and shove him up against the masterpiece mirror. My rage-filled face stares at me over the Help's shoulder; my pupils are dilated, my fair hair's a mess, and Selene's lipstick is on my neck. I look powerful.

I grin, leaning harder into the Help. "What is wrong with you?" I push my forearm up under his chin, placing more pressure on his neck. "No one else is scheduled to arrive this evening. You know I like privacy when I'm doing business. Your job is to bring us dinner—which you have—then *leave*." I press the Help harder on my final statement, so he really gets the message. "Do you understand?"

The Help's face starts to purple. "Yes, M. Hugo."

"Good." I release my grip.

I spin away from the mirror and back to Selene. She's watching me, twirling a lock of permed hair around her slim finger.

My body electrifies.

I jerk my head at the Help. "Get out."

I don't notice him leave. I'm too intent on my appetizer.

After Selene has been thoroughly satisfied and *I've* been thanked, several times, we return to our meal. The food is delicious, but Selene's presence is far more engaging. Her flattery, praise, and toes in my lap are just what I need after a long week of work.

There's a knock on the salon door.

Selene wiggles her toes, then looks over her shoulder. "He's persistent, isn't he?"

"They're trained to be," I say. "It's probably time to clear." I pat Selene's foot. "We can finish this scintillating conversation in the lounge, if you'd care to stay?"

"How could I say no?" Selene lowers her leg—and her bared breasts. Her smooth curves of flesh hover an inch above her barely-touched plate. "I have a scintillating topic in mind." She bites her lower lip. "Did I say scintillating? I meant titillating."

Selene arches her back. My ardour rises, but I tamp it down: I have to deal with the unplanned intruder rapping on the door before I can deal with Selene. I raise my voice—impatient. "You can come in. We're done."

"Almost done." Selene reattaches her clasp as the Help opens the door.

I'm contemplating how comfortable I am revealing my giant erection to the Help when he places a silver, dome-covered tray on the dining table.

"What is this?" I glare at the covered tray, then at my cowering servant. "We finished our meal."

"M. Hugo, this was delivered earlier this evening." The Help straightens his torn collar.

"Well?" I adjust my pants, glaring. "What is it?"

"M. Hugo." The Help swallows, then lifts the cover of the tray. "I'm so sorry."

Selene screams.

As my date leaps to her feet and runs from the salon, my entire body freezes. Bile rises in my throat and the room spins. The Help covers his mouth, then falls to his knees, vomiting behind Selene's overturned chair. I can't look away from the platter.

A severed boar's head, sitting in a pool of thick, clumpy gore, rests on the tray. The dead animal's black eyes stare at me and its snout curls up in deceased distaste. The stench rising from the beast is equally as horrifying as the steady drip of blood running off the tray and onto my lap—but that isn't what makes my stomach heave and my body shiver.

Shoved into the pig's opened snout is a scroll of paper, stamped with the government's seal of subpoena.

I've been served.

I sit on one of the wooden benches that lines the hallway of the judicial courts. The boar's head sits on my shaking lap, wrapped in plastic and slowly decomposing. The subpoena sits on the bench beside me, deeply creased from the many times I've opened, read, then folded it since receiving my summons the night before. Other accused citizens pace the hall, or shake on their benches. I watch them pace and shake; anything to distract me from the gelatinous accusation rotting in my lap.

Loud footsteps stomp into the courthouse—louder than the muttering 'accused.' I turn my head towards the sound, and I'm not the only one. Every lawbreaker summoned that day has been waiting for the assistance we all dread and need: our assigned lawyers, coming to defend our crimes.

Seven pairs of sensibly-shoed feet stomp down the hallway. The lawyers stare straight ahead, not wanting to make eye contact with us—the vermin—until they have to peel away from their colleagues to greet their assigned client. Since I'm sitting at the far end of the courthouse, on the last wooden bench, my lawyer is the last to stomp over.

She's a hard-looking female. She's looking down at me, hard. "You Hugo?"

I nod. The knot in my stomach releases ever-so-slightly.

My lawyer jerks her pointed chin towards my lap. "Which one did you get?"

"The pig." I don't look down. "I got the boar."

My lawyer sighs, then sits next to me. "Oh, that's not too bad." She offers me her hand, reaching over the plastic bag to shake it— hard. "I'm Lib. My friends call me Libby, but you can call me Lib. Your court session starts in twenty minutes. You will sit quietly while I plead your case and you will stay quiet while the judge delivers her verdict." She cranes her neck, scanning the hallway. "We'll be in the small court this morning. You're lucky."

"Am I?" My hands shake. "You sure?"

"I know the law backwards and forwards." Lib taps her temple. "Top of my class at university. You're in trouble, but the penalty for Gluttony is nothing."

"Is that what the boar means?" I nod at my lap. "I was greedy?"

"No, Greed is something different. If you were charged with Greed, they'd have sent you the head of a crocodile. Didn't you pay attention in school? 'Sins Against The Government' is in the elementary curriculum." Lib eyes me up and down, taking in my rumpled suit and tie—the same clothes I'd worn the night before. "I figured someone like you would be familiar with the Sins. You work in business, right?"

"Money management." I puff out my chest. "Foreign finance."

"Right," Lib says. "Nifty."

My chest deflates. I place the severed head on the floor between my feet. "What's going to happen? In the small court? What do I need to do?"

"I told you. I'll plead your case, then the judge will determine the parameters of your penalty. You don't have to do anything. Except tell me what happened." Lib tilts her pointed head. "What did you do that was gluttonous?"

My gaze lands on an accused and lawyer duo walking by my bench on their way to a courtroom. The accused holds his severed subpoena under his arm—the beady eyes and thick tongue of a goat press against the side of his plastic bag.

I point to the goat head, then whisper to Lib, "What did he do?"

"Oh, the goat?" Lib's loud voice rings out in the hallway. "That's Lust. That criminal committed a Lust crime."

My nausea increases as the Lust Criminal glares at me before entering his courtroom. I mutter to Lib, "Way to embarrass the guy."

Lib snorts. "He's way past embarrassment. Lust Crimes are humiliating." She smooths her stiff trousers, then smiles at me. "You're lucky you were charged with Gluttony. Your status in society can survive a Gluttony penalty."

"There's a different penalty for each Sin?" I nod at another duo making their way to another courtroom. "That criminal's carrying a wolf head. What did she do?"

"That's not a wolf. She's got the lion," Lib says. "Sin of Pride. She was probably caught bragging about an accomplishment. She'll have to work in the government's Public Relations department until her Sin is purged. That penalty's cushy, if you ask me. My undergrad was in propaganda, so if I was served for Pride I'd complete my sentence faster than any—" Lib slaps her hand over her mouth. Her eyes dart around the emptying hallway, then she drops her hand and laughs, quietly. "That was close."

"Is that how it works? The penalties match the crimes?"

"Well, yeah," Lib says. "How else should our legal system operate?"

"You don't need to be rude," I say, staring down at my sloshy bag of pig. "I was just asking."

"Sorry," Lib says. "You're right. But representing Sin Criminals gives me anxiety."

"I'm not a criminal," I say. "I didn't do anything wrong. Not really."

"I'm sure you think you're a nice guy, but be real," Lib says. "You're scum, dude. At least, you are according to the government."

"That hardly seems fair."

"Sin subpoenas aren't about fairness. They're about right and wrong." Lib scowls at a female; the accused clutches her subpoena to her chest as she sobs on the shoulder of her lawyer. "See her? That's a wolverine in her bag. You can tell because the teeth are tearing through the plastic."

Lib is correct. Liquified soft tissue drips from the ripped wrapping and onto the weeping female's handbag.

The acid in my stomach roils violently. "What Sin does a wolverine represent?"

"Wrath."

"Wrath?" I can't help but laugh. "She was violent? Her? That tiny, older lady? Not possible."

"Nothing's impossible, Gluttony guy." Lib reaches into her briefcase, pulls out her ArmCom, then snaps the communication device around her wrist. With a swipe of Lib's thumb and a beep from the screen, the ArmCom starts recording. "Tell me what happened yesterday. Go through the whole evening."

"Fine." I pick up my scroll of paper and twist it in my hands. "A date came over to my house—"

"What kind of date?" Lib raises her pointed eyebrow. "Business or romantic?"

"We had sex before the first course."

"That doesn't answer my question."

"It was a romantic date." I blush—the last thing I want to do is discuss my work relationships with a lawyer. "I prepared dinner for a friend named Selene."

"So, Selene came over for dinner," Lib says as she scans her ArmCom. "You had sex. Then what happened?"

"We ate dinner. I got served." I shake my head as I stare at the portraits of Parliament members past and present hanging on the hallway's walls; the paintings are pathetic compared to the pieces in my salon. "This whole thing is insane."

"You're keeping something from me." Lib grabs her briefcase. "This will go a lot quicker if you let me access your thoughts."

I scramble across the bench, away from Lib—shocked. "I hardly know you!"

"I'm a Sin lawyer, Hugo. I've seen it all, so I know humanity sucks." Lib rifles through her briefcase, then pulls out a tube labeled 'eyelink.' She places the clear, circular, connective device over her cornea. "Let me access your memory of last night."

Muttering under my breath, I reluctantly slide over the bench, back to Lib and my rotting retribution. I slip on my own device, then make eye contact with Lib. As our gazes lock, our minds connect. I feel Lib's presence shuffle through my thoughts; she selects the sequence from the night before, then retracts.

Lib removes her eyelink device. She stares at me. "You *are* scum."

I grin. "Not to Selene."

"Gross!" Lib kicks me in the shin. "You should've been served multiple subpoenas for last night. I'm surprised you're only here for Gluttony, and that Selene wasn't served, too." She raises her hand, ticking off a list on her fingers. "You had intercourse with a stranger: Lust. You boasted about your influence: Pride. You flaunted your wealth: Greed. Your date coveted your privilege: Envy."

"What's the animal for Envy?"

Lib points at the second-to-last couple in the hallway: the accused drags a long, thick plastic bag along the ground as he and his lawyer enter their courtroom. "An anaconda."

I stare down at my pig, suddenly grateful for its macabre sneer.

"It's time, Hugo." Lib stands, brushing invisible dirt from her perfectly pleated pants. "Let's go."

"Wait." I nod at a courtroom door closing behind the last accused. The sin perpetrator could hardly stay on their feet, so their lawyer had to carry their animal head into the room for them: a bulky plastic tarp had been wrapped around the creature. "What did they do?"

"Oh." Lib pales. She heads for our courtroom. "Don't worry about it."

"Tell me." I grab Lib's arm. "Their predator was huge. I need to know. I don't want to come back here."

"Oh, well…" Lib swallows, staring at the floor. "Their Sin was Sloth. Their subpoena was a shark."

"A shark?" I stare at Lib. "Why a shark?"

"Oh, you know," Lib says. "Sharks are the laziest predator. They swim around the ocean with their mouths open, eating and sleeping without any effort. The government considers Sloth to be the most grievous of Sins. You don't want to be subpoenaed for Sloth."

"Not possible." I try to regain my usual swagger, but my hands won't stop shaking. "I'm the hardest worker in—"

Lib slaps her fingers over my mouth. "That's Pride, Hugo." She drops her hand, then heads towards our courtroom.

The Honourable Judge Meris presides over my hearing. She hunkers behind her mighty bench like a black-clad walrus, watching me with pursed lips from under her white wig.

Lib whispers, "Meris values efficiency. We'll be out of here in no time."

"M. Lib?" Judge Meris grunts from her bench. "What are the charges?"

Lib walks up to the judge and hoists the pig's head onto her bench. "Gluttony, *Madame*."

Judge Meris sniffs at the rotting boar. "What did your client do?"

"He served an overly lavish meal to a dinner guest, *Madame*."

"Disgusting," the Judge spits through her puckered mouth. "You should be ashamed."

"He is, *Madame*," Lib says. "Very ashamed."

"Hmm. Well," Judge Meris says. "I need to go through your client's records—see his remorse myself. Bring them here."

"Yes, *Madame*." Lib slips on her eyelink device.

The Judge places her own device over her cornea. Her eyes catch Lib's. After a second of electric silence, the judge and my lawyer shiver, then Lib stomps away from the bench. She sits next to me, behind the hearing table. "This shouldn't take long."

"What's going on?" I hiss at Lib. "What did you do?"

"I did my job, Hugo."

"Did you show her my memories? Everything that happened last night?"

"She's watching everything you've done your whole life."

"Lib!"

"It's standard protocol in criminal court."

"I didn't say you could read *all* my thoughts!"

"I didn't. I snatched them."

"You *snatched* my thoughts!?"

"Assigned lawyers don't need permission from criminal clients to access their life story."

"But my privacy!"

"You gave away your right to privacy when you committed a Sin Against The Government."

I leap to my feet. My pupils dilate, my stance widens, and I loom over my lawyer. "HOW DARE YOU—"

Lib pulls me onto my seat. She nods towards the Judge's bench. "You want to get charged with Wrath, too?"

Sucking in air through my nose, I cross my arms. My hands shake within my armpits. I mutter under my breath.

Lib pats my leg. "Cheer up. You've been charged with Gluttony, and that's all the Judge will penalize you for."

"What will my penalty be?" I glare at my stoic lawyer. "You might as well tell me, if it's *so* basic."

Lib rubs her invisible trouser creases. "You'll probably have to give your belongings to the government for wealth redistribution. That's the max penalty."

"My mansion? My staff? My mirror?!" I pout. "Let's hope I get the minimum sentence."

"I told you. The maximum sentence is an easy sentence." Lib ticks another list off on her fingers. "The penalty for Wrath is eight years serving in the military. Envy? You'd have to work in the Department of Innovation. Greed? You'd have to become a pirate, negotiating backdoor financial deals with the Global Governments." Her lip twitches. "Though you might like that. It'd be easy for you to complete your sentence, like PR would be for me."

"What about Lust?"

"They're still refining the penalty for that one but, right now, the government is creating a special department where criminals work off their sinful ways—" Lib whispers, "—using their bodies. I've seen the uniforms they're prototyping. Red, sparkly things." She pats her grey trousers. "Way worse than lawyers' uniforms."

I straighten my rumpled grey tie. "Or business suits." I glance at the Judge's bench; Maris' eyes are still glazed. "What about the last Sin? The worst Sin."

"Oh." Lib shivers. "Sloth. It has the worst penalty. Criminals are banished from the country and forced to infiltrate international governments the Prime sees as a threat. To spy." She stifles a laugh behind her fingers. "I shouldn't find it funny, but it is interesting that the Sin Crime penalties are catered to utilize the worst parts of humanity to serve the greater good."

"M. Lib?" Judge Meris calls to us from her bench. "I'm finished." She tucks her eyelink device in its tube, then stands.

Lib and I climb to our feet.

"M. Hugo?" Judge Meris spits her words. "For the Sin of Gluttony, the Court of Oakland in the Province of Union finds you guilty. Your luxury goods will be confiscated by our redistribution staff and you will never—never!—pursue a lifestyle of excess again. Do you understand?"

I lower my eyes, contritely. "Yes, *Madame*."

"And furthermore—" Judge Meris raises her finger. "If you ever—ever!—commit one of the other Sins I witnessed in your memories you will be imprisoned, immediately—for life! Do you understand?"

"Yes, *Madame*." I stare at my feet. "I understand."

"Good," Judge Meris says. "If you want to stay free, get out."

My metal cutlery clinks together as I eat the modest meal I've prepared that evening.

Selene stares at me from her place across the table. She scrunches up her petite nose. "Hugo?"

"Yes, Selene?" I look up. "Is something wrong with your steamed grains of rice?"

"Nooo…" Selene pushes her metal plate across the empty tabletop. "I don't understand. Where are your things? Why did you move? When did you fire the Help, and how long do I have to wait before you put your dick in my—"

I lunge out of my seat and around the table, slapping my hand on Selene's mouth. "Careful." I shake my head. "That's Lust."

"What the hell, Hugo?" Selene pushes me away, then stands on her sparkly stilettos. She throws her paper napkin on the floor. "I can't believe I walked to this shithole apartment in the middle of downtown nowhere to do nothing."

"I know this place isn't as nice as my home in the suburbs, but Lib—my lawyer—said—"

"Shut up!" Selene's green eyes glitter. "Here I am, looking hot as Hades—"

She did look hot, in an orange catsuit that hugged her curves, though I was trying not to notice.

"—you force me to eat this terrible meal *you* made—what?!—

and now you're telling me we can't even fuck—"

I place my fingers in my ears. "I'm not listening." I start singing loudly over Selene's sinful exclamations. "La la la la laaa! La la la la laaa! La la la la—"

"HUGO!" Selene pulls my hands away from my head. "I'm leaving."

As she storms out of my modest living-slash-dining-slash-bedroom-slash-bathroom, I follow Selene meekly to the door. Not wanting my date to hold a grudge—or accuse me of being proud—I offer her a food box made out of recycled cardboard. "I baked brownies."

Selene knocks the box of pastries out of my hands, and wrenches open the door. She places her dainty foot on the upcycled doormat that covers the stoop, then turns for one last jibe. "I used to think you were interesting, Hugo; powerful and competitive. I thought you were sexy, and rich, and confident—but now?" She sneers at my modest apartment. "Now, I know you're LAZY."

Selene slams the door.

I stand in my entranceway-slash-closet-slash-foyer: terrified.

There's a knock on my door.

My hand shakes as I place it on the knob. I slowly open the door, then look down. Resting on my mat is a giant tray covered with a silver dome. As I reach for the dome, my legs give way and I crumble to the ground. The silver lid tilts off its tray. A toothy grin on a severed shark head smiles up at me.

I've been screwed.

THE ABYSS

4

You know what's the strangest thing about being alone? You aren't. Ever. Not really. I learned that lesson the hard way. I learned that lesson the way Squirrel learned to stay out of the cold. The way Goose learned to fly during the Suffocate season. The way Lizard learned that rains flood and Earth nests get stolen.

I learned that lesson the same way Friend learned that people are cruel.

Cruel feels like too simple a word. Too shallow a word. Cruel is the time Squirrel had her acorns snatched out of her sleeping sack by Goose, who had her wing tips bitten by Lizard, who had his Earth home stolen by the floods.

People aren't cruel. People are monsters. Friend learned that lesson, then I learned the lesson about being alone. I learned that lesson the day the leaves fell. The day Friend was stolen.

Leaves falling is a strange thing. They cling to their branches, attached to twigs, stuck on by… I don't know, a plant goo. I'm not a science person.

The leaves stick to their trees after pushing out of their buds during the Haze and the Suffocate. After that, most of them fall to the ground. Then they all fall to the ground. The winds rise, and one morning the leaves are missing from their trees. They've fallen from the branches, been ripped from the twigs, are torn from the goo.

Except they aren't on the ground where you expect them to be— where they've been every Snap for thirty years. The cyclones have stolen them, leaving nothing but cracked, broken rocks. The same cracked, broken rocks you've stared at every morning. Every morning since you ran to the abyss, Friend's hand grasped in yours, hiding from what you thought were the monsters.

You thought the monsters were the giant seabound beasts with their radiation shooters and slingshot firebrands. You thought the monsters were the behemoths that clawed their way out of the depths of the boiling oceans, armed to the teeth, their teeth arming their mouths, row upon row of scraggly, slanted stickers. You thought the monsters were the Creatures, the species that destroyed the world.

But the monsters aren't the Creatures. The monsters are the people who set them free.

That morning when I stepped out of the abyss, thirty years after Friend and me escaped into the mountains to hide, the leaves were gone. The cyclones whipped up during the night to steal them. The trees that stuck out of the rocky landscape were barren.

"We missed it again." Friend patted my head.

She didn't have to do that. My hair was coarse and rough. Barely hair at all. But Friend always patted my head. I don't know why.

Friend let her hand linger behind my lopsided ears, then she crouched on the ground in the abyss' mouth. "What has it been? Three years? Four? We used to catch the seasonal shifts, but now…" Friend trailed away. "I miss our tradition. I keep forgetting the day the leaves fall. I'm losing the flow of time."

I watched the wind shake the trees' empty branches. "I lost time a long while ago. Longer than I can remember."

Friend laughed. Her laugh lingered. "We'll catch the Snap shift next year. Even if we forget time, I'll always remember the seasons." She walked to the edge of the flat plateau that stretched in front of the abyss—and looked down, down the mountain. "Strange there aren't any leaves that stayed, though. Usually a few are trapped in the cave crevices, or…" Her eyes scanned the ground as her voice trailed away.

Her voice was like music. It felt hot in my old shrunken chest.

I lost the heat from her song a long while ago.

My mind clung to Friend's voice, trying to stay in the moment. I walked to the edge of the plateau, then grunted to get her attention. There wasn't any music in my gruff, guttural noise. "Time to feed the Others."

"Hey." Friend touched my face. "Don't be sad about forgetting. Sometimes, out here, that's better."

I blotted out the image of Friend's hopeful expression—the

hope I couldn't forget, the hope that ate me up inside—and watched the wind twirl. I was wary of the wind: it wanted to eat up my outsides.

Friend's voice carried over the sound of the spinning air, pulling my mind out of my head. "Try to remember the good things. It's okay to forget everything else."

I grunted. "What good things?"

"There are always good things," Friend said, like a chime. "We have shelter. Food. Company."

The wind died.

Friend's voice trilled. "We have love."

"I definitely forgot love a long while ago," I said. "Longer than I can remember." I cupped my hands around my mouth. My cracked fingers caught on my stubble; I hadn't been able to grow a beard since we ran. I turned to the abyss and hollered into the darkness. "YAWHEEEEE!"

At the sound of my hollering, Squirrel, Goose, and Lizard scampered, waddled, and slinked out of the abyss' gaping face.

"Get on." I waved at the Others.

They scampered, waddled, and slinked away, over the rocky ground, down the side of the mountain—following the trail that led to clear water. The only clear water.

Friend tugged on my ear. "You got the canteen?"

"Gave it to Goose last night."

"Good on ya." Friend rested her head on my shoulder. "I might stay here a bit, then. To teach you how to remember love."

"Don't." I put on my smile, the best I could scrounge up. The one I reserved for her. "Go with them. Enjoy the moon. We'll get less glowing now that the leaves are gone."

"Not all of them." Friend knelt, reaching out her fingers.

The wind picked up—another cyclone on its way—and an orange leaf fluttered in the air. Friend caught it then stood, showing me. The veins in the leaf were blue—deep blue, brittle blue. Its short stem was infused with wild, virulent purple.

Orange, blue, and purple. Those colours stayed with me, long after Friend was stolen.

See? You're never alone. Ever.

Friend laughed. Laughed like a song. The wind caught her music as it caught the leaf in her hand. We watched the orange, blue, and purple spiral up and away, over the abyss, over the top of the mountain, disappearing into the glow of the moon. Friend's music brought my eyes homeward, back to Earth.

Friend's face disappeared in the moon's glow. "I should go." She nodded at the trail. "Last time they went for a swim, Squirrel rode on Goose's back and she almost got drowned."

"Good thing you're here," I said. "I'd let them leave."

"You wouldn't." As she passed me by, heading for the clear water, Friend patted my head. For the last time. "You're a good person. And you need us. You'd hate being alone."

"You don't know."

"I do know. I know you." Friend's voice was music. "And you know I'd never leave you. My love."

When I found her body later, mangled by the monsters leading a caravan of Creatures to the water—the only water—I remembered

Friend's voice. When I kissed her face—with the bruises, and swelling, and orange and blue and purple—I thought about loneliness. And when I buried Friend's body—when I shoved it into a deep, cave crevice—I remembered her words: Next year, during the Snap shift, when the leaves fell, I'd be there.

But Squirrel wouldn't.

The thing about squirrels is that they're rodents. Nothing more, nothing less. They're cute—they have fur and fluffy tails—but at the end of it all, at the end of the world, they're just rodents. Flesh. Blood. Bone. Under the fluffiness, they get cold like any other living thing.

I didn't see when it started snowing. Friend always saw. Despite the bitter frost, Friend said snow was her favourite. She used to dance in the early drifts. She'd whirl her arms above her head—singing and trilling—and Squirrel and Goose would follow behind, playing in the snowy paths Friend carved out of the snowy bank with her snowy body. Friend would 'Yawheeeeeee!' to the frozen heavens, her voice bouncing off the mountains' face to hit me in the chest like a blast of hot air. She'd dance in the snows before the ice came. Before the wet tornados.

Have you ever seen a wet tornado? Not the ones from before, not the air and tunneling wind. No. Wet tornados came after. After the oceans rose, and humidity rose with it.

Wet tornadoes aren't cyclones. They aren't wind at all. They're columns of rain, mixed with hail and choking snow. They come at the end of the Freezing—after the rocky ground is covered—and they push grooves into the foothills below the mountains. They push everything in their path.

We'd sit in the abyss, peering over the break—the solid wall where snow ended and sky began—and we'd watch the wet tornadoes push their way towards us.

Squirrel would sit on my shoulder. Goose would sit in Friend's lap. Lizard would hide in his Earth nest at the back of the abyss because Lizard was always smarter than the rest of us. He knew his cold-blooded body wouldn't survive the show.

But we'd watch the columns. We'd watch them push, howling as they moved like a grate of giant icicles, spinning down from the azure sky, coming out of nowhere. No clouds, no sleet—just white, towering pillars that wanted to eat us, inside and out.

Friend would laugh when she saw them. We aren't in any danger, she'd say. The wet tornados split when they hit the mountain range; they always stop after the foothills, she'd laugh. And Squirrel would chirp on my shoulder. And Goose would flutter her feathers.

Then Friend would sing. Flake-a-bies, she called them. Soft, and low, and smooth. The music soothes Goose, she'd say. Do you want to shovel bird poop out of the abyss in the Haze? she'd chastise. When Goose gets scared, her offal is unbearable, she'd admonish.

We learned that the first year.

After Friend was stolen, I hid from the early snowfall. I didn't want to see Friend's absence leaping in the drifts, tossing Squirrel and Goose into the larger banks, lifting her pale white eyes to the azure sky. I stayed in the abyss with Lizard to tend the garden. I trimmed the legumes that climbed the cavern's walls. I changed the water filters so our cells wouldn't dry out. I combed burrs from the bison fur that insulated our sleeping sacks.

Friend was a science person before the Creatures came. She knew how to create things like food, and heat. I kept her science projects running that year. I kept them working that Freezing. I stayed in the abyss with Lizard.

Lizard was a science animal. His job was to manage the finer details of Friend's projects. He and Friend grew our crawling legumes, wove the water filters from mountain weeds, and harvested the fur from the bison that died in droves during our first year.

The sound of Lizard's talons skittering over the walls as he managed the projects used to be a comfort. Friend would sing melodies—Flake-a-bies—to the rhythm of Lizard's skittering. Now there was no singing. I stopped listening for Lizard's talons.

But there was something new. Something fresh. Something almost as comforting as song—the smell of bright, sharp citrus, bursting from the garden.

That Freezing, our pine blossoms bloomed.

Lizard tended the aromatic needles, squeezing their sap into our water. Friend told me, once, that she'd been looking forward to the pine blossoms' blooming for a long while. She'd said the vitamins in the pine would make us strong—help our bodies rally so we could leave the abyss to search for a home.

She never saw them bloom, but Lizard tended the blossoms just fine. Every morning, that Freezing, I woke to the smell of bright, sharp citrus. My water burst with flavour. My body became strong. Goose, Squirrel, Lizard, and me moved with more energy—more purpose. It became easier to remember the good things and force away the bad.

Until Goose nudged me with her beak one morning at the end of the Freezing season. The wet tornadoes were coming. I stumbled to the mouth of the abyss, peered over the break between snow and sky, and searched for the columns of ice. But they hadn't come. What had come, instead, was another absence.

I can say that now. Squirrel wasn't a rodent anymore. She wasn't anything anymore. She was like Friend. Squirrel's body—a miniature column of ice—was what stayed. Her rodent hand clutched a leaf that had survived the Freezing by getting trapped in a snowbank, trapped in the break. It stuck to her rodent fingers. Squirrel died because she held onto the orange, and blue, and purple.

Goose crawled into my lap when the wet tornadoes came. I didn't know the Flake-a-bies, even after thirty years, so she had to make do with me patting her head. Her feathers were soft and smooth. Lizard slept in his Earth nest. My shoulder tingled from Squirrel's absence.

But I wasn't alone. Not yet.

Not ever, really. But I was starting to feel like I was.

Feel.

I could only feel. Thinking was over. Thinking was forgotten, for a long while.

You shouldn't think. It isn't helpful, not at the end of everything. You definitely shouldn't think about the 'why.' Why was my friend was stolen? Why did the rodent get cold? Why were the Creatures set free, and why did the monsters start the chain of events that led to it all being over?

If you think about the 'why,' you think about what you might have done differently. If only you'd noticed the melting bergs. If you'd only paid attention when the autocracy came into power. If you'd only looked up at the nighttime stars and tracked when the moon grew brighter—if only you'd seen its swollen glow.

If you hadn't thought about full hair and shaved cheeks and strong chests and blood pulsing through your wife's living body, filling her throat with song and her hands with heat... if you felt more, sensed more, saw more—knew more—maybe you wouldn't be in an abyss holding a broken leaf in your hands and trying not to remember the thoughts you should have thought when you still had the ability to think.

If I thought about the 'why,' it would've been impossible to feel. And at the end of everything, all you can do is feel. Because if you think too hard—too long—you obsess over the 'why.' And trust me: You don't want to spend thirty years not knowing answers.

That Haze, after the snow melted and the water ran in clear waterfalls down the mountainside, I stepped out of the abyss and into the dim moonglow. The moon was still weak because of the Haze. But the moon would be suffocating, soon.

Still. It was better than snow.

Goose and me buried the rodent with my friend. We threw her down the cave crevice. I couldn't see anything inside the mountain's broken face. The split between the rocks was deep, and the Haze filled the depths of the burial site. The swirling mists made me thirsty.

We left my friend and the rodent to fill the canteen. Goose waddled by my side. Absence weighed on my shoulder, but we made our way to the clear water. The only clear water.

The trail was slippery. The downpour had started, drowning the sky. It would stay for the Haze season. But our thirst for fresh water overcame my desire for dryness. The downpour ran along Goose's back like pine oil squeezed from blossoms; every time we walked under an empty tree she'd shake her feathers, like it was possible to dry off.

Not me. I wore the rain like I wore my nudity. I didn't think about it anymore.

Dripping and shivering, Goose and me slid down to the lake to fill our canteen. I've never once questioned how Goose filled the void my friend and the rodent left. Goose had no hands, yet the canteen was opened. Goose had no arms, yet the canteen got full. After Goose took care of our water wants, we slopped back to the abyss. Me dripping and Goose shaking her feathers.

"Lizard!" Time for my skittering science animal to wake up and do his part. "Lizard, you cold-blooded bastard. The Haze is here.

We have water for your garden."

Goose honked, then waddled to the back of the abyss where Lizard's Earth nest rested.

Had rested. While we were at the lake, a flash flood cleared the space, carrying away our belongings—taking our legume seeds and water filters, sleeping sacks and pine blossoms. And Lizard's Earth nest. And Lizard.

There was no absence to throw into the crevice.

Just as well. The split was running out of room.

In the Suffocate, Goose and me sat. We waited. For what, I don't know. I'll never know what we waited for. Another ending? It felt like something was coming. Almost thirty-one years we'd survived, but we couldn't last much longer—which felt too terrible to be true. We sat in the mouth of the abyss, beneath the burning moon. The biting flies buzzed around our sweating heads. Goose ate the stray ones that flew by, sticking out her long black tongue and plucking them from the air.

In the Suffocate, we waited. Soon, the caravans would come, and we'd have to hide until the Snap. The caravans with their Creatures towing the monsters in their mighty wheeled domes, traversing the countryside looking for water, protein sources, and people like me who'd run.

After thirty-one years, the monsters still sought us out. They had to hunt. They had to force us into servitude, apply the lash to our scrawny bodies the way they used them on the Creatures. The Creatures did their bidding, but the monsters wanted the world to bow down.

She hated the Creatures, but she felt bad for the monsters. Those poor people, she'd say. Think how sad they are inside. They do those things because their insides hurt. Aren't we lucky our insides are filled with love? Aren't we lucky we care for each other?

She didn't know that my insides hurt. She didn't see my outsides either, otherwise she wouldn't have patted my scraggly hair. If I ever caught one of the monstrous people alone, away from their fusion whips, and fusion tasers, and fusion slings and guns, I'd kill 'em quicker than a flood clearing out an abyss.

She wouldn't like it if I told her that.

Funny. When I sat in the Suffocate with Goose by my side, thinking vengeful thoughts about the monsters who stole my sanity, I couldn't remember her name.

Just her face. Orange. Purple. Black.

No.

No, that wasn't right. It was blue. Her eyes were blue, her voice was music.

Her eyes were white.

Her voice was gone.

Goose pecked my knee. I looked up, pulled out of my moon dreams. I watched her nod towards the freshwater trails. Clanging sounds carried up the mountainside: the caravans had come.

Sliding my body into the abyss' shadow, I huddled behind a rock until the clanging sounds went away. I waited until the monsters left. I waited for silence. Then I crawled out of the abyss, into the Suffocate moonglow, Goose by my side and—

Goose wasn't by my side. There was a single feather sitting on the rock, roasting in the heat—but no Goose. Just a feather, resting beside a leaf, burning in the pre-Snap shine.

The strangest thing about being alone, is that you aren't.

I never found out what happened to Goose. Maybe she got stolen by the monsters and was roasted over one of their fires. Maybe she tried to hide and fell into the crevice with my memories and the other one. Or maybe she flew away, stretching her wide wings towards the Suffocate sky to leave me with my loneliness.

But I wasn't lonely. 'Cause you aren't. Ever.

I'm sitting in the abyss on the last day of the Snap, waiting for the cyclones to strip the trees. I'm waiting for them to twist the leaves into columns, denser than the wet tornadoes, hurtling towards the stars, painting the foothills with splashes of orange, and purple, and clear, luminous blue. I sit in the abyss with a feather in one hand, absence on my shoulder, the scent of sharp citrus in my mouth—which I open. To sing.

I sing music. Some song, made by some person. A melody I don't remember from a time I never think about. I sing the lullaby and my hand feels soft. My shoulder feels strong, my mouth feels alive, and my old, sunken chest feels hot. It's strange.

It's strange that after a lifetime, after losing everything I ever had—in the depths of my abyss—that this is the moment when I remember. I remember thoughts. I remember Friend.

I remember love.

You aren't ever alone. Ever.

A LITTLE GOES A LONG WAY

5

I wanted to go home.

As I laid back on my reclining beach chair and stared at the sands that smudged up against the achingly sapphire sky, I crossed my arms—and pouted.

Anna peered at me from under the wide brim of her sunhat, then looked at the ocean and sighed; pleased. "You're such a twit."

"I know." Ignoring the roar of jet engines as an airplane soared across the sky—taking passengers from island to island—I flicked a sand bug off my leg. "You don't need to remind me."

"Sweetie. Baby. Honey. Look around." Anna swept her arm across her swim-suited torso, gesturing towards the multitude of vacationers relaxing on the beach. "Open those sweet brown eyes of yours and take it all in. We're on holiday, honey! Holiday!"

"My body might be on holiday, but my brain is at school." I shook my sandalled foot angrily. A shower of sand rained out of my last-season Birkenstock. "Finals don't disappear, you know. Even when you're in a different country."

"Sweetie." Anna pulled on her cherry-red braid as she pursed her cherry-red lips. "Finals are eons away. Months and months."

"*You're* months away." I plucked the straw out of my cocktail and flung it at my friend.

"Don't do that." Anna retrieved the straw then handed it to a passing server, who threw the plastic tube into a recycling bin. "We're literally in the capital of baby turtle land. Don't be the lady who kills baby turtles. You are not she. She is not you."

"Right now, I don't care if the whole island gets swallowed by the tortoise goddess Enki."

"We aren't in Mesopotamia, honey. You need to brush up on your geography."

"*You* need to brush up on your—be quiet!" I glared at the sea, hoping any goddess turtle would pull herself out of the ocean's depths to swallow me down her snapping maw.

Anna tucked her legs onto her beach recliner. Sweeping her sunhat off her head, she grabbed her coconut cocktail. "Listen to me."

I glared at the sand. "No."

"Brielle?" Anna swirled her coconut. "Listen to Anna. Has Anna ever done you wrong?"

"No."

"That's right. Because I care about you. With my big, muscular, veinous heart."

"Ew."

"Listen to me, honey, and listen good." Anna placed her drink on our seashell table, then leaned over my recliner. Her shadow covered my body.

Goosebumps broke out on my arms—I shivered.

Anna tapped my knee with her cherry-red acrylic. "You're at the top of your class at university."

"So?"

"You have an incredible family that loves you."

"And?"

"You have an ass that could stop a swarm of Bee-bots."

"I only let Evelyn out of the backyard that one time. And she didn't go anywhere near the autohives."

"Ha, ha." Anna dumped her cocktail ice on my belly. "Enough with the 'I have an imaginary pet donkey named Evelyn' jokes. Be serious. Listen to Anna."

As the rapidly melting ice filled my belly button I shot a disdainful glance at my best friend. "I am serious. What's your point?"

"My point, sweetie-baby-honey, is that you have a wonderful life." Anna swung her legs to the sand, her hat onto her head, and her gaze out to the ocean. "You just can't see it."

"*You* can't see it," I said. "You don't get it."

"Explain," Anna said. "What can't I see?"

I brushed the water out of my belly button, then glared at a speck on the sea. A bobbing speck: a floating, fluorescent speck. I aimed all my frustrations at the buoyant bobble, bouncing up and down as the waves curled towards the beach. "Being top of my class means

I'm under a lot of pressure. Having an incredible family means I want to make them proud. Evelyn the donkey was a cute concept in theory, but her imaginary upkeep is astronomical and I haven't been able to find an adequate fake facility in which to deposit her fanciful feces—"

"No 'imaginary donkey' jokes, sweetie. Be serious. Serious."

I sighed. "It doesn't matter if I'm good looking. No one cares if I'm a hot doctor. My professors don't grade my rockin' butt."

"A partner would care." Anna tilted her sunhat away from her eyes. "When was the last time you went on a date?"

"I don't have time to date—and I'm not going to shackle myself to someone who's turned on by killer abs and well-toned glutes. The people I like don't care about that stuff." I flicked away another sand bug. "Looks are fleeting. Asses come and go—except for Evelyn."

"Oh my lord," Anna said. "Holidays are wasted on you. Life is wasted on you. Baby—you need help."

"I need to go home." A brisk sea breeze blew a gnat into my eye. "Ow." As I rubbed out the ocular intrusion, I redirected my ire at Anna. "Since when are you so peppy? Three months ago you were saying your lifelong dream was to become a permanent cave girl. I had to lure you out of your apartment with pedicures and mochas. What's up, duck?"

Anna's lips blew me a cherry kiss. "It's all up, duck."

"But why?" I spun around on my recliner. "You used to be more pessimistic and paranoid than that band that went viral because they killed their lead singer."

"What?"

"That high school band. In the '20s. They killed their lead singer and covered it up."

"You mean, The Slugs?"

"The Slugs, or Bugs, or something related to insects," I said. "You used to be like those girls: The Bugs. You thought everyone was out to get you. But now, you're—" I frowned at Anna's lounging, sun-drenched body, "—you're this. What happened?"

"I have no idea what you're talking about."

"You do," I said. "Over the last three months you've quit your job, started your own business and—next week—you're accepting an award for Entrepreneur of the Year."

"I know," Anna said. "I'm amazing."

"You are amazing, but none of those things are you," I said, grabbing my cocktail. "Not the old you, anyway. It's your turn to be serious. What changed?"

Anna stared at the sea for a veinous heartbeat—two veinous heartbeats—then glanced my way. "I was shown something."

My whole body broke into goosebumps, despite the humid ocean air. "What do you mean, 'something'?"

"I met someone, and—" Anna looked over her shoulder, then at my face. "I met a guy. He gave me something that flipped my life upside down. I can show it to you. If you want."

"Whoa." I leaned back, waving my hands. Cocktail splashed on the fist gripping the coconut. "I don't take drugs, Anna. And neither do you."

"It wasn't a drug. It was a miracle. I can show you." The seaside sun lit Anna's face, turning her cherry cheeks gold. "You could be happy."

I swallowed the last of my icy drink in one gulp—and bit my tongue so I couldn't complain about the sudden icy headache. "I am happy."

"You're not happy," Anna said. "Trust me. You need to change."

"I trust you, but I don't need to change. I need a break."

"You're on a break."

"A bigger break. A break after I've graduated. And got a job placement. And—"

"Honey. Sweetie. Baby," Anna said. "You *do* need a change. A little change. And with this miracle, a little goes a long way."

"But Anna—"

"Brielle." Anna held up her lacquered fingers. "Stop talking." Anna showed me the miracle.

A smile slowly spread across my face. "Whoa."

Anna nodded, smiling back. "You're welcome."

Climbing cliffs is hard. Recreation junkies don't tell you that, but it's true. Fecking cliffs. Fecking hiking. Fecking trip in the Rockies when I could be relaxing on a beach with a coconut cock—

"Whoa! Cleo!"

I look up. Brielle is waving her fingers in my face. Fecking Brielle.

"Give me your hand," Brielle says. "I can pull you over the

ridge. It's a bit awkward."

Grumbling, I grab Brielle's fingers. She yanks me to the top of the cliff we're climbing. No, she's climbing. I'm trying not to fall. Fecking cliff.

Brielle swings her backpack off her shoulders and onto the ground. She takes out a water bottle, gulps down the drink, then offers me the refresher. "Here. Your cheeks are more flushed than Evelyn's when she's busy not existing. You need electrolytes."

"Stop treating me like a child, Brielle. I'm sick of hearing about Evelyn." I slump onto a boulder. It's covered in moss, which stinks. Fecking, stinky moss.

Brielle's deep brown eyes catch the sun. Fecking Brielle and her deep brown eyes. She's always been the prettiest in our group. She doesn't even care.

"Cleo?" Brielle plops down next to me. "Tell me what's wrong. You used to like Evelyn. You've been grumpy this whole vacation."

"Some vacation." With a snarl I pick up a stone. I'm going to hurl it over the edge of the cliff. Maybe it'll hit a goat—or, better yet, a bear. Fecking wildlife. "Anna took you on an island holiday. You dragged me to this frozen hellhole."

"It's 35 degrees outside."

"I know!" I tug on the scarf wrapped tightly around my neck, then pick at pimple that's broken out on my chin. "It's freezing."

"35 degrees Celsius, love."

"Don't call me that." Fecking love. "I hate when you call me that."

Brielle sighs. "I know the last few years have been hard, but did something happen recently? I haven't seen you this gloomy before."

"Gloomy?" I laugh. A trickle of rocks spill down the cliff. I throw my stone after the rocks and watch it bounce down the hiking path. The stone disappears into the aspens clumped at the bottom. "Gloomy is a fecked-up word, Brielle."

"Cleo?" Brielle's eyes go dark—an airplane passes overhead—then they light up as the shadow from the aircraft moves on. "Talk to me."

I grit my teeth; Brielle doesn't give up once she wants something. Fecking persistence. "It's horrible being me. Especially when I have friends like you. And Anna. And Dom."

"What did Dominic do now?"

"Nothing." I pick at my pimple. "Dom's the only person I can stand. Ever since you and Anna—" I stop. I'm not saying another word, no matter how deep Brielle's eyes look.

Brielle's deep eyes sparkle. "Ever since what?"

I snarl. "I knew you wouldn't understand."

"I'd like to understand."

I grind my teeth. Fecking compassion. "It's hard hanging out with you. Anna changed last year—she's really annoying, and you've started acting like her. You used to be kind of normal—not a hundred percent normal—but in the last three months you've gone nuts. You fast-tracked your doctorate, you opened a private practice, and you saved that kid from that nasty deer in the middle of your first international elk rehabilitation competition *and* won the Golden Hoof award while the kid was getting his antler injuries stitched. Dom and I never see you anymore. When we do, you force us to do stuff, like climb cliffs and drink water." I pick up another stone. "Cliffs suck. Water sucks."

Brielle stares at me. "You can be happy, you know."

My laugh is harsher this time. More rocks trickle down the hill; bigger rocks. "No, I can't."

"You can," Brielle says. "I can help you."

"No, I can't," I say. "No, *you* can't. I don't have a charmed life like you and Anna. I flunked out of college, even though I bought the best AI essay-writing app. I got banned from Swindler for posting pics of my cleav, even though Kimmy K flashes hers every day. My ma won't talk to me, even though I've apologized a million times for falling asleep when I was driving her EV and crashing it into that bush." I toss my stone down the path. "I'm cursed."

Brielle nudges my shoulder. "I can give you something for that."

"Give me something?" I sit up. "Give me what?"

Brielle chuckles. "You really want it?"

"What is it?" I clutch her leg. "Is it a new drug? Something only doctors can get? Is it an antidepressant? Or an energy booster? Or a beauty enhancer? Or—"

"Cleo!" Brielle's laughter doesn't dislodge rocks; it's too light. "It isn't a drug—but it is something. Would you like it?"

"Wait." This is too good to be true. "How much is it? I'm not rich, like you and Anna."

"It's free," Brielle says. "It's a miracle. And a little goes a long way."

"Give it." I shift on the boulder so I can hold onto both of Brielle's legs. "Give it to me good."

Brielle gives me the miracle.

A smile slowly spreads across my face. "Oh, wow."

Dominic runs to the limousine. The pouring rain soaks his canvas jacket. An AquaJet passenger plane thunders into BHO-II airport and Dominic hops into the back of the driverless limo, slamming the door. "Oh, wow!" He grabs a towel from Cleo's outstretched hand and rubs it vigorously over his blue-tipped hair. "This is the only day with bad weather, right? On our trip?"

Cleo's clear skin shines in the limo's overhead light. "This isn't bad weather. This is adventure weather."

Dominic snorts.

The limo pulls onto the street. Soon the airport is swallowed by skyscrapers as it recedes into the distance.

Dominic shivers as cold air pumps through the vehicle's vents. "You have to drop this can-do attitude of yours. I've put up with it for three months, and I can't handle it on my only vacation." He glares out the limo's tinted window at the water-logged town. "We're in Old York City, for chrissake. Cynicism is an expectation of the culture. You want us to blend in, right?"

"I want to have a good time," Cleo says. "That's all I want."

"Sure, you do. Hey!" Dominic taps the window. "Did you see that woman? What a click-bait copycat. Kimmy K wore that exact outfit when she was on holiday last year. I hate mediocrity mimics." He spins his blue fringe of hair across his forehead. "People should own their style."

"Or they could wear what they want."

"Or they could wear what they want." Dominic's high-pitched imitation of Cleo is a tad too whiney to be realistic. His tone modulates into its typical timbre. "Grow up. Nobody does what they want."

"I do."

"You're different," Dominic says. "At least, you are now."

"Where do you want to eat tonight?" Cleo places her finger on her temple—her eyelink device flashes and a list of local restaurants appears in the air, hovering behind the limo's front windowpane. Cleo's pupils scan the 3D list as it scrolls upwards. "My treat."

"Doi, biotch." Dominic searches the street for more fashion faux-pas. "This whole trip is your treat. I can't afford your lifestyle." He flutters his sequined eyelashes. "Your new lifestyle, I should say."

"What about KuYu? The food looks awesome."

"What happened to you, anyway? You used to be salty. I miss it. Why'd you change?" Dominic frowns. "Is it the menopause?"

Cleo laughs. Her eyelink list scrolls faster. "I'm twenty-four, you dingus."

"Periscope-pause?"

Cleo rolls her eyes. The list of restaurants freezes, then scrolls upwards as Cleo's eyes refocus. "What about Crispy Canard's? It's supposed to be good, and I've never had French food before."

"Clueless—"

"I'm done with that nickname, Dom. Please call me something

else."

"Clueless," Dominic says. "Why are you acting high? Since the summer you've been granted an engineering fellowship, become the youngest person to smash fifty-three pumpkins in under a minute, developed the cure for chronic bronchitis, and solved world hunger—all while designing your sustainable Klęer Skeên brand."

"I also bought my ma a new EV," Cleo says. "She still hates me, but I'm allowed to come home at Christmas."

"Are you on something? Meth? Crack?" Dominic gasps. "Flakka?"

"Sure." Cleo blinks and the list shudders. "I'm a 1980s business executive."

"Clueless. Share."

"Ooo, Tapas Flagrante looks good. I love erotic dining."

"Clueless!"

Cleo shakes her head. The 3D eyelink list disappears. "Okay—I'll share. But it's a secret."

Dominic presses the back of his head against the limo's window. "Spill. Spill, now."

"You'll love it," Cleo says. "You'll become obsessed. You'll never get enough."

"Darlin', you sold the store—don't smash down the door," Dominic says. "I'll take it all."

"You don't need it all," Cleo says. "Just a little."

Dominic's blue hair bristles as his patience implodes. "Share it, you snark."

A smile slowly spreads across his face.

Cleo beams. "Welcome to the light side."

Dominic sat in the airport, waiting for his connecting plane to take him home. A girl passed his terminal. He smiled at her. A sexy artist-type walked by. Dominic smiled at him. An elderly couple made their way to their gate. Dominic smiled at them.

Dominic sat and smiled, dreaming about his limitless life.

The girl smiled at a man selling magazines. The man selling magazines smiled at a customer buying a packet of gum. The customer buying a packet of gum smiled as they answered their cell, cheerily chatting with their friend.

The sexy artist-type smiled at the server taking his drink order. The server smiled at the dishwasher working her first shift. The dishwasher went home and smiled at her roommate, who suddenly found it easier to complete his schoolwork.

The elderly couple boarded their plane and smiled at their flight attendant. The flight attendant smiled at the captain as he delivered her tea. The captain's heart lifted as she steered the airplane through a difficult patch of turbulence: the plane handled easily in her hands.

Anna received a smile. She showed her smile to Brielle. Brielle gave her smile to Cleo. Cleo shared her smile with Dominic. Dominic boarded his flight, smiling. The smile continued to spread.

A little goes a long way.

PILL POPPERS—POP POP POP

6

Mr. Billings opened the door to the den. Ms. Bifi, Ms. Lactis, and Ms. Breve shuffled past, settling on the chairs that surrounded a long, oval table belonging to Mr. Billings' late client. Mr. Billings gently placed the will on the table and said, with the appropriate amount of sympathy, "You have until nine o'clock."

"Nine, Mr. Billings?" Ms. Bifi loosened her silk scarf. "Just nine?"

"Yes, nine." Mr. Billings inched towards the door. It was inappropriate for him to remain in the room. "My client didn't want his family to be inconvenienced longer than that."

Ms. Lactis rubbed her greasy chin. "We are... his family."

"Must you call him your client?" Ms. Breve bit the tip of one of her long, lustrous, completely natural nails. "He had a name, you know."

With a *bang!* the opened door hit the wall and twelve mourners shuffled into the den, shrouded in veils of grey satin. Ms. Breve squeaked as the veiled mourners stood in a loose circle around the table. Mr. Billings stared at the carpet, shaking his head—he'd forgotten about the Closure Choir.

As one, the hired mourners raised the bottoms of their shrouds, lifting their heads towards the ceiling and wailing, "Poor Longum!"

Ms. Lactis rubbed her distended belly. She glared at Mr. Billings through her close-set eyes. "Will they be here until nine?"

"Yes. Unfortunately." Mr. Billings took another step towards the opened door. "My client spared no expense. They won't interfere with the division of the assets. Just…" He waved his hand limply. "Talk over them."

Ms. Bifi squinted. The mourners stayed still, waiting for their next interjection. A drop of sweat beaded on Ms. Bifi's temple. "This seems awfully impractical, Mr. Billings."

The lawyer shrugged. "My client wanted the best. I had to ensure his wishes were followed for the funeral, during the wake, and throughout his bequeathment. If you have a problem with how the assets are ceremonially divided, blame your deceased friend."

The mourners swayed to the side, then raised their veils. "Poor, poor Longum!"

Mr. Billings rolled his eyes. "The assets are on the table. After you decide who gets what, place your shares in the marked containers. I'll be back to collect them at nine."

"Mr. Billings?" Sweat slithered down the back of Ms. Bifi's neck. "When will we receive our assets? After they're divided?"

"Must you say it… so emotionlessly?" Ms. Lactis huffed.

"Show some care for the departed."

"Poor Longum!" The mourners swayed. "Poor, poor Longum!"

"Nine, ladies." Mr. Billings left the den, closing the door after he stepped over the threshold. It was inappropriate for his client's family to hear the bargaining—they were still in the living room with the coffin.

Ms. Bifi, Ms. Lactis, and Ms. Breve glanced at the oval table.

The mourners stayed still, waiting.

Ms. Bifi picked up the will. "Are we honestly supposed to do this? It feels so wrong."

Ms. Lactis poked her container. "Let's each say which assets we need. How we should... divide them."

"Yes, let's not draw this out. It's bad enough that we lost our friend and club compatriot. I would hate to fight over the gifts he's left us," Ms. Breve said. "Poor Longum."

The mourners raised their satin veils. "Pill Poppers Pop—Pop Pop Pop!"

Ms. Bifi pulled on her scarf. Her raspy breath invaded the silence that filled the den. She squinted, then ran her blue and white fingers through the loose pills that covered the oval table.

Bottles filled to bursting sat beside the pills; tubes and vials, greens and reds, orange-striped and purple-dotted and yellow-streaked and pink-flecked. Probiotics heaped in piles, stacked in columns, amassed in mountains.

The assets.

Ms. Bifi eyed the silent mourners draped in their shades of grief, then retied her silk scarf. "I'll go first.

"Listen. Ever since Longum died, I've been a mess."

"Poor Longum!"

Ms. Bifi scowled at the mourners, then muttered under her breath, "I'm a mess. The biotics inside my body are out of balance. There are too many cons and not enough pros. Without Longum, I'm totally lost."

"Poor, poor Longum!"

Ms. Bifi glared at the Choir. "I need the biotics." She pointed a white finger at the other two women. "And I need them more than you. I didn't want to say this, because it's awfully awkward, but— you both have a lot of privilege. I've had to fight my whole life to survive. And you two are—well—look at you! I need Lon—"

Ms. Bifi's eyes flickered to the mourners, then back to the table. "I need the pink-flecked biotics that belonged to our friend. Just the pink-flecked. I need to balance out my internals and externals. The biotics are my internals. The Poppers are my externals."

The mourners swayed. "Pop! Pop! Pop!"

Ms. Bifi coughed into her scarf, then continued with a rasp. "You two have so much. Giving me the biotics would just be fair. You know how important fairness was to—" She wiped her brow. "The Departed. Honestly? The Departed would agree with me. Longum was—"

"Poor!"

"—totally fair," Ms. Bifi said. "It's not my fault he's totally dead." She sniffed at the heaping pile of pills. Her blue and white fingers quivered. "Oh, this is awful. I can't believe I have to say these things. Honestly. Lactis? You have the most incredible family. And Breve? You have your wealth, your fame, your beauty; all I have is this club. I had Longum—"

"Poor Longum!"

"—but now he's dead and I can barely breathe; my cons and pros are out of balance. Give me the pink-flecked assets. That's all. Then we can keep meeting. Every week. For the club. The Poppers."

"Pill Poppers!"

Ms. Bifi clawed at her scarf. "Honestly?"

The mourners dropped their veils, then turned to the right. In a seamless series of sways, they moved around the circle, chanting as they marched:

> "Pill Popper One seeks balance
>
> "The assets split in three
>
> "To keep the Poppers running
>
> "With fair equality."

The mourners' voices rang out in the corners of the den. "Pill Poppers Pop!" Their voices dropped, barely above a whisper. "Pop Pop Pop."

The Closure Choir completed the circle, then halted their march, turning to face the oval table. The three women stared incredulously at the veiled chorus. The mourners stayed still.

Ms. Lactis rubbed her greasy chin. She belched and her bloated belly fell as the gas released. Her close-set eyes ran over the containers where their assets would be placed—after they were divided. Her name was scratched on the smallest box, scratched in red pen. Her thick fingers twitched convulsively as her greedy gaze counted the probiotics on the table. She was going to get her share. She was going to get the assets.

Ms. Lactis eyed the mourners, then she smirked. "My turn. I'm dying." She waved away the surprised expressions on the other two women's faces. "I know, I know. It's sad. I've known about it for a while. I have a sickness. In my... downstairs place. Longum was giving me the right combination of pills to stop it."

The mourners raised their veils. They lifted their chins towards the ceiling. "Poor Longum."

Ms. Lactis sneered. "Yes. Poor Longum." She shifted her close-set gaze to Ms. Bifi and her sneer widened—large, blunt teeth protruded under her top lip. "I'm not saying this to... shock you. I'm saying it because I need the right combination of pills to keep the sickness small. That's... it."

"Pill Poppers Pop! Pop Pop—"

"Pop." Ms. Lactis chuckled. "Poor, poor Longum." She patted her belly. "I'm not trying to be a problem or... anything. My needs aren't an issue or... anything. I just need the right combination of pills to stay alive."

"Pills!" The mourners swayed. "Pop!"

"Here, I'll line them up." Ms. Lactis leaned over the oval table. "I'll show you the combination so you can see what I need." Her swollen fingers pushed the pills into piles. Her thick tongue stuck out the side of her mouth. "See? Three greens, five orange-striped, and one yellow-streaked. I take them six times a day, every day, and the sickness stays small."

"Poor, poor Longum."

"I don't want to die." Ms. Lactis leaned back in her seat. "You don't want me to die. My kids would be... sad. You letting me die would be... mad. How will the Poppers club keep going if only two members are left?"

"Pop! Pop! Pop!"

Ms. Lactis ignored the mourners. "Just... give me my pills." Her sneer twisted as the mourners began to march.

> "Pill Popper Two seeks living
>
> "Her share divided twain
>
> "To keep her children happy
>
> "And her body free from pain."

The mourners' voices soared:

> "But watch out, gentle Bifi,
>
> "And Breve in her chair,
>
> "If Lactis gets her assets
>
> "Yours aren't going anywhere."

The mourners raised their marching knees higher—their veils swayed back and forth. "Pill Poppers Pop!" The mourners breathed, "Pop Pop Pop." They completed the circle, then turned inwards.

Ms. Lactis glared. Ms. Bifi yanked on her scarf.

The chorus stayed still.

Ms. Breve bit the tip of one of her long, lustrous, completely natural nails. Her thick, voluminous hair fell to her shoulders in waves. She pursed her plump lips, then snuck a look at the other two women. They were lost in their thoughts; Bifi was sweating rivulets and Lactis was huffing at the mourners.

Ms. Breve's lips widened as she gazed down at the pink-flecked probiotics. She didn't care about the rest. Let Lactis take the others, the pink-flecked ones would be hers. She put on a frown. This was a game, and she knew how to win. She always won. Stupid, stupid Longum.

The mourners shifted. Their veils swayed, as though touched by a breeze.

Ms. Breve didn't notice. She bit her nail, then shot a tremulous smile at her Popper club compatriots. "Oh! Is it my turn? Oh, okay. Here I go—I guess."

Her thin voice wavered: she played her part perfectly. "I have listened to you today. I listen every week. All I can do is listen because I've never had disadvantages like Bifi or hardships like Lactis. I have a beautiful life, and I've dedicated it to serving others. If there's a way to—"

Ms. Breve leaned towards Ms. Bifi, the sweating Popper. "Are you alright? You're looking blue. Would you like a probiotic? Try one of our dear friend's black tablets. I always carry a bottle in my purse for emergencies. Lactis, can you grab them? Thank you. There, Bifi. That's better. Poor Bifi."

The mourners whispered. "Poor, poor Bifi."

"What?" Ms. Breve turned to the mourners. She narrowed her black-lashed eyes, then shook her long, lustrous hair. "Where was I? Oh, right."

Her voice wavered. "If there's a way to support both of you, I'm happy to help you find it. I'm happy to mediate, as Mr. Billings has apparently abstained from that task this evening. I'd never ask for any of the probiotics for myself—I'm happy to take what's left over—but I can, instead, see if I can help you divide the assets in a way that works for both of you. I didn't know Longum as well as you did—"

"Poor Longum."

"I only joined the Poppers a month ago—"

"Pop, pop, pop."

"—but—" Ms. Breve's eyes widened as she leaned towards the other two women, "—I grieve just as you grieve. For the loss of our dear friend, our mentor, our confidante—the person we all aspired to be. We didn't say it enough, but our dear friend was courageous, every day: showing up before the rest of us, and putting in more time than everyone else combined. Often, it's the people who give the most that are the most invisible. Well, I saw Longum."

The mourners breathed. "Poor, poor Longum."

"I will try my best to fill the emptiness left in our group—left by our dear friend."

The mourners' voices soared. "Pill Poppers!"

Ms. Breve said, more loudly, "The dear, wonderful—"

"Pop!"

"Enough!" Ms. Breve rose to her feet. She glared at the mourners as she pointed one of her natural nails at Ms. Bifi. "Look what you're doing to her!" Ms. Breve knelt by Ms. Bifi's side, whose face was turning white. "Take another black probiotic. Longum gave them to me to help my breathing. Swallow it. There, there—you'll be fine in a minute." She stroked the woman's back with her talons. "Poor Bifi."

The mourners' veils fluttered. "Poor, poor Bifi."

"What was I saying?" Ms. Breve stood. "Oh. Yes. How I'd like to fill the emptiness left by—our dear friend." She scowled at the mourners as she returned to her place at the oval table. Ms. Breve's practiced voice wavered. "I know I'll never be good enough to replace him. I'm weak, I—sorry. This is hard for me to say."

She let out a flawless sigh as tears cascaded down her flawless face. "I know how my life seems: accomplished, successful. But I push people away because, deep down, I know they'll never be able to accept me. I would love to be vulnerable all the time; share my authenticity all the time. But this world made me hard. It made me bitter. It made me afraid and—"

Ms. Breve covered her perfect eyes with her perfect hands. "I'm sorry. I never cry like this. You must think I'm weak. But—for Longum—"

"Poor, poor Longum."

"—I'll keep going." Ms. Breve dropped her hands in her lap. "Despite the distractions."

Ms. Lactis pushed herself out of her chair. "Bifi?"

Ms. Bifi gasped and clawed at her throat.

Ms. Lactis poked her shoulder. "Your face is turning blue." She looked up, into Ms. Breve's perfectly concerned face. "She seems…"

Ms. Bifi slumped to the floor.

Ms. Lactis growled. "Bifi! Bifi, get up! Get up!"

The mourners breathed, "Pop."

Mr. Billings opened the door: it was nine o'clock. Ms. Lactis and Ms. Breve shuffled past, leaving the den. They hustled into the living room that was now empty of the wake's attendees, though the family still gathered around the coffin as they waited for the bequeathment ceremony to conclude.

Mr. Billings scanned the den, then said with an appropriate amount of confusion, "Ms. Breve? One moment."

The completely natural woman paused on the door's threshold. "Yes, Mr. Billings?"

"Where is Ms. Bifi?"

The mourners swayed.

Mr. Billings eyed them uneasily. Their contract was complete—it would've been appropriate for the Closure Choir to leave, not hang around like ghouls. He frowned, then said to Ms. Breve, "My client wanted the three of you to sign the asset distribution amendment."

Ms. Breve's plump lip twitched. "There was an incident."

"An incident?" Mr. Billings' frown deepened.

The mourners breathed. "Poor Bifi."

Mr. Billings turned his back to the chorus. "Where is Ms. Bifi?"

"We divided up the assets." Ms. Breve inched further into the living room. "When will the containers be shipped to our homes, Mr. Billings? Ms. Lactis and I completed our final obligation to your client."

"There are only two containers." Mr. Billings pushed through the circle of hired mourners. He picked up the will. "Where's the third? Where is Ms. Bifi's?"

The mourners closed the circle, trapping Mr. Billings inside. Their voices echoed in every corner of the den. "Poor, poor Bifi!"

Mr. Billings stood on his toes, peering over the top of the swaying satin veils and trying to get a clear view of the doorway. "Ms. Breve?"

The doorway was empty. Ms. Breve had gone.

Mr. Billings shoved his way through the Choir, then spun around, searching for the third container. The chorus marched in their circle. Their chins lifted towards the ceiling, veils swaying as they chanted. Mr. Billings pressed his back into the den's wall, watching the mourners with the appropriate amount of horror.

The Closure Choir's voices poured into the living room through the opened door.

> "Pill Popper Three craved power.
>
> "She paid the potent price.
>
> "Without remorse she bargained
>
> "And tossed the devil's dice."

The Choir marched faster.

      "With Lactis on her shoulder

      "And Longum in his grave

      "The assets were divided

      "To profit life, not save."

The satin swung from side to side.

      "The Poppers sought perfection

      "With dark, biotoc aid.

      "They sold their souls to Longum

      "With death part of the trade."

The mourners shrieked:

      "Beware dependent living!

      "Beware the cost of life!

      "Beware the terms of vanity—

      "They only lead to strife!"

The mourners marched towards the doorway, hollering as one, "Pill Poppers Pop! Pop Pop Pop!" Their voices dropped. The mourners stopped. They breathed, "Pop. Pop."

After the Closure Choir shuffled out of the den, Mr. Billings shut the door. He twisted the will in his hands, then proceeded to scour the room, looking for the missing asset container; an inappropriate task for a lawyer to undertake.

He shuffled around the room—finding nothing—then crouched on the floor, peering under the table.

Mr. Billings leapt back, banging his head against the underside of the table in the process. As he crawled to the door on his hands and knees, he cursed. Mr. Billings clutched his throbbing head, threw open the door, then ran into the living room—shouting for the family to come!—come, quickly!

This was most inappropriate! Terrifically inappropriate!

In the den, under the oval table, two flat feet protruded. They belonged to a blue and white corpse: the woman who used to be Ms. Bifi. Her face was swollen. Her body was stiff. She was dead from asphyxiation.

On the table sat the containers that held the division of assets—one filled with tubes and vials, greens and reds, orange-striped and purple-dotted and yellow-streaked. The second was stacked with bottles of pink-flecked probiotics. The third container rested on top of the blue and white body.

A breeze fluttered in through the opened door as shouts filled the home which, all day, had suffered in silence. A sigh rolled into the den. It whispered a single word:

"Pop."

KIDS THESE DAYS

7

"Okay, gang. Here's what we gotta do." Faith pulled on the strap of her ribbed tank top as she glanced around Queenston Park.

The girl wrinkled her freckled nose as she watched the drones circling the nature sanctuary's tire swings. Faith's gaze slid away from the flying robots and landed on the public waterpark: the pool was overflowing again. She patted her messy hair bun as she counted the construction materials her crew had gathered.

A shrill cry trilled within the poplar trees that ringed the sanctuary, and Faith looked back at her gang. "I know time's tight—the Theorists have been kicking our keisters all morning—but I believe we can do this. We can reclaim the park. Today!"

The crowd of teens around Faith cheered, raising their sweaty hands in the air and pounding each other on the back.

A shaggy girl with long, unkempt locks pushed through the group, making her way to Faith's side. She jammed her hands in her sweatpants' pockets, then said, "Heya. I don't want to be a downer, but I didn't bring the hammers."

The crowd of teens groaned, but Faith simply smiled and patted the scruffy girl's shoulder. "It's okay, Norah. We'll find a solution."

"Wowza." The shaggy girl—Norah—grinned with sheep-like docility. "Thanks, Faith."

With a low bark, a Great Dane bounded across the sanctuary to plop on the grass at Norah's feet. The shaggy girl patted the dog's head, who gazed at Norah through adoring eyes.

Faith offered her hand to the dog. He licked her palm, then lifted his paw—begging. Faith laughed. "Sorry, Dooby. I didn't bring your Meaty Treaties."

The dog dropped his paw, then rolled on his back.

"Don't mind him," Norah said. "Doobs knows he gets plenty of snacks after the day's battles are done." She smiled at the canine, who was softly whining as he rolled around on the ground. "That is, if we win."

"We'll win. Don't you worry your shaggy little head," Faith said. "But what happened with the hammers? I thought your gear guy was solid?"

"I didn't get to his shop before it closed." Norah shrugged. "You know me."

"Yaar, Norah." A boy with a bowtie clipped to his shirt collar pushed through the crowd.

The group of teens gave way with good-humoured eye rolls; the bowtie boy—Virgil—sauntered up to Faith without too much jostling.

He stepped over Dooby—who was chewing on a clump of sod—then held up a duffle bag. "I found this in my pater's garage: leftovers from when he used to volunteer for Houses By Humans. Look! Bonus supplies, with more hammers than we need. Our apartment building will be assembled in no time." Virgil turned his fresh face toward a half-assembled structure standing beside the pool. He lifted the duffle bag higher. "Furthermore, these happen to be hydraulic hammers. Furthermore, I brought something that will help us tackle *them*." He pointed at the circling drones.

The biggest drone divebombed the pendulum swings, knocking the primary-coloured, plastic discs around on their chains. Dooby rolled to his feet, then barked at the drone until it rejoined the rest of the sky spies. With a satisfied snuffle, the dog settled at Norah's feet.

Faith took the bag from Virgil and pulled on the zipper. "Jeepers!" She rifled through its contents, then removed a long wooden staff. "How is this supposed to help, Virgil?"

"It's for Dylan." Virgil pointed at the back of the crowd.

The teens parted again, revealing a lanky redhead who stared at the clouds with an empty expression on their beautiful features.

"Dylan!" Virgil waved his arms and the redhead's eyes shifted to the boy.

Dylan—the redhead—beamed. "Hey, gang!" They lumbered through the gathered teens, who watched the tall Adonis with admiration as they trotted to Faith's side. Dylan nudged Faith's shoulder. "What's up, buttercup?"

"Oh, you know—the usual." Faith nudged Dylan back. "Saving

society, one battle at a time. How're you feeling, Dylan?"

"Slinky." Dylan's smile spread across their pearly cheeks. "Ready for positive action."

"You're just the person we need." Faith pointed at the drones. "Your first task? Swat those suckers from the sky."

"Yaar. Check it." Virgil snatched the staff from Faith's hand, then waved it in the air above his head. "With your tall frame and awesome aim, those devil-drones will be down, lickety split."

Dylan blushed. "It's always nice when my height can be useful."

Smiling sheepishly, Norah shuffled closer to Faith with Dooby at her heels. "Heya. What about me, boss?"

"You should stick with the Theorists," Faith said. "Their raving rants won't have any effect on your mellow mind—and Dooby can win over the hardest of heads."

The dog gave a *ruff!* then licked Faith's fingers.

The blonde leader called to her team of youths. "Okay, gang! You know the drill. Split into your separate squads so we can battle the baddies, section by section. Squad A—the Unicorns? Go with Norah to the trees to tackle the Theorists."

Faith gestured to Virgil. "Squad B—the Frugalists? Head to the apartment complex and get that building built."

She readjusted her tank top strap, then nodded at the lanky redhead. "Squad C? The Anti-Techs? Follow Dylan and start disabling those drones. The rest of you—Squad D—come with me."

Faith looked across the wide, expansive sanctuary, then frowned at the circling drones, the half-constructed apartment building, the yells still sounding within the poplars—and at a fountain nestled in the centre of the waterpark pool. Sludgy, foul-smelling water squirted high into the air before falling to the ground in sheets, overflowing onto the grass. The earth around the fountain sagged under the weight of the soiled water, which chugged down a series of paths that wound away from the pool and towards a sandy beach.

Faith squinted at a line of tiny, green saucers that floated on top of the chugging water. "We have some turtles to save."

A high voice yelled from the back of crowd. "What are we called, Faith? What's Squad D?"

Faith planted her hands on her ribbed waist. "The Bio-Crusaders."

Dooby barked. The teens cheered, then headed for their various battle stations.

Faith grinned, watching the youths huddle around their squad leaders as they got down to business—then she fell to the ground, knocked over by a woman.

A strong woman. A whip of a woman. A woman in a tight, corduroy tracksuit. A woman whose tight brows stormed over her dark lashes; lashes that framed eyes radiating with hatred.

The woman looked Faith up and down, then sneered. "Watch it."

Faith crawled backwards over the grass. "Jeepers! I'm awfully sorry."

The whip-like woman shook her head, then pushed her way through the remaining teens who scrambled to help Faith to her feet. The woman ambled up a high hill that rose beside the sanctuary's parking lot. She stopped at a picnic table that rested on the mound.

The woman glared at the teens—who ran around the park, intent on their tasks—then she plunked a plastic cup brimming with sugary-sweet Coffuccino on the table's top. Beads of condensation slid down the side of the cup, collecting on the table's surface.

"Excuse me. Pardon me. Oh! I'm so sorry, that was my fault." A stooped woman in a jean jumper maneuvered through the teens still clustered around Faith. She plodded over the ground, huffing as she trundled towards the hill—bumping into Faith, too. The stooped woman gasped. "Oh, goodness. I did not mean to step on your toes. Do you want my number? You can text me, and I'll reimburse you for the damage I did to your shoes—"

"Lissa!" The whip-like woman called down the hill as she sat on the bench behind the picnic table. "What are you doing?"

"Sorry! Coming!" Lissa weaved her way through the teens—carefully avoiding any touching—then fluttered her fingers at Faith as she reached the picnic table. "You can give me your number later. We'll be here a while. I'm happy to set up your shoe replacement whenever it's convenient for you—"

"Lissa!" The whipping woman wrapped her lips around the green straw sticking out of her Coffuccino, then slurped loudly. "That girl doesn't care if you step on her shoes. Her daddy will buy her three new pairs tomorrow."

Lissa watched the teens disperse, then she shot a wavering wince at the woman. "Sorry, Mason. I just thought—"

"Don't think." Mason—the whip—slurped her drink. "You're not here to think. Or make friends with teenyboppers. You're here to help me."

"Help you. Of course." Lissa swung her jean-jumpered legs over the bench and under the picnic table, leaning towards Mason. "What happened? When you called me, I assumed you were upset about your date last night." Her eyes widened. "Wait. *Is* this about your date last night? Did it not go well? Oh no. Mason! Tell me everything—"

"It went fine." Mason cut off Lissa's simpers. "The girl I hooked up with was totally ridiculous. I'll never see her again—but it went fine. No. I need you because I had the worst day, and I don't know what to do."

"Oh no." Lissa whimpered. "Oh, geez. Tell me what happened."

Mason sighed. Her brows relaxed a hair as she frowned at the picnic table. "Alright. So, my day started out fine—"

A drone whizzed overhead. Mason glared at the interruption, then at the redheaded supermodel who chased it.

Dylan's teeth shone in the sunshine, perfect and white, as they loped up the hill. "Sorry to interrupt, but I'm trying to disarm the drones. They're making a heckuva mess down below. I'd move if I were you. Catching copters can be challenging." They climbed onto the bench beside Lissa, brandished a long staff at the flying vehicle.

Mason shrieked and jumped to her feet. "What are you doing?" She pushed the lanky teen off Lissa's bench and snatched the wooden staff from their hands. "You can't play with this here! This is a public space!" She shook the staff. "And this is a weapon! What's wrong with you?" She threw the staff onto the grass.

Dylan watched in dismay as the staff rolled down the hill and into the parking lot. A Volkswagen Mantis pulled out of its spot, then spun over the staff. The domed car popped its tire, and the VW Mantis swerved. Curses streamed out the car's open window. Dylan looked at the Anti-Tech Squad—who were still battling their drone battle, chucking rocks at the flying robots—then said, "Slinky." They loped down the hill to rejoin their team.

"Kids these days are so stupid," Mason said. "What kind of person does that sort of crap?"

"I don't know." Lissa's eyes followed the redhead. "It seemed important to them, though."

"Doesn't matter." Mason wrapped her lips around her straw. "Back to why I need you."

"Need me. Of course." Lissa spun around, nodding. "So, your day was fine?"

"Started fine." Mason glared. "Gawd, Lissa. Pay attention. So, my day was fine. I got up at noon, as usual, then tried to order a new cable adaptor off Shamazon."

"Because the lady you dated last week borrowed your old one." Lissa nodded. "And you can't get it back."

"My date two weeks ago," Mason said. "And no, I can't get it back. And my date wasn't a lady, she was a hag. I'm not going to see her again. Anyway, I was on Shamazon, but I couldn't place my order. Every time I went to pay, the vendor said they were out of stock." Her tight brows furrowed. "I'm heartbroken."

Lissa reached out to pat Mason's hand.

Mason jerked her fingers away.

"I'm so sorry," Lissa said, sitting on her hands. "Did you talk to a Shamazon representative?"

Mason's tight lips trembled. "I called Shamazon's hotline, but I had to wait two minutes—two whole minutes!—before I could talk to a service guy. He fed me some story about a drone uprising. Apparently, Shamazon's delivery devices revolted and started attacking people. That's what he said. Or something. I wasn't really listening. He had this nasal voice that gave me a headache. They shouldn't allow people like that to work in their service department."

"I'm so sorry."

"I know. Anyway, because of Shamazon's stupid drone war or whatever—I think the guy said they were attacking public parks?— my cable was out of stock, so I couldn't place my order." Mason pulled her straw up and down through the hole in the Coffuccino's plastic lid. It gave a *squeak!* and a *squeal!* as she pulled and pushed. "The whole thing ticks me off. It wasn't that long ago that humans did deliveries. I don't understand why they can't do them again."

"Nobody takes those jobs anymore," Lissa said. "Everybody's penning the next screenbuster."

Mason scowled at Squad C, who stood on each other's shoulders to snatch drones out of the sky with their bare hands. Mason whirled her Coffuccino in its cup. "You're telling me those teenyboppers couldn't deliver my cord? They don't have anything better to do?"

Lissa frowned as she watched the redhead shout orders at the tower of teens. "They seem busy to me."

"They aren't!" Mason chomped on the plastic straw, grinding the tube between her back teeth. "Anyway, that wasn't the worst part of my day."

"Oh, geez. It wasn't?"

"No." Mason bit down—hard—and her straw gave a *squeak!* "So, after my disastrous convo with Shamazon, I thought it would be nice to clear my head and take a break. You know, go to Astrobucks and grab a refresher." She held up her Coffuccino. "I needed a pick-me-up."

"A pick-me-up. Of course." Lissa nodded vigorously. "You did need a pick-me-up."

"That's what I said!' Mason slammed the half-empty drink on the table. "So, I get to Astrobucks, order my Coffu, and guess what?"

Lissa's eyes grew larger. "What?"

Mason's lips trembled. "They were out of spicy dolce syrup."

Lissa gasped. "No!"

"Yes."

"That's awful!"

"I know."

"Spicy dolce is your favourite!"

"I know what my favourite syrup is, Lissa. Gawd!"

"Sorry." Lissa's hands twisted in her lap. She picked at a thread in the seam of her jean jumper. "I'm so sorry—"

"But that wasn't the worst part." Mason gazed up at the sky. Smoke trailed from the wings of a drone as it streaked over the sanctuary. A cheer rose from the towering teens. Mason sneered at the noisy youths. "When the barista put my vanilla Coffu into my to-go cup—"

"Oh no! Vanilla?"

"Don't interrupt me. Yes. Vanilla," Mason said. "So, when the barista put my Coffu in my to-go cup, she gave me one of those lids without a straw hole—just a mouth hole!"

Lissa gasped—then paused. She tilted her head. "But—you *have* a straw."

"I know I have a straw. Gawd, Lissa!" Mason slid the straw out of its plastic hole with a piercing *squeal!* She flicked the end of the tube at Lissa.

A bead of drink landed on Lissa's nose.

Mason scowled as Lissa wiped away the sugary frost. She spun the straw in her fingers. "I had to ask the barista for this. It was so embarrassing. She made a huge deal about it, like I was unreasonable or something. She said they don't stock straws anymore. Gawd." She flicked the straw and it fell on the grass. "Now that I think about it, I'm pretty sure the barista was that girl I dated three weeks ago. She seemed vindictive." Mason wiped her wet fingers on Lissa's sleeve. "Anyway, after I spoke with the manager, the barista sent a different caffeine jockey to a different store—downtown—where the staff was smart enough to keep straws stocked. The whole experience took ten minutes. It was traumatic. It ruined my morning." She stared at her empty cup, then sighed. "Not much of a pick-me-up."

"That's awful," Lissa said. "It *has* been a terrible day for you."

"That wasn't even the worst part," Mason said. "So, I'm going through my DMs, when—"

"Check it."

A finger tapped Mason's shoulder. She recoiled, glaring at the bow-tied boy standing beside the table.

Virgil clutched his hands behind his back, then rocked forward on his toes. "I don't mean to be a bother, but I thought I should inform you that we're about to make a rather large noise over there." He pointed towards the half-built building swarming with teenagers. "We're attaching the siding, and our hydraulic hammers make an awful ruckus, so—"

"Excuse me?" Mason stood, yanking on the waistband of her corduroy pants as she towered over the child. "What are you saying to me?"

Virgil took a step backward, then nodded down the hill. "We're building affordable housing. For the future." He smiled at Mason. "This neighbourhood is terribly overpriced, so my squad is creating a handcrafted—"

"No. Not that," Mason said. "I don't care about your teenybopper project. I'm asking what you're saying. To me. About the noise."

"Oh, uh." The boy hesitated. He looked at Lissa.

The stooped woman smiled encouragingly.

Virgil turned back to Mason. "So, uh, we use hydraulic hammers? To put up the siding? And they're noisy, so you might want to move to a different part of the—"

"I knew it!" Mason slapped the tabletop. "You brats want this picnic table. It's got the best view of the park and you're trying to scam it. Kids these days are liars." She scowled. "Whatever. We're not moving."

"Mason?" Lissa leaned over the table, whispering, "I think they *are* building affordable housing. I've been watching them. They've been working on it since we arrived—"

Mason turned on Lissa. "You've been watching the teeny-boppers? I thought you were talking to me. What, do you have a kid fetish or something?"

"Oh no!" Lissa shrunk into her shoulders. "That's an awful thing to say. I would never hurt a child. I was listening to you, I promise, but I was also—"

"So, which is it? Are you here to support me? Or are you here to pick up a bopper?" Mason drummed her fingers on the tabletop. "Or did you come here to tell me I'm an awful person?"

Lissa trembled. "What?"

"That's what you said." Mason sneered. "You said, 'that's an awful thing to say.' Only an awful person would say an awful thing, right?"

"What? Oh no!" Lissa stammered. "That's not what—"

"So, you *think* I'm awful." Mason raised her brows. "Is that what you think, Lissa? Is that why you came here? To make me feel bad? On the worst day of my life?"

"I'd never do that," Lissa said. "I'm here to help you. I don't think you're an awful person. You're my best friend. I think you're a wonderful person."

Mason's tight eyes bored into Lissa's widened ones. Mason nodded, then flicked her fingers at Virgil. "Go away."

He adjusted his bowtie. "I mean no disrespect, but it would be best if you—"

Mason lunged at the boy, snarling, "Get out of here!"

Virgil shrugged, then ambled down the hill; back to Team Frugalist.

"So." Mason sat heavily on the bench. "Where was I?"

"Um." Lissa swallowed. "You went through your DMs."

"Yes." Mason took a deep breath, then smiled—a tight smile. "I did. You know that lighting fixture I ordered from Eurasia?"

"The Modern Flush Six Spiral Ceiling Lamp by Dini Dakini that comes in bronze, gold, chrome, and crystal?"

"Yes, that one." Mason's smile softened. "Thank you for paying attention."

Lissa blushed. "Of course."

"Anyway, I was supposed to receive my chrome light this morning, but the delivery drone didn't show up. I have no idea why. It's totally frustrating."

A flaming drone plummeted to the grassy earth.

"Turns out," Mason said, "Dini Dakini doesn't make the chrome Modern Flush Six Spiral Ceiling Lamp anymore."

Lissa wrenched her eyes away from the drone to blink at Mason. "Dini Dakini doesn't make the Modern Flush Six Spiral Ceiling Lamp?"

"Yes. Isn't it tragic?" Mason picked at the paint flaking off the tabletop, ruined by the water ring from her Coffuccino. "I might have to buy the gold one."

"Wait," Lissa said. "Dini Dakini makes the ceiling lamp, but only in gold?"

"No!" Mason snarled. "Dini Dakini makes bronze and crystal,

too, but those fixtures would be stupid. You've seen my basement bathroom. There's no way bronze or diamond could work with my wallpaper. It has lilies on it, Lissa. Lilies!"

"Of course." Lissa's eyes darted around the park. "Bronze and diamond would clash with your lilies."

"Exactly," Mason said. "So, I have to decide. Do I go with a different brand? It could take hours to find a reputable designer. Plus, I'd have to place another order, then arrange for someone to pick it up—"

"I can pick it up."

"Don't interrupt me," Mason said. "Or do I settle for the gold? I don't know." She sighed. "It's so stressful."

Lissa watched a teen climb a ladder that leaned perilously against the side of the apartment building. His hammer jacked against a slab of siding, then quieted. Lissa picked at her jean jumper. "Why doesn't Dini Dakini make the chrome anymore?"

"Here." Mason removed her phone from a pocket sewn into her corduroy pants. She tapped the screen, then slid it across the table to Lissa. "You read it. I can't relive the trauma."

Lissa scanned the message. With every hammer—and flaming drone crash—her eyes darted to the teens before shifting back to the phone. Lissa pulled on her jumper thread as she read Mason's DM, mumbling key phrases out loud: "...due to inflation... fires down South... political unrest... economic upheaval... chrome no longer in stock."

"I wish people would do something about this global chaos." Mason licked her finger, then ran it across her tight brow. "I'm not comfortable taking a chance on my lighting fixture—gold is so temperamental. Especially with lilies. It might be okay: I mean, it's just the basement bathroom and if I don't like it my parents promised they'd get me something else for this month's moving-out anniversary—but what if the lily stems are a touch too green and the gold fixture looks more amber than white? It could be a disaster!"

"Hmmm." Lissa watched the teens scramble over the apartment building, climbing scaffolds and stapling translucent fabric across empty window frames. "Yes. Someone should do something about our global economic inequity."

"They should," Mason said. "Anyway—"

Yells pealed out from the poplars. The treetops shook, and branches broke off their knobby trunks before crashing to the ground. The teens froze, then returned to their battles.

Lissa spun around on the bench. "What was that?"

"Huh?" Mason looked up; she'd been picking a hangnail. "What?" She scowled at Lissa. "My weekly manicure appointment was cancelled. My nail place shut down. The staff got radiation poisoning from the shellac hardeners. It was a whole thing. Totally stupid. Anyway, I haven't told you the worst part of my day."

"There's more?"

Screams pealed out from the trees again, and the teens abandoned their squadrons to run—en masse—towards the poplars. As the sanctuary emptied, silence descended upon the hilltop.

Lissa trembled.

Mason stared around the quiet park, grinning. "That's better."

The cluster of poplars shuddered.

"So, the worst part of my day was when—" Mason stopped. Water beaded along her dark lashes.

"Tell me," Lissa said. "I can handle it."

Mason took a slow breath, then wiped her lashes. "I woke up this morning and—" She rubbed her eyes. "My allergies have returned. My seasonal allergies. And there's a shortage of tissues at my grocery store. I don't know why. It's totally—"

A roar filled the park as dozens of adults burst from the poplar cluster. Their torn trousers and dirty shirts stood out like mud splatters against the park's green landscape. Faith hurtled between two poplars, followed by the rest of the teenagers. The youths nipped closely at the adults' heels as the blonde shouted words that were swallowed the grownups' yells.

Lissa gasped as a mighty battle commenced. The adults darted around the sanctuary, hurtling insults over their shoulders as the teens followed close behind, trying to hug them. Several kids waved pamphlets over their heads, but the adults batted them away.

A scruffy teen with a dog by her side chased a wheezing adult up the hill. The trio hurtled around the picnic table; the teen shouted, the dog barked, and the adult screamed curse words as they ran.

Mason picked at her hangnail as she continued her story of suffering. Lissa tried to focus on her friend's distress descriptions, but the shouts of the adult, teen, and dog were too loud—and much more interesting.

"—the newt overlords are here—"

"—heya, sir, if you read this information, you'll see you've been tricked by the—"

"—there are implants in our heads! Chips in our heads—"

"*Ruff! Bark, bark!*"

"—I'd love to send you some online resources that might help you feel better—"

"—my life, my privilege, my mine mine mine mine—"

"—in a holistically interconnected society we all support each other's equitable needs—"

"*Bark! Ruff, ruffity! Ruff-ruff rrrrrrruff!*"

"—the aliens are here! They've demonized our nation's leaders! Nole Scent is their pod overlord—"

"—my sibling has a fantastic counselor. I can give you her contact info, if you want. She's reasonably priced and your insurance could probably cover it—"

The trio ran down the hill, disappearing into the larger melee.

Lissa shivered. She wrapped her arms around her body. "I want to go home, Mason."

Mason's jaw dropped. "Were you paying attention, at all?"

The noise echoing around the sanctuary escalated: the teens were creating a human wall that slowly corralled the adults into a clump. The blonde shouted orders, waving her arms and running behind the youths.

"I'm sorry." Lissa stuck her fingers in her ears. The cacophony down below muted slightly. "Oh! Um, yes. I can drive you home. You've had an awful day and I completely understand you need time to yourself."

Mason's expression softened. "Thanks, Lissa. You're a good friend. After you drive me home, can you pick up some takeout?

Maria's Pizzeria is going out of business, so her prices are super discounted."

"Maria's?" Lissa tilted her head. "That's too bad. I love that place."

"I know, but Maria's been pushing pronouns, so—obviously—her restaurant got boycotted," Mason said. "I wish people would leave politics out of real life. It's not like anyone cares about... whatever. Oh! Can you order a couple of appies? And a dessert? Maria makes a killer tiramisu. Or—" Mason gave a tight laugh. "She did."

"And I'll pick up some wine." Lissa scrambled to her feet. She pointed to the parking lot where her electric scooter charged in its power base. "Is it okay if we take my transport?"

"We aren't doubling up on your scooter."

The adults streamed out the front entranceway, hobbling and bent—and each holding a crumpled pamphlet in their hands.

Mason glared at them, then at Lissa. "Go get your car. I'll wait until you get back."

"Um—" Lissa pointed at the sun, which neared the horizon. "It's dangerous after dark. The Warrior Rebellion patrols the streets at night. I heard they're recruiting for their—"

"Gawd, Lissa!" Mason stomped down the hill. "Why do you have to turn everything into a problem?"

The kids hugged each other, then gathered around their blonde leader.

Mason kicked her Coffuccino straw at the teens as she passed them by, heading for the lot. "Kids these days don't take anything seriously."

Lissa adjusted her jean jumper, then scurried after the whip-like woman. The parking lot gate slammed shut behind the pair and the teenagers were, once again, alone in the sanctuary.

"Wow, gang! What a day!" Faith waved at Norah, who hung on the outskirts of the group. "Unicorns? Wanna wrap?"

The crowd turned to Norah, who smiled sheepishly under her shag as she rubbed Dooby's head. "You know me. The Unicorns threw a little kindness at the crazies, kept them away long enough for y'all to take on your tasks, then let 'em loose once I got word you'd beat the drones and slapped on the siding. Wowza. Not too shabby."

Faith grinned. "Not shabby at all."

"Shaggy is more like it!" Virgil shoved his way to Faith's side. "The Frugalists did astoundingly well, too, I must admit. We assembled the southern side of the structure, which means our residence will be ready for occupation this winter. Furthermore, we attached the environmentally-friendly transparent sheets. When the rains begin the interior of the domicile will stay dry."

The teens cheered, and Virgil flushed a light pink. He grinned, then pointed to Dylan. "But the Anti-Techs are the real heroes."

"Dylan?" Faith patted the redhead's muscled shoulder. "Ready to report?"

"We were slinky," Dylan said. "We took down the drones with a bing, bang, boom."

"Yaar!" Virgil clapped the supermodel on their back. "You were right to keep fighting after that woman stole your staff."

"That's what resiliency and quick thinking will getcha," Faith said. "Nothing's gonna stop Dylan's stride."

"Or slow me down," Dylan said. "Feeling blessed about this height."

Dooby barked. Norah raised her dog-slobbered hand. "What about you, Faith? How did the BioCrusaders do?"

Squad D shouted with joy. Faith shushed her team, then patted her messy bun. "I'm happy to share that the rehabilitation effort for our endangered turtles was outta sight. Because your squadrons succeeded, the BioCrusaders were able to patch the hole in the waterpark pool. Now, the baby turtles won't die when Queenston's sanitation system clogs the fountain. The turtles can hatch in the sanctuary, then travel to their ocean home by the natural paths."

Faith pointed at the dry trails that wound towards the beach. A cool breeze brought on by the quickening evening rustled the grass. She raised her hands and the cheering teens quieted, gazing at their leader—enraptured.

Faith cleared her throat. "Now. Today was a good day."

"Check it—it was a great day!"

Faith grinned at Virgil. "A great day." Her smile drooped. "But even though we won today's battles, the war isn't over. I say we celebrate tonight, then take the fight to the capitol in the morning. There's a lot more destruction that threatens our society— like the rising tides, the unregulated rare earth mines, and the hyper-intelligent AiTrolls. But you kids are the most amazing people I know, and if anyone can take on the scary stuff, it's us. So, let's head home, relax, and refresh. Tomorrow's another big—"

"Faith!" Norah pointed over Faith's shoulder, her mouth gaping. "Look out!"

Faith spun around. She gasped, then screamed, "NOOOOOO!" She started running, as fast as she could.

Faith sped across the park—legs pumping, lungs heaving—then dove through the air with her arms outstretched. Her body hit the grass and slid three feet before slowing to a stop. Faith rolled onto her side, then crouched on the balls of her feet. She stared at her cupped hands, which were wrapped around a small object.

Protecting a small object.

Slowly, Faith uncurled her fingers. She gazed tenderly at the tiny turtle resting on her outstretched palms. With a delicate touch— a loving pluck—Faith reached down and removed Mason's plastic straw from the turtle's mouth. She tucked the straw in her back pocket, then placed the baby turtle on the beach pathway. Faith watched it crawl along the trail and disappear into the shadows cast by the setting sun.

The teens watched Faith—horrified—until she reached into her pocket and removed the straw, thrusting it into the air above her head. The youths exploded into happy shouts, jumping with glee.

Faith grinned, then ran back to her allies. She handed the straw to Virgil. "You know what to do."

Virgil gave her a high-five before running over to the apartment building. He placed the straw in a cardboard box with the other bits of found plastic waiting to be repurposed.

Faith smiled, satisfied, as Virgil ran back to the group. "Well, gang? Time to celebrate!"

As the sun set, the teenagers ran into the parking lot. They hopped on their bikes, then sped onto the street. Despite the darkness lengthening behind their pedaling feet, every child felt their hearts lift as Faith led them home. Even though there were battles they had to fight, and a war that needed to be won, they couldn't be prouder to be a kid these days.

SHAME ON YOU, SLUT!

8

I run down the sidewalk, staying on my toes—prancing along the pavement like I'm the prima in an opera. I lift my arms to the side, flitting from shadow to shadow like the dancers in the vids my mother used to show me—before she was exiled. I leap from one concrete slab to the next, hardly daring to breathe, holding onto the image of a graceful ballerina in my mind so the fear bubbling in my belly doesn't rip out my mouth in a scream. If they hear me, I'm done. If they hear me, I'm dead.

It's two in the morning. It's warm outside, even though winter arrived weeks ago. The nuclear lamps hum on their street poles, casting a blue pool of light in the middle of every block. I run a-round the pools, avoiding their edges so the light won't catch me in their beams. I stick to the shadows. It's safe in the shadows.

As I run down the sidewalk, balanced on my toes, Jennifer's bungalow appears in the darkness. Her lights are out—good—and she's left her gate open: once I reach her property I can slip into her yard, unnoticed.

A siren blares behind me. I don't stop running. I don't even turn to look. The Toggletank is on patrol—it's Tuesday, after all—but I've taken the proper precautions. I'm wearing my grey jumpsuit with the hood pulled over my head to hide the shine of my hair. I match the grey stone pavement, grey stone walls that surround the city, and the grey stone Sentinel Towers that stand on every street corner.

I pretend I'm invisible—a grey performer no operettist would ever invent—but even with my concrete camouflage the likelihood of being caught is almost certain. I knew the risk of leaving my bungalow after dark, but running is better than the alternative.

The siren grows louder. The Toggletank turns onto Jennifer's block. I skit across the street and stop, hiding behind the Sentinel Tower that presides over the neighbourhood like the Queen of the Night from Mozart's *Die Zauberflöte*. I press my back into its cold, grey stone as the siren wail reaches its peak. Carefully, I peer around the tower's trunk and watch the Toggletank drive past the row of beige bungalows. The siren's wail dims to an eerie yowl, then quiets as the patrol leaves the suburbs. I pull on the cord that hangs from my hood, hiding my face within its encasement: something's wrong.

The Toggletank on its Tuesday route isn't the typical midweek patrol. The Tuesday tank is driven by a Complot underleader, and underleaders are masochistic perfectionists so their tanks are always clean and polished; they sparkle when they pass under the nuclear lamps. Tonight's tank was dirty. It was dusty, seemingly unused.

There was only one tank in Canuckia's Complot that didn't patrol—because it was only brought out in emergencies. Tonight's tank belonged to Trenton.

He knows I'm not home.

He's looking for me.

"Strumpet on a crumpet," I swear under my breath—then smile at the rhyme. Creative curses come from my mother's vids. I loosen my hood and hurry along the sidewalk, heading for Jennifer's.

Trenton looking for me changes nothing. I knew I'd have to face him eventually.

"Jen." I hiss through the crack in Jennifer's back window: she left it open, like we agreed. "Jen, it's me."

The light in Jennifer's bedroom flicks on—it shines through the space between her floor and her door—then the light goes out. Her bare feet pad across her faded floorboards, then disappear as she heads towards her mudroom. I pull my face away from her window and creep to her back door, waiting for the code.

"You're not supposed to be outside. I can't let you in." Jennifer's voice carries through her door's solid frame. Jen's articulation is crisp, and she projects well—a skill she learned working for the Informers her whole adult life. Jennifer increases her volume. "This is your official warning. If you don't return to your bungalow, I'll report you for trespassing."

I wait. I count to twenty. The wind swirls around my feet, pushing small stones from one side of Jennifer's yard to the other. Jennifer's door opens a centimeter—several centimeters—and I turn sideways to slip inside.

I walk further into the mudroom as Jennifer locks her back door, then sets her alarm.

"What are you going to say?" I kick off my shoes. Jennifer hates when I bring the outside world into her safe place.

Jennifer shrugs, then nods at her alarm panel. "I heard a sound outside. I turned off the alarm so I could investigate. Turns out, it was a racoon. They'll send officers to look for traces tomorrow, but—"

"They won't find any." I smile. Animals are a myth—though the official Complot line says they still exist. The lie works in our favour: Jennifer and I use the Complot's deceit against them when we can. I walk through the mudroom and into Jennifer's attached kitchen, calling, "You haven't reported a rodent before, have you?"

The Complot scans for patterns: too many similarities sets off their security systems and they immediately investigate.

"Nope. We're fine." Jennifer guides me through her darkened house. "But we're more fine downstairs, so stay quiet until we're protected."

Jennifer steers me into her bedroom, then releases her grip. She walks across her carpet—towards her closet—then pauses. There's a *woosh!* of air as she throws open her closet door.

A yellow light flickers inside the clothing locker. I walk towards the light, then look down the long staircase that descends from Jennifer's closet to the secret room underneath her bungalow. The light grows stronger; a pleasant heat emanates from the closet's depths. I turn to Jennifer—and grin.

I gesture to the light. "Informers first."

Jennifer laughs, softly, then nods at the bedroom behind us. "I have to lock up. Fugitives first."

Rolling my eyes, I start down the stairs. The light, and the heat, grow stronger as I step down the wooden staircase and into the bunker our mothers built for us years ago. A fire crackles in a hearth set within the cement walls. My favourite armchair—covered with a pile of my mother's thick, river reed blankets—sits in front of the fireplace, facing the warmth. Jennifer's armchair stands besides mine. It's made of cactus leather; her grandmother made it for Jen when she was a baby. The chair rocks on its base: fortunately, it's sturdy. Jennifer really gets going when her anxiety takes over, but the chair hasn't given up—yet. Our elders knew how to create things.

Shame they weren't able to teach us.

I settle in my chair and pull the thickest blanket around my shoulders. Jennifer shuts the closet door and the room warms another few degrees. I stare into the fireplace flames as my friend—and co-conspirator—descends the staircase and enters the bunker.

Jennifer rocks in her chair. "My supervisor sent me a message. About you."

Strumpet on a crumpet. This is bad. I push the blanket down to my waist as I sit up. "When?"

"Right after you left your house." Jen's black hair glows like coals in the firelight. "Officers are inspecting your bungalow, right now."

"Strumpet on a crumpet." I close my eyes. I can see the fire's flames through my lids. "I knew the Complot flagged me, but I didn't think they'd run a raid so soon."

"Are you going to tell me everything?"

I open my eyes. "I already told you everything."

"You did not. The message you sent me this afternoon didn't say you'd broken any laws. What did you do that caused a raid, Beth?" Jennifer rocks, faster. "And what do you mean, you 'knew they flagged' you? Be honest, or I'm not going to help."

I stare at the floor. Telling Jennifer the truth is going to be hard enough without her wicked stare shaming me into submission. But I need to be strong. For both of us.

I worry the river reeds in my hands. "Just—don't say anything until I'm done. Okay? Don't interrupt me."

Jennifer rocks.

"Jen. We promised our mothers—and your grandmother—that we'd take care of each other. I need your help, but if you don't listen to the whole story you won't be able to help me properly."

Jennifer grunts.

"I know you think I'm being finicky, but I'm not. I'm being—"

"Bossy," Jennifer says. "I know."

"I'm not bossy." A spark leaps from the fire and lands on the wooden floor. It burns a bright, scorching blue, then turns black. "I want to tell you the whole story, and I don't want to forget anything. Your judgement is distracting."

Jennifer stops rocking, then stares at a picture on the fireplace's mantle; one from when we were kids. "She never wanted this for me."

"Who?" My eyes shift to the photograph. "Your mom?"

"Yeah," Jennifer says. "She wanted me to be like her."

"You are like her." I smile at the picture. "You're inventive. And strong."

"Strong?" Jen grunts. "I serve the Complot's spy network—how is that strong?"

"You use your connections to help people," I say. "You only report the bad guys. Integrity is powerful, Jen."

"That's where my strength ends, though. My mom had so much courage. Nothing stopped her. Until—"

"Jen." I scratch the side of my face; my hood is tickling my jaw. "You're brave. Like your mom. And it's not her fault—or yours— that she was exiled."

Jennifer's eyes gleam in the firelight. "It's the government's."

"Yes." I nod towards the photo, where Jen and I stand with our once-happy family. "And I don't want to be exiled either, so…" I sit taller, straight and steady. I can be brave, too—like Jen, and our elders. I can tell my friend the whole truth. "Yesterday morning I was at school, helping my class get into their recess gear. You know how hard it is to fit eighty six-year-olds into daytime pollutant protectors. I was distracted."

Jennifer stays quiet, rocking in her chair.

I look back at the photograph, at my mother's defiant face. "So, I'm in the middle of shoving Buster Nightingale's arm into his raincloak when Isaac walks into my classroom."

"Isaac?" Jennifer's voice rises an octave. "Why?"

"You said you wouldn't interrupt."

"No, I didn't." Jennifer's voice settles into her typical alto range.

"But, sorry. Keep going."

"So, Isaac comes into my classroom." I grin—I can't help it. "Picture this, Jen: Buster's squirming in my right hand, his cloak is in my left, I've got seventy-nine other kids in various stages of undress, and the good old principal himself waltzes into my room like he visits every day."

"Instead of once a year when he evaluates your teaching to find reasons not to promote you."

"Exactly," I say. "But I wasn't worried about a promotion—for once. I wasn't even worried about how unprofessional I looked with the kids yelling, and hitting each other with their gamma ray gloves, and running around the classroom like Bot-hunters—"

"That's not unprofessional," Jennifer says. "That's education."

"Exactly." Heat spreads up my neck and sets my ears on fire—hotter than the embers in the hearth. This is the moment I've avoided: telling Jen the truth. "Anyway, I wasn't worried about that normal stuff; salaries, or screaming students, or Buster Nightingale's arm. When I messaged you after work, I told you I'd been fired."

Jennifer grunts.

My vision blurs as I force out the next sentence. "Yesterday was the first Monday of the month, so we were allowed to wear our—"

"Casual uniforms." Jennifer's chair stops creaking on its rocker. "Oakland public employees can wear their jumpsuits."

"Exactly," I say, blinking rapidly. "So, I wore my jumpsuit, except—" I stare at the hardwood floor, trying to clear my eyes. I don't know if I can say this.

Jennifer's hand grabs mine. Her grip is mild. "Except what?"

I look up. "The last time I wore my casual uniform it got dusty on the walk home, so I washed it. I didn't realize, but the fabric shrunk. A little. So, the pants were a little short. And when I was kneeling on the ground, helping Buster—" I sigh. "I exposed the skin between the cuff of my boot and the hem of my pant leg."

Jennifer hisses. She lets go of my hand. "No."

"Yes." Tears stream down my cheeks. "I'm so sorry, Jen. Because Isaac was there—"

"He had to fire you." A growl rolls out of Jennifer's body: a growl of shame. "Which was the right thing to do."

"Jen!" I scrub the tears off my cheeks. "Please don't be angry with me. I didn't want this to happen—"

"Stop it." Jennifer purses her lips. She speaks out the side of her mouth. "This is just like you. You've always been irresponsible. You break bylaws all the time. You never arrive for the Purity Checks fifteen minutes early, you don't keep your eyes on the ground when Complot Members are present, you wear your hair untied during Bondage Week, and you always—always!—forget that Informers are watching us." She hits the arm of her chair with her fist. "Damn it, Beth! I knew you'd be the death of me. Before my mom was exiled, she warned me you'd be the one to get us in trouble—"

"Jen!" I leap to my feet, shaking with anger. "I don't break bylaws on purpose, and I would never intentionally put you in danger. I didn't mean to shrink my uniform. I don't want to be flagged—it's humiliating. If you don't get that, you don't have to help me." I throw my blanket on the floor, then stalk towards the staircase. "We've been careful—nobody knows we're friends. I can leave here now, and you'll never see me again."

"Beth." Jennifer is on her feet, beside me. She grabs my shoulder. "Stop. I'm sorry I judged you. I want to help."

I believe Jennifer's being honest—if only to get me out of her house so she can go on with her uncomplicated life.

"I don't need a lot," I say. "I just need one of your contacts to take me to a safe place, outside the city. I don't know anyone with your connections."

"What about Trenton?"

I walk back to the fire, then sink into my chair. "Who do you think ordered the raid, Jen?"

Jennifer shakes her head and falls onto her rocker. "So that *was* his tank I saw earlier."

"Yup."

"I told you not to date a cabinet member."

"You told me *to* date a cabinet member, Jen. You said it would be helpful to have someone in the government looking out for me."

"I told you to become a Slut for a Member, not date a Member. Those are very different things."

"Well, too late. We dated, I fell in love, and he betrayed me. He chose his position over real intimacy."

"Of course he did." Jennifer tucks her legs up onto her chair. "This isn't one of your mother's opera vids, Beth. We don't live in a world with dancers, and heroes, and happily-ever-afters."

I bite my lip—I hate when Jen shames me. Quiet consumes the

bunker, broken only by the snap of the fire and squeaking rocking chair. I squirm in my seat. The only thing I hate more than Jen's shame is her silence.

So, I break it. "I wish we lived in one of my mom's opera vids. Each one told a different story about a different world, filled with endless possibilities."

"Your operas aren't real, Beth," Jennifer says. "They were filmed a hundred years ago."

"But they felt real, when I watched them." I stare at my mother's face, smiling confidently in the photo on the mantle. "My mom used to tell me that human originality stopped existing before she was born, but human possibility—our choices—meant it was impossible to repeat ourselves. My mother had countless vids about ballerinas—dozens of stories about music, and theatre, and the stage—and they never played the same way twice; their endings were variations on a theme."

The fire snaps. I cradle my mother's blanket in my arms. "The Complot controls our lives—the government tells our story—but that doesn't mean we shouldn't try to change how it plays. We're more than servants, Jen. We could find a happily-ever-after." I smile at my friend, then reach for her hand. "We can choose—to try."

Jennifer doesn't take it. "We don't have choice, Beth. We'll never be free. There's just us. And Canuckia's Complot. That's never going to change, no matter what we do."

The fire crackles. We stare into the flames.

"Then I have to leave," I say. "But how?"

Jen untucks her legs. "*We* have to leave."

I sit up. "What?"

"You're right," Jen says. "I'm sick of curtsying to the Complot. I'm done being an Informer. I want out, too."

"Yay!" I leap to my feet and run to my friend, giggling as I wrap her in a hug. "You mean it?"

"Absolutely," Jen says. "With my connections, escaping will be a piece of cake."

"I love you!" I squeeze Jen tightly. "Yes, let's eat cake."

She squirms in my grip. "First things first, Beth."

"Right." I let her go. "I'm excited."

"Uh huh." Jen grins. "Here's what we have to do. You need to become comfortable with uniformity. I'm happy to leave the country, but I don't want to challenge my Canuckian values." She tugs on my sleeve. "No exposed skin, no looking for real romance, and no sex without a bigger agenda. Got it?"

"Deal." I squeal, then hop up and down. "What next?"

"I'm going to message Isaac. He's tired of being shamed, too."

"Isaac?" I shake Jen's shoulder. "My principal, Isaac? The male who fired me?"

"Yes, Isaac. He's an educator, *and* an Informer. And my friend," Jen says. "Between the two of us—"

"Three of us."

"Three of us," Jen says. "With Isaac's status, my connections, and your spirit, we can get out of here."

"How?"

"We're leaving," Jen says. "Tonight. There's an asylum on Oakland's southern border that houses dissenters, like us. It isn't the nicest place; the supplies are minimal and the accommodations—well, they're different—but the Complot doesn't know about it."

"That's amazing!" I jam my hands on my hips. "How come you never told me about this asylum?"

"In addition to the giant list of bad habits you perform on a regular basis, you can't keep secrets."

I blush. "So, you still haven't forgiven me for letting it slip in my staff meeting that you thought Isaac's thighs were juicy?"

"There's a time and place for advances, Bethany. I was making progress with Isaac before you—" Jen purses her lips. "Never mind. It doesn't matter now. Isaac and I are fine being friends. He'll lend us a coptercyle so we can fly over Trenton's Toggletank." She starts for the stairs. "You pack while I message him on the Informers private channel. As soon as Isaac gets my code, he'll head here. We need to be ready."

I wave my hand in assent, and Jen disappears through the closet door. I hear her footsteps walking across the floor above my head—she's in her bedroom, she's moving into her kitchen, she's heading for her office...

Her steps stop. Jen must be messaging Isaac.

I gaze around our basement shelter. Years of conversations happened down here, planning for a future neither one of us thought was possible. We reminisced about the days when our mothers were still with us. We commiserated over failures we hoped one day wouldn't get us into irreparable trouble.

Trouble had arrived, but Jen and I were going to be okay. The two of us were going to get out of there. We could change. We could

escape. We just had to try—

Jennifer rocks her chair. "This isn't an opera vid, Beth. There aren't heroes, and happily-ever-afters. The Complot controls everything. That's never going to change."

The fire crackles. "How do I get out of here?"

"There's an asylum," Jennifer says. "A place where you'll be safe."

"A what?" I rise out of my chair. My mother's blankets fall to the floor. "Why didn't you tell me about this?"

"Do you want the long explanation, or do you want to leave?" Jennifer's face blazes in the light from the fire. "I promised I would help you, Beth, but we don't have much time." She paces back and forth across the bunker. "For the past few years, groups of dissenters have been quietly leaving the city and building a refuge along Oakland's southern border. They created a sort of basic paradise. It isn't much—there's still lots of work to do—but it's safe. People aren't forced into Slutitude when they break laws." She stops pacing, then smiles at me. "You can be who you want to be—you can be free."

"That's incredible." I can hardly believe it. "You'll take me there?"

"Isaac will take you there." Jennifer grins as I lift my hand to my mouth: shocked. "Isaac's an Informer, too. He isn't the classiest male, but you can trust him. But I need to stay here. I'm in this too deep. If you disappear and I disappear, the Complot will know something big is happening behind the scenes. I'm one of their top Informers, after all."

"You want me to leave you?" I take a step towards my friend. "After all this time?"

"I don't want us to separate, but the second you exposed your ankle, your life here was over," Jennifer says. "You know that. As much as I hate the hypocrisy within Canuckian society, I have to abide by it. I have to follow the rules. And you need to follow Isaac."

Isaac and I walk along the grey sidewalk, close to the wall that rings Oakland. My principal is a short, round male who looks a lot like my mother—if she were twenty years younger and comfortable groping the asses of her staff.

I bat my ex-supervisor's hand off my rear for the third time since Jen led me to the Sentinel Tower where Isaac was waiting. He looks at me as we trundle along the sidewalk: a smirk fills his round face. "You're pretty when you aren't surrounded by a hoard of screaming children. Did you know that?"

I watch the ground. I watch my feet stepping one in front of the other. "So I've been told."

"Sure you have," Isaac says. "A lot, I bet."

"Where is this asylum?" I walk close to the wall, away from Isaac. His leering grin makes my stomach churn. "Jen said it was somewhere safe."

"It's more than safe," Isaac says. "It's outside of Complot control."

We pass another Sentinel Tower. Isaac uses the forced proximity to 'accidentally' brush my butt again.

I slap his hand away and my cheeks burn red—my face cheeks, not my behind. Educators were exempt from having to Slut, but now that I'm fired—and flagged—I'm fair game. Still, I try to fend off Isaac. "I'm leaving. I can't Slut for you."

Isaac chuckles as we continue down the walkway. "There's plenty of time, and plenty of dark corners, before we reach the asylum."

He's wrong: there isn't time for after-dark escapades. Before leaving, Jen told me I had to reach the asylum before sunup, and the sky is already starting to turn a misty grey—like my hooded uniform that covers my body from ankles to eyes.

I pinch Isaac's wandering hand. "Seriously. Stop."

"Come on, Slut." The word slides out of Isaac's round mouth. "Don't you want one last chance to serve your superior?"

"I'm good, thanks."

"Alright, Slut."

Along with being a service job—and punishment—'slut' is a term of endearment in Canuckia. Even though Isaac's using the word as a compliment, it makes my skin crawl. Luckily, we're nearing a door, set in the wall. It's small and muddy brown—hard to see—but, as we draw closer, Isaac slows.

I stop. "This is it?"

"Nice, huh?" Isaac places his hand on the door's knob. "Looks like a maintenance closet."

It does look like one of the dozens of Complot closets built within the wall. "The asylum is in there?"

"Sure is, Slut." Isaac turns the knob. "But don't take my word for it. See for yourself."

He opens the door. I step over the threshold, and my breath catches in my throat. Isaac waves at me before he shuts the door, enveloped by the boundaries of the city. Hopefully forever.

I grin.

The asylum is incredible. Colourful streets with brightly lit carriages trundle past. Jovial 'hello's reach my ears. The smell of baking bread and stone-cooked whitefish wafts on the wind. A female dressed in a pink, knee-length skirt and a yellow tunic jogs out of a two-story home and across the street, heading my way. Her smile is as bright as the day and her chin is held high. I like her instantly.

"You must be Beth!" The female raises her hand as she reaches me. "Let's get you out of that drab old uniform and into something fun, okay? We want you to feel your absolute sluttiest while you're with us."

Despite the slur being used in this new world, my heart pounds —with hope. The people in the asylum are filled with energy and purpose. They're different.

This place is different. Here, my life could finally cha—

Jen stands. "This isn't a vid, Beth. Our lives will never change."

The fire crackles. "How do I get out?"

"There's an asylum." Jen turns and her face disappears in

shadow. "Isaac can take you there. Don't ask questions." She holds up her finger. "Do you trust me?"

I nod.

"Good." Jen heads for the stairs. "Pack your things. Isaac will explain on the way."

Isaac and I walk along the grey sidewalk, close to the wall that rings Oakland. Isaac glances at me, and sneers. "You're pretty, Slut. Did you know that? Slut?"

I watch the ground. "Yup. I've been told that. A few times."

"Sure you have." Isaac snickers. "Being pretty will help you a lot in the asylum. You're lucky. Slut."

"Where is the asylum?" I walk close to the wall, away from Isaac. His leering grin makes me sick. "Jen said it was safe?"

Isaac chuckles. "Jen doesn't know everything."

We near a door in the wall. I expected something hidden, out of sight, but this copper monstrosity is anything but discreet. Its audacity flips my stomach.

I stop in front of the door. "What do you mean, 'Jen doesn't know everything'? Where are we?"

The door opens. My principal steps behind me, then pushes me through the opening. The copper door slams shut. Rough hands grab me from behind. I try to scream, but soft fingers cover my mouth.

"Hey, Bethy." Trenton's smooth voice whispers in my ear. "I missed you."

I squirm in my ex-lover's embrace.

He chortles; his breath is hot and heavy. "Finally, a place where you belong. Slut."

My eyes take in the room behind the door—the room within the wall. Underneath wire-strung lamps, rows of metal tables line the space. Behind the tables sit half-naked citizens. Pasties cover their nipples. Thongs stretch over their hips and wind around their bottoms. The citizens work in unison—in tandem—oblivious to the newcomer in their midst. They sew as one: stitching, pulling, threading. Working on a pile of grey fabric. They're making uniforms. Grey uniforms.

My eyes widen. "What is this?"

Trenton presses a set of pasties and a bright red thong into my hands. He steers me towards the nearest table. "This, Bethy, is your new life. Hope you're ready for a chang—

Jennifer stands, then walks towards the fireplace. She flips over the picture of our family so it lies face down on the mantle. "This isn't one of your mother's vids, Beth. Canuckia isn't going to change."

The fire crackles. "How do I get out?"

"You don't." With a *bang!* the closet door bursts open and a horde of males trundle down the stairs. Within seconds, Jennifer and I are handcuffed together and standing in the middle of a ring of officers, back-to-back.

I pull on the restraints, then stop as Jen gives a startled shriek. "Sorry." I press my back into my friend. "I'm so sorry, Jen."

"Save your sorries for someone who cares." A pair of heavy beige boots clomps down the staircase, followed by beige-clad legs, a gleaming beige belt, a formal buttoned shirt, and a trim waist under thin shoulders—all attached to a familiar face.

"Trenton." I snarl through gritted teeth. "You crumpety strumpet."

"Hey, Sluts." Sneering, Trenton pushes through the officers, then places his soft finger on my chin. "You're looking well, Bethy."

"Let us go." I jerk my head away from Trenton's all-too comfortable touch. The back of my head hits Jen's; we both yelp.

Trenton moves his finger to caress his neatly trimmed beard as his eyes scan our cuffed wrists. "Jennifer. I expected more from you. Beth has been on our watch list for weeks—we knew she was close to breaking a major infraction—but I had no idea you were working with her."

"Shut up, Trenton."

"No, Jen. Don't." I wrench my head around so I can see my friend. "Don't say anything. Let me tell him the truth." I glare at Trenton, who's watching my fractured movements through his gentle eyes.

Even though I hate him, the impulse to stay lost in his gaze consumes my feelings: the attraction is so strong.

I bite my lip—hard—to break my ex-lover's manipulative spell. "Jen and I hardly know each other. I broke into her bungalow when she was asleep. I was trying to find a private channel so I could secretly communicate with the Southern Shelter, an asylum for people trying to escape this horrible city. You and your officer friends don't know what you're doing. Jen isn't part of this."

"Oh, really." Trenton clomps over to the fireplace. He picks up the framed picture, then shoves it in my face. "You two look like you know each other here."

"Beth—"

"Be quiet, Jen!" I take a deep breath. "I can explain. We were friends when we were little. A long time ago. That's how I knew she lived here. But we haven't spoken in years. You're making a mistake."

"Beth." Jennifer groans. "Stop."

I wrench my head around to yell in Jen's ear. "They are!" I lean towards Trenton. "You are. You don't know what you're talking a-bout. Take me, leave her. She's innocent."

The light from the fire dances in Trenton's eyes. He doesn't blink, doesn't move. Then his fingers snap, and an officer steps out of the circle.

Trenton addresses his underleader. "Do you know who this is?" He jabs the image of Jennifer's mother.

The underleader nods, curtly. "Yes."

Trenton sneers. "Who is she?"

The underleader nods at the picture. "That is Slut 735. We took her into custody in 2117 and she's been serving His Majesty's Royal Autocracy ever since."

"Thank you." Trenton's finger moves to the side. "And who is this?"

"That is Slut 741," the underleader says. "We took her into custody shortly after Slut 735."

"And who is this?" Trenton's smile grows as his finger slides again. "Who is this female?"

"The elder standing between the two girls started service in His Majesty's Royal Autocracy in 2107. She served as a Member Slut until her retirement in 2120."

Trenton drops the photograph on the ground. The glass shatters on the worn wooden floor.

"Your grandmother's Member wore her out, Jenny. But both of your mothers are still going strong." Trenton hits the side of the fireplace with his fist. A panel pops open, revealing a camera stamped with the crest of the Complot. He chuckles. "We've known about your family for years—and your mom *is* powerful, like you said. She's been a strong Slut. For years."

"No!" Jennifer wiggles in the cuffs, pulling me to the side. "You're lying! My mom isn't a Slut, she would never serve you! She was exiled after exposing her wrist at a Chastity Ceremony in 2117! Beth's mother told us! And my grandmother died in the aftershock from the Comet! How dare you say she was a Member's Slut! How dare you say she retired! How *dare*—"

Trenton backhands Jennifer's face. Blood spurts from her mouth. It sprays across her mother's rocking chair, staining the cactus leather. Jen spits, and a tooth lands on the rocker. She looks up, then smirks at Trenton through her red-stained mouth. "So… I'm going into service, too?"

Trenton starts to laugh. His laugh turns into a roaring guffaw as the officers in the circle join the raucous mocking. The laughter lasts a long time before Trenton raises his hand, cutting it off.

"That's right, Jenny." Trenton grabs our cuffs, dragging Jen and me to the foot of the staircase. As he pushes us up the steps, Trenton leans over and breathes in my ear. "You've both got reunions with mommy to look forward to. The other Sluts will love hearing *that* story."

Trenton drags us out of Jennifer's bungalow and throws us into his dusty Toggletank. He drives us out of the city's suburbs, to the business district—the heart of Oakland. Jen and I stay silent the entire trip. Even when we're pulled from the tank and hustled into His Royal Majesty's palace—the Royal Offices of the Autocracy— we keep our mouths shut.

There's nothing to say.

"Beth?" An elderly servant stumbles down the palace hallway.

The Royal Offices of the Autocracy drip with signs of wealth— gold leaf instruments, white marble poetry scrolls, plinths topped with nude sculptures of Wagner, Stravinsky, Verdi, and Gershwin. The elderly servant is naked, like the statues, except for a red, spandex toga draped loosely around her shrunken body.

Still held in the grip of the underleader who escorted me and Jen into the palace, I stop at the sight of the broken female. "Mom?"

My mother reaches out her hand. "Bethany." Her spandex shines under the red-tinted light of the Complot's shaded lamps.

The officer slaps my mother's hand away. He shoves her out of my reach. "Don't you have duties to attend to, Slut 741?"

"Yes, sir. My apologies." The elderly female—my mother— stumbles away. She staggers up the palace hallway and around a corner.

Tears fill my eyes as I whisper to Jennifer, "Your mom must be here, too."

"Shut up, Slut 1805." The officer pushes me and Jennifer into a room that branches off the main hallway. Once inside, he drops our cuffed wrists, then marches over to a gilded cabinet. He removes two wrapped parcels from the cabinet, then tosses them at us.

I open my parcel. Diamond-studded nipple pasties and a jewel-encrusted thong fall into my opened palms. I blink the tears from my eyes. "What are these?"

"Your uniform, Slut 1805." The officer unlocks our cuffs, then marches into the hallway, calling, "After you and Slut 1806 dress in your new attire, report to the Head Slut's headquarters for your service detail."

I look at Jennifer, who's staring at the crimson clothing in horror. I shrug, then unzip my grey jumpsuit. "Could be worse."

Jennifer looks up. "Could be worse?" She shakes the sparkly thong. "We are Sluts for the Complot!"

"You always tell me sex can be useful." I slide my jumper off my hips, then step out of the suit. I peel the sticky backing off one of pasties and press the diamond accessory onto my nipple. I attach the second pastie, then turn my bared breasts towards Jen. "This isn't so bad. Our moms are here, and your grandmother is alive…" I shake my shoulders; a comical shimmy. Jen looks like she could use a laugh.

The pasties catch the light from the room's chandeliers and spatter red dots across Jennifer's grey uniform.

I shrug again. My new uniform jiggles. "What's the problem? These are better than the casual jumpers. I won't be shrinking this uniform any time soon." I grin as Jen's jaw drops. "Even if I did, I doubt I'd get fired. I'd probably get promoted."

Jennifer shakes her head, then groans.

I bend over, step into the jeweled thong, then strike a pose—hip cocked, arm raised, breasts and pelvis jutting forward. I feel great. "Of all the ways our lives could've changed, this isn't so bad."

A gurgling sound erupts from Jen's throat. Her face turns red, redder than my G-string. "It *is* bad, Beth. Really bad—

Jen tucks her legs onto her grandmother's chair. "Our lives aren't one of your mother's opera vids—"

Trenton bursts through the closet door. He stamps down the stairs with a fleet of uniformed officers at his heels. Before Jen and I can move, Trenton raises an electric-blue blowgun to his lips and takes a breath. He exhales, and a fusion darts shoots out of the gun to bury itself in Jen's neck. Her eyes bulge and she slumps to the ground. Her arm dangles off the side of the rocker's base.

I back away, hands in the air. "Trenton. Don't do this, please. I can change. I'll serve the Complot. I won't fight anymore—"

A second fusion dart leaves Trenton's blowgun. I duck and it narrowly misses my body. I pick up my mother's pile of river reed blankets and throw them at the approaching officers, but it only slows them for a second—and I have nowhere to go. Trenton raises the blowgun, and I grab the framed picture of my family off the mantle. I hurl it at Trenton's smug, authoritative face.

And I miss.

The fusion dart does not. It burrows into my—

Jennifer stands. She walks to the foot of the stairs. "This isn't one of your mother's opera vids, Beth."

The fire crackles. "How do I get out of here?"

Jennifer turns. "Can you keep a secret?"

"No," I say. "But tell me anyway."

Jennifer walks up the stairs. I hear her footsteps overhead as she walks through her bungalow. Then, without warning, her steps are joined by a second set—heavy bootsteps that clomp. Soon the two sets of steps are marching into the bunker. Jennifer stands by my side as Trenton steps into our shelter.

I can't move. "What are you doing here?"

"He's a double agent, Beth," Jennifer says. "He's part of the revolution."

"I'm sorry I never told you." Trenton's mouth quivers behind his perfect beard. "And I'm sorry we broke up. I had to call it off. We were getting close—too close. You would have found out the truth and—"

"I can't keep a secret." Relief floods my chest. Trenton doesn't hate me! We might get back together! I fall to my knees, weak. "Oh, Trent!"

"It's okay, Beth." Jennifer crouches by my side. "We're going to protect you."

"There's more." Trenton kneels on my other side. My heart

flutters as his gentle voice says, "There's an asylum where the revolution operates. On the southern border."

"You mean the Southern Shelter?" I look into Trenton's eyes. "I know about that. I overheard Isaac talking about it in the staff room."

"No, that place doesn't exist. It's a lie we use against the Complot," Jennifer says. "Like the racoons, Beth."

"Oh." I breathe. "But there's a southern asylum?"

"Yes. It's our base." Trenton stands, then hoists me onto my trembling feet. "I'm going to take you there. Jen's going to gather the others—she has connections in every level of government—then she'll join us."

"Isaac's one of us, Beth." Jennifer clutches my arm. "We've been in a romantic relationship for months."

"You and Isaac? In love?" I gape. "I didn't ruin your chance with him?"

Jennifer laughs; it's good to hear her laugh. "Not at all."

"Your mother is in the asylum too, Beth," Trenton says. "And Jen's mom, and her grandmother, and all the people the Complot say have been exiled or retired. They're waiting for us to join them so we can dismantle the Autocracy."

I raise my shaking hand to my mouth. "My mom?"

"Yeah, your mom," Jennifer says. "She's there. She'll show you her vids again, Beth. Like before."

"So, operas are real?"

"Pretty much." Trenton pulls me into a gentle hug; the buttons on his uniform scratch my cheek. "We're going to live happily ever after, Bethy. We'll have real love. Romantic love. You'll only Slut for me, for the rest of your life. Nobody can touch you." He sighs, deep in his chest. "You're my Slut. Mine."

I can't believe it. I start to cry.

"It's everything we dreamed of, Beth," Jennifer says. "I'm Isaac's property, and you belong to Trenton. We'll serve our males as we take down the Complot. Change is—

Jen tucks her legs onto her chair. "There aren't dancers, and heroes, and happily-ever-afters. There's just you and me. That's never going to change."

We stare into the fire. It crackles.

I shift in my chair. "How do we get out?"

Jen leads me up the stairs, silently. I follow her into the mudroom. She turns off her house alarm, then leads me out into her darkened yard. We walk along the sidewalk without saying a word—she leads me past shadowed bungalows, giant Sentinel Towers, and nuclear lights. The dusty Toggletank drives by, but it doesn't see us in our grey uniforms that blend in with the stone city.

Jennifer doesn't pause, never hesitates; she just keeps walking.

I don't pause. I don't hesitate.

I follow my friend.

We near the southern border. The Oakland wall looms over our heads. A brown, dingy door stands before us, embedded in the grey stone.

Jen places her hand on the door's handle. She turns to me. "Ready?"

I shrug. "Sure."

She opens the door.

The sun rises over the horizon and floods the space beyond Oakland with light. A female dressed in a pink, knee-length skirt and a yellow tunic jogs out of a brightly decorated bungalow, heading our way. Her chin lifts towards the illuminated sky. I like her instantly.

She raises her hand as she jogs over. "Hello, you two!"

Jen nods, solemnly. "We're here."

"About time!" The female in the yellow tunic laughs. "We've been taking bets on how long it would take you to give up."

"Give up?" I look at Jen. "What is this place?"

"This is where you come when you stop caring." The female pinches my chin, then steers me towards her house. "When several of us were exiled years ago we decided to screw the Complot and build our own world. Now, whenever Canuckians have had enough of the government's controlling ways, they come here to live in a proper city." She gestures around the space beyond the wall.

The lighted area looks exactly like the city we just left, except there isn't any grey. It's all colour, energy, and light. The air smells fresh. Fearless.

"We do have a few rules to follow—but nothing too scary," the female says. "We expect you to contribute, but I'm sure you'll be able to find jobs suited to your abilities."

"Wait," I say as we enter the female's home. "What about the others?"

Jen hisses. "Beth."

"The others?" The female's face darkens. "Oh. You mean the Sluts."

The word is a curse in her mouth. It leaps off her tongue and hits me in the chest, overpowering my heart with hatred and loathing.

My hands shake. "What?"

"Yeah, the Sluts." The female's smile jumps back into place. She grabs my forearm and pulls me inside. "Anyone who serves under an Autocratical regime is a Slut. We don't waste our time worrying about people who refuse to fight for change." The female spins into a side room, muttering 'sluts' under her shame-filled breath and leaving Jen and me alone in her foyer.

I turn to my friend.

Who shrugs. "Our moms are here. And my grandmother. Other citizens might join us. Eventually."

"How long have you known about this place?" I grab Jen's arm. "Why didn't we come here sooner?"

"I'm an Informer, Beth. I know everything," Jen says. "And you know me. I don't like taking a risk unless it's absolutely necessary." She steps further into the foyer. "And it's not great here, Beth. But it's better than the alternatives."

"What are the alternatives?"

"You don't want to know." Jen stares out the opened door, at the brightly-lit community.

The female re-enters the foyer and hands us two wrapped parcels. "Get out of those drab clothes." With unexpected vigour, the female whips off her yellow tunic and throws it on her floor. "Now that your official welcome is over, we can really let loose."

With a whoop, the topless female runs out of her home to dance in the street. Dozens of nude and half-naked people join her, cavorting along the sunlit road. A male slaps a male on his bare butt. A female grabs a person and kisses them on the mouth. Couples and small groups frolic, filled with erotic ecstasy in the cold, crisp, fearless air.

I open the parcel. It's empty.

Jen sighs, then strips off her uniform. "By the way—in this colony, paired intimacy is outlawed, and communal intimacy is expected." She shrugs. "Change comes with consequences. Hope you're ready to—

Jennifer tucks her legs onto her chair. The fire crackles. "We don't have a choice, Beth. We'll never be free. Our lives won't ever change, no matter what we do."

"So—there's no hope." I stare into the flames. "How can you be sure?"

"I've never told you this, but the Informers have a database that analyzes patterns," Jennifer says. "It contains vid evidence of citizens throughout history who rebel against their governments. I've watched the vids, Beth. Based on what I've seen, there are a few ways our story could end." She frowns at the fire. "But nothing really changes. We always serve—we're always Sluts. We sell our autonomy over and over for nothing but the promise of security. We accept the shaming—and the judgment, and control—for the illusion of love or the delusion of peace. But it's not real, Beth. We never have any power, or any choice."

I watch my friend as she rocks slowly in her grandmother's chair. Looking at the picture on the mantle and remembering the stories our elders told us—and the opera vids—I grip my mom's sheltering blanket in my hands. "We always have a choice, Jen— and I choose to try."

I stand, then extend my hand. "Will you join me? Or will you stay here? Hiding, and sitting in silence; rocking on your chair while the people in power make us dance—and keep telling our story."

Jennifer grunts—then smiles. She grabs my hand, and I pull her out of the rocker. Jennifer squeezes my fingers as the fire-warmed air in our shelter hugs our united bodies. "Shame on you, Beth: for being right. For our mothers—and our grandmothers—I'll try, too."

Excerpt from FIXING IT by Stefanie Barnfather
YOU KNOW WHAT I THINK? (Barnfather Books, 2022)

'*Grasshoppers chirped within the wheat fields. The alien ship landed on the lawn that stretched out in front of the farmhouse. Old Denny rocked on her porch chair as she watched the extraterrestrial climb out of its spacecraft. Old Denny turned, then yelled over her shoulder, "Kim! Your turn…"*'

'*…Grasshoppers chirped on the balcony. Ava stuck her head into her children's bedroom, watching as her husband tucked the boys under their coverlets. "Sugar? The ship's here."*

Lucas straightened. "Tonight? Where?"

"In the foyer."

"Inside the building?" Lucas jogged out of the boys' room, then grabbed his coat from the front closet. "I didn't think they came inside…"'

'*…The grasshoppers hummed as Agnes slowly made her way through the retirement complex's garden. She smiled at Benji and Gael, who'd fallen asleep in each other's arms as the sun set. Agnes removed a spray can of DEET from her purse and made her way over to the bushes. With a focused and thorough spraying, she killed the grasshoppers that filled the garden's foliage.*

"There." She placed the lid back on the spray can. "That'll teach you for Evil-Making. Damned chirping keeps me up all night. Now I can finally sleep." She smiled. "I needed to Fix-It, real bad."'

PART 2: FACING IT

9

Lightning bugs zipped around the spaceship's nutrient distribution cafeteria. The line of orbitorgs—'*orbit*ing *org*anics'—shuffled forward as they collected their afternoon meal. G.O.R.D.O.N. shoveled food into their trophic hole as their friend, E.L.L.E.N., shuffled into the cafe. Gord whoomped, then yelled at the electrified orbitorg. "Elle! Saved you a seat!"

Elle blinked her luminescent eyes, then shuffled over to the table. She fell onto the bench beside Gord with a sigh.

Gord smiled around his mouthful of protein-enriched carbo-hydrates. "Long pulsar set?"

Elle shrugged. "It wasn't too bad."

"You seem more crepuscular than usual." Gord nodded at Elle's minimized voltage fronds. "Anything wrong?"

"I'm not waiting in that line." Elle shut her eyes. The light in the cafeteria dimmed. *Yota?* she thought. *Can you bring my rations?*

"Read your mind. Here you go." N.Y.O.T.A. squished down on the bench next to Elle, then slid the electric orbitorg's ration tray across the table. "Suck it down while it's hot."

"Thanks." Elle pulled the tray closer. With another sigh she unfurled her consumption rope and burrowed it into the meal. The tray shivered, then lumps of warm carbohydrates chugged up the rope and down Elle's throat. She sighed louder, this time content. The light in the cafeteria brightened. "That's better."

"Who did you have this pulsar set?" Gord swallowed and their digestive system let out an extrusive roar. "Sorry 'bout that. My third stomach can't process polycyclic beans."

Elle stayed silent. Yota's exoskeleton squirted secretion onto the bench as she turned to absorb Elle's energy.

Gord's digestive system roared louder. "Okay, something's wrong. We can tell." He sloshed his belly from side to side. "Was your humanoid high maintenance?"

"No, she was simple." The lumps in Elle's rope chugged faster. "I'm just tired. This pulsar set has been rough. It's a stressful time on Earth: lots of healing sessions to do."

Yota nodded and her exoskeleton ooze spilled onto the cafeteria floor. "My schedule's packed, too. Good thing the 89th pulsar is almost here. I'm going to Beta Pictoris b for the 101st pulse to take pictures of dying organisms." Her ooze smiled. "I'm almost done my collection. You should see how big my snapshot gallery has grown."

"Another pulsar." Elle waved her glowing fronds. "Maybe on the 102nd?"

"Tell us about your humanoid." Gord shoveled more protein-carbs into their hole. "Mine was boring this pulsar set."

Elle retraced her rope, then pushed her tray across the table. "She wasn't that interesting. Her Evil-Maker did something terrible, but facing her four-year-old self didn't seem to faze her." Elle's eyes dimmed. Her body tube turned translucent, as did the cafeteria's lighting. "She was a calm little thing. A teenager, I think. Took her Evil in stride. She said her younger self didn't require healing. Apparently, she's been managing fine."

"Hmph." Gord opened his maw, revealing rows of sharp, spade-like teeth, which he picked with his boil-encrusted digit. "That's good. Cases like hers make it easy to meet our quota."

"I guess," Elle buzzed. "Except, she got me thinking. Sometimes I wonder why the Face-It program exists. Not everyone requires a deeper look into their past. Wouldn't it be more efficient to bring the humanoids here on a case-by-case basis? Instead of pulling every abuse victim on board without their consent?"

"I was thinking that, too." Yota sloshed on the bench. "If the humanoids applied for Face-It, we'd have less work to do and more time to do it."

"Careful." Gord looked over their bumpy shoulder. "Don't let the big gals hear you say that. This is a cushy job with intergalactic benefits. You don't want to get fired for grumbling. You'd have to take a gig on an OutPost planet."

"Kling and Klung aren't here." Yota oozed across the bench, closer to her colleagues. "They jetted off on a shuttle last pulsar. They're pitching the Face-It program to other star systems. I read their minds: they're hoping more humanoid aliens sign up."

"They didn't consult with us before making that decision?" Elle's eyes flared. The orbitorgs in the ship's cafeteria winced as the lights beamed brightly. "Sorry!" Elle raised her frond in apology. The orbitorgs went back to their meals. Elle buzzed, "I need to lie down before my next client." She unfurled her bottom-fronds and shuffled towards the exit portal, calling to her colleagues, "I've got twins in my next session. I can't imagine the Evil they're about to Face."

Lightning bugs zipped around the balcony overlooking the Flomp Courts. C.L.A.R.A. stuck her thought cell into the playing zone and her ears spun in circles as her colleagues finished their match. A bell chimed within her cellular core. Lara silenced the ringing, then flushed her core yellow in warning. "Team? That's break time."

The Flompers grumbled. They threw down their netquets. The energy ball flickered, then expired as the Flomp Court powered down for the ten mass-length-time-Plank break.

E.D.G.A.R.—the first Flomper—hissed as he steamed off the court. "Did you see that last goal? Did you? I slammed it. Slammed it!"

Lara's expression cell flickered, indicating pleasure. "Howa didn't see it coming."

"He sure didn't. Sure didn't!" Gar steamed onto the floor, then massaged his atoms. "I'm going to get 'im in the Final. Get 'im!"

"Not likely." H.O.W.A.R.D.—the second Flomper—scraped the sides of the court's exit portal with his geode shoulders. With a rocky groan, he settled on the floor beside Gar.

Gar hissed. "Just you wait. I'll getcha, Howa. Getcha!"

Lara rolled over the hydration sacks, then indicated her amusement as the Flompers consumed their recovery calories. "You're going hard this pulsar set. Any reason you're blowing off—" She indicated irony, "—steam?"

Howa clacked his pleasure stones as Gar gurgle-hissed. "Very funny, very funny." Gar absorbed his snack sack. "If you must know, our humanoids were especially frustrating this pulsar set. We're annoyed, so we thought we'd take it out on the court."

"Mine was average." Howa's stones clacked. "He accepted his younger self pretty fast."

"Mine was mean." Gar's atoms swirled. "He took forever to forgive his younger self. His eighteen-year-old persona practically begged him to apologize." Steam rose from Gar's energy centre. "It really burned me up."

"You have to be patient with humanoids." Lara indicated tolerance. "I know it's hard, but every one of them handles their Evil differently. Once you've done the job longer, you'll see."

"She's right." A stone tumbled off Howa's shoulder. He replaced it with a bemused *clack!* "Lara and I have been here 25,067,489 pulsars. We were part of the first orbitorg hiring phase. Trust us. We've seen it all."

"Once your client attacks their younger self—once you watch them deny what happened to them—you'll realize that a little resistance is nothing." Lara indicated compassion as she turned her thought cell towards Howa. "Remember that humanoid who went into shock when they met their abused persona?"

"Ohhhhhhh." Howa rumbled. "That was bad."

Gar's steam puffed. "What happened?"

"My client's younger self witnessed a terrible Evil." Howa shuddered; stones fell from his shoulders. "Poor thing."

"She completely froze." Lara indicated sadness. "She stopped talking, didn't eat, wouldn't sleep—she couldn't even move. We had to put her in the health capsule until she started showing signs of conscious thought. She was on the ship for multiple pulsars."

"No!" Gar hissed. "That's against policy!"

"It didn't used to be." Lara's thought cell slowly shook from side to side. "Not during the beginning stages of the Face-It program."

"But how?" Gar gurgled. "Our clients have to be returned home within twelve Earth hours. That's the deal."

"Earth's humanoids hadn't accepted the extraterrestrial partnership back then," Howa clacked. "It was easier to offer flexible healing systems—there wasn't any bureaucracy mucking up the process."

"I bet the big gals hated that," Gar hissed. "Kling and Klung love structure."

The orbitorgs grinned at each other, then spoke in unison: "Structured supports spin the solar systems symbiotically." They expressed, steamed, and stoned their laughter, then took a swing from their hydration sacks.

Lara's cell bell chimed and her core flushed orange—a warning that the next Flomp match was about to start. Howa and Gar groaned and hissed as they unfurled from their break positions, then headed for the court's entrance.

Steam rose from Gar's shoulders as he turned to Howa. "So—what happened to the humanoid? The one who stayed here for multiple pulsars?"

"Earth's Leaders invented a series of lies about my client when we returned her home," Howa cracked. "It was innovative, actually. They created a cover-up to justify the pulsar frame. Earth's Leaders built an entire area so humanoids would believe them. They call it '51.'"

"Why didn't Earth's Leaders tell the truth?" Gar steamed. "It seems more complicated to lie."

Howa paused, stuck within the court's entranceway. "The galaxy was different back then, before the Universal Government officially acknowledged the existence of Many Beings." As he pushed through the doorway, the frame ripped out of its casing. Howa shrugged, and the frame shattered. He clacked. "Things changed."

"Well, sure." Gar's atoms swirled. "After the Tyson meteorite hit the lower southeast quadrant of the planet, the humanoids needed our help—they had no choice but to let go of their superiority ideology."

"Precisely." Lara indicated amusement. "There was less resistance to the program after that. The big gals were able to negotiate terms with Earth's Leaders that allowed us to do our jobs effectively."

"Can we play now?" Howa clunked. "My geodes are getting crumbly."

"I'm gonna slam you! Slam!" Gar steamed over the broken doorframe and onto the court. "But—" Hot air swirled around his atoms. "Do you think my client will be alright?"

"No reason why not." Howa's stones rumbled. "After they accept their Evil, humanoids return to Earth and live lives without fear. They let go of their pain. They're happy."

"You'll see, once you've done the job longer." Lara's thought cell indicated joy. "The Face-It program brings a lot of peace to Earthling society. We're doing great work here. Don't worry."

Lightning bugs zipped around the bushes that lined the space-ship's greenhouse. The orbitorgs harvesting the hydroponic gardens went about their work slowly, trimming and managing the vitamin sources without any fuss.

M.A.R.V.I.N. and A.U.D.R.E.Y. cut side by side, chatting with each other quietly so they wouldn't disturb the other harvesters: gardening restored equilibrium to the Face-It staff after long pulsar series.

Arv rotated his metallic slice-saw. "She was a calm old lady. Real grounded."

"How lovely." Rey plucked a flower bud from a radish stem. "How lovely."

"I really enjoy healing humanoids like her." Arv watched the lightning bugs zoom around the greenhouse, pollinating as they went. "The reasonable clients remind me why I took this job."

"They make it worth the stress. For sure."

"Did you hear about the group of younger employees who are petitioning to have humanoids like her eliminated from the Face-It program?"

Rey slithered closer to Arv, winding her tail around a column of tubers. "I saw the draft. They're giving it to the big gals next pulsar set."

"No way." Arv's metal shell hardened. "I didn't know they were that far along with the digidoc."

The tip of Rey's tail twitched. She smiled, showing her venomous canines. "It's complete. The younger crowd are pitching it to Kling and Klung when they get back from their intergalactic marketing meeting."

"The young ones will be fired into the stratosphere." Arv shook his spears, which gave a *ting!* as they clattered together. "What are they thinking?"

"They believe the program requires too much work." Rey purred; her fur bristled along her claws. "They want more time to play Flomp and hack the EyeSpy network. They don't realize how important our job is."

"They *should* be fired into the stratosphere, then." Arv settled back on his aluminum haunches, then resumed his bud trimming. "Immature youngsters."

"Was your humanoid really that great?" Rey unwound her tail. "I mean, she was practically dead. How interesting could she have been?"

"She was lovely." Arv stroked a leaf with his spear. "She was sweet, and very kind. Very forgiving of her younger self. Very respectful." His platinum irises contracted, then spun out of his sockets as he gazed at the other orbitorgs in the greenhouse. "We don't heal enough humanoids like her anymore."

"Such a shame. Such a shame." Rey licked the padding between her claws—they were muddied with clumps of dirt. "But clients like her make the work worth it."

"They do." Arv's protruding irises followed the lightning bugs' flight. "They really do."

"Hey!" R.I.P.L.E.Y. stuck their ice block into the greenhouse. Frost crystalized over their nose as they glared at Rey and Arv. "The Flix's starting in a pulsar—you two are on sucrose duty."

"Coming, Ley." Arv's spear flashed as Ley retracted their ice block into the spaceship's travelling corridor. Arv's metal shell sparkled in the greenhouse's leafy light. "Immature youngster. So impatient. They have no idea how to be respectful. They have no idea that it was employees—like us—who built this organization. Without us, Face-It wouldn't exist."

Rey flexed her claws. "So disrespectful."

"Let's go." Arv shook his metal slats, then clanked towards the corridor. "We need to show the youngsters how to do their jobs properly—otherwise the human race is doomed."

"That we do." Rey purred as she loped after Arv. "That we do."

Lightning bugs zipped around the spaceship's dormitories. The orbitorgs asleep in their bunks were oblivious to their glow—except for one.

E.L.L.I.O.T. watched the bugs flitter around the silent sleeping space. He felt sadly reflective.

A probe rippled out from D.I.L.L. and I.O.N.—the sixth-dimension siblings—and Liot sighed. "I can't sleep."

Dill rippled.

Liot turned on his side and faced the rippling orbitorgs. Liot rubbed his bottom with his worry tendon, then launched into his explanation for his restlessness. "I know I haven't been here very long, but I've been thinking. You know how the new staff wants to make changes to the Face-It program? The way we do things up here?"

Ion rippled.

"Right. Well, does anyone know what happens on Earth after we return the humanoids to their homes? We don't do follow-ups. How do we know the program really works?"

Dill rippled.

"I know the big gals tell us that the humanoids let go of their pain and live in peace for the rest of their lives." Liot paused, deep in thought. His worry tendon rubbed his bottom more vigorously. "But do we actually know? Kling and Klung *say* that's what happens, but we've never seen happy humanoids."

Ion rippled.

Liot snorted. "Don't use that line on me. I like evidence. Faith isn't part of my genetic assembly." His worry tendon trembled.

"What if the humanoids don't let go of their pain? What if they do something different?"

Dill rippled.

Liot frowned. "I don't know. Something. Revenge." His worry tendon sparked. "The human race doesn't have a history of being particularly forgiving. How can we trust that the Face-It program is doing real good? I'm worried the program creates more Evil."

Ion rippled.

"I know we can't manage what humanoids do." Liot rolled onto his back, watching the lightning bugs dance. "But if we're supposed to be helping them, shouldn't we make sure the program works? I don't want to work for a company that makes the universe worse."

Dill and Ion rippled in unison.

Liot laughed. "Don't worry. I'm not going to request an inquiry. Those things never work."

Dill rippled.

"Yeah." Liot's worry tendon sparked again, flaming in the darkened dorm before settling against his bottom. "You're right. The only thing I can manage is how I heal my clients. I have to trust Earth's humanoids. I have to trust Kling and Klung. I have to believe in the Face-It program and believe it's doing good." Liot's tendon snatched the remaining lightning bugs out of the air, then wound around his firebrand body, extinguishing his flame and plunging the dorm into total darkness.

Dill and Ion rippled.

"Good night to you, too." A final spark ignited on Liot's bottom; he snapped it out with his tendon. "See you next pulsar set."

SCARS

10

"I don't want to do this." Pamela stumbled as the fluid sack pulsated under her feet. She held out her hand to break her fall, and caught herself on the lining that curved up and around her body. The warm sack vibrated under her touch—Pamela felt her stomach lurch. Keeping close to the membrane, which swelled around her frame like a gelatinous globe, Pamela stumbled over the blue-veined floor to her brother's side. "Jake? I changed my mind."

"You can't change your mind." Sweat matted her brother's ragged, black hair. "It's too late."

"Jake." Pamela pinched her nose: the inside of the fluid sack smelled like sour milk. It heaved and Pamela fell into Jake's sturdy frame. "We don't have to do this. I don't need the scars. I can survive in the outside world without them."

Jake absentmindedly patted her back. Tension rippled through his gaunt arm. The scar running across his wrist looked white; the mark of trauma was stretched across his skin, pulled taught. Jake kept his eyes on the sack's entryway: the orifice. The sacrifice was going to enter through its puckered hole.

The sack's floor heaved, but Jake held his stance as Pamela stumbled away from her brother. "I'm serious, Jake," she said. "I don't want to do this. It's not right. It's not fair."

"What's not fair is that we were both born in the 22nd Century." Jake's voice took on the steely tone that only sharpened right before he yelled.

Pamela stepped further away, leaning into the sack's lining.

"What's not fair is that people like you—" Jake swung around, "—are forced to choose between pain or death. I didn't get to choose, so I'm choosing for you." Jake's black hair looked red in the bloody glow emanating from the sack's membrane walls. "I choose death."

"Well, I don't." Pamela pulled her long ponytail over her shoulder. "I didn't give you permission to choose for me. I'm strong enough to earn my own scars."

"You aren't strong." Jake's voice dropped; it took on his softer edge.

Pamela paled—she was in trouble, now.

Jake whispered. "You can't survive what I went through. You aren't better than our dads, and the thousands of adults before them. You're only twelve. I love you, so I'm choosing for you." He turned back to the orifice. "I choose death."

With a *squelch!* and a loud pucker, the orifice began to open.

Jake grinned at the widening entranceway. He rubbed his hands together. "She's coming."

"Jake!"

Clear salient fluid squirted out of the orifice, spraying the inside of the sack. Pamela wiped the lubricant off her face, then squeezed the thick liquid out of her ponytail. The transference fluid smelled worse than the sack's lining; like sour milk that had curdled.

"It's not too late," Pamela said. "We can undo this—you can return the money. I don't give my permission. You don't have my consent. I don't want to be any part of this, Jake."

"She's here." Jake pointed at the orifice, which had unfurled until it opened half a meter across the sack's lining, leaving a dark, glistening maw in the wall. Jake turned his head: his black eyes swallowed Pamela's defiant figure. "It's too late."

The soggy head and lubricated shoulders of a nude female squeegeed through the orifice's blue-veined opening. Pamela scratched her fingers along the sack's side, fumbling for something to hold onto so she wouldn't fall if she fainted—but the muscular sack bulged, then slipped from her grasp. Pamela groaned; her eyes stuck on the terrible scene before her.

The nude female's torso passed through the hole. Jake slid forward and placed his hands under the female's armpits. With a grunt, he fell back on his knees and began pulling the female the rest of the way through the orifice, into the sack. Her hips slid through the hole with a *slurp!*, then she fell on top of Jake as her thighs, legs, and feet rapidly followed.

The orifice shuddered. The veins pulsed purple and the arteries throbbed red, then the entryway squeezed shut—enclosing Pamela, her brother, and the female inside.

The female started crying.

"That's enough." Jake squirmed out from under the weeping female, then scrambled to his feet. "That won't help you here."

The nude female lay on her side, knees pressed into her chest and her hands cradled under her head.

"We're doing you a favour," Jake said to the female. "Look how many scars you have. You wouldn't have lasted much longer—and you've had enough chances to redeem yourself."

The nude female continued to weep. The sack pulsed and flowed around her, oblivious to her sadness.

Pamela pushed herself away from the sack's siding. She grit her teeth, then slid to Jake's side. "I don't want to be like her. If we leave her alone—let her go and leave here, now!—I might have a chance. I could be better than her. Come on, Jake. You have to give me a chance."

"You think you could be better than her? You?" Jake shot a glance at the female, then grabbed Pamela's elbow. He spun his sister around so she had no choice but to stare at the sacrifice. Jake shook Pamela's arm. "She's one of the better ones, Pammy. Look." His finger hovered an inch above the female's skin as Jake traced the sacrifice's scars in the air. "See the size of this wound on her calf? Dad's was twice as big after he helped cover up Prime Billadeau's extortion racket." Jake's finger moved. "See this scar on her thigh?" He nudged the female with his foot.

She whimpered but stayed still.

"It's hard to tell, but it looks like this scar is only a few centimetres long," Jake said. "When Pop had to choose between keeping us over Alice—"

Pamela winced. Jake never said their sibling's name, not after their father forced Alice to join Ollivier Billadeau's revolution in exchange for food.

"—his scar went all the way around his body. Pop showed me." Jake knelt on the bottom of the membrane, then placed his hand on the female's shoulder. "Do you see this scar? Do you?"

Pamela leaned over. A brown, puckered line wound around the female's neck, from the base of her ear to her collarbone. Pamela raised her hand to her own neck, then stepped back, staring at Jake's face.

"I've never shown you mine." Jake stood, towering over his sister. He pulled down his shirt collar. "When I shot Dad for treason this appeared the next day." Jake's scar was thick; it hadn't completely healed. It wound twice around his neck, over his shoulder, then stopped above his heart. Jake let go of his collar. "You think this female's life was bad?" He looked down at the nude sacrifice, whose cries had subsided into quiet sniffles. "She got off easy. You'd be lucky to have her scars."

Pamela gripped her ponytail. "Jake—"

"Don't you get it?" Jake's voice thundered. "You have held us back for years. If you weren't so weak—so small—we could've escaped Canuckia. But, to protect you, we had to stay. I've had to become a monster to keep you safe. I've carried the burden of your incompetence our whole lives—and I can't do it anymore."

The female rolled on the floor, moaning.

Jake ignored her. "If you steal her scars, you'll be strong. Then we can leave." His voice softened. "Isn't a little discomfort worth a lifetime of freedom? For me?"

Pamela's eyes filled with tears. "Jake—"

"We're done talking about this." Jake's voice rose, stern and loud. "I had to give all our credits to ScarCorp to arrange this for you. Only rich kids get luxuries like this. You will steal this female's scars, and you will be grateful." He raised his hand, palm extended.

The scar in his flesh that wound around his wrist looked shockingly like the maroon, pulsating membrane of the sack.

Jake raised his eyebrow. "Got it?"

Pamela shrank back into her wall. "Yes."

"Good." Jake dropped his hand. "I love you, Pammy. I'm doing this because I love you."

Pamela slid to the bottom of the membrane. She drew her legs to her chest, then dropped her forehead on her knees.

"Stay there," Jake said. "I'll get you when it's time."

Pamela sat with her head on her knees for what felt like an hour but was probably only a few minutes. She listened to the female cry, to Jake's laboured breath, and to the whizzing sound of uterine cords rubbing together. After Jake grunted and huffed for longer than Pamela could stand, she raised her head.

The female was on her back, stretched across the floor of the sack like a starfish. Four cords protruded from small orifices that pulsated in the membrane—Jake had tied each cord around one of the female's limbs. Her ankles and wrists were bound, and the smaller orifices pulled each cord tightly. The female lay flat—limp.

Exposed. Sweat ran between her breasts, down her stomach, and onto the sack's floor. Her breath was shallow. Her skin was pale. Her eyes were closed.

Her scars began to pulse, wickedly.

Jake frowned. "It's time."

The lining, bottom, and ceiling of the sack pulsed in time with the female's scars. The four orifices opened and shut, mimicking the rhythm of the sacrifice's breath. The female began to moan, pulling on the cords and writhing on the floor. The cords held. Her scars burned brighter.

"Come here, Pammy." Jake held out his wounded hand without looking at her. His eyes were on the sacrifice. "You have to sit by her head."

Pamela stood, shaky on her legs. She slid to her brother, then clutched his outstretched, puckered palm. Jake guided her to the transference spot. Pamela sat behind the female, legs crossed, then—following Jake's silent command—she lifted the female's head and placed it in her lap.

The female opened her mouth.

"You ready, Pammy?" Jake stood over the sacrifice. Sweat poured down his cheeks. "You remember what we practiced?"

Pamela nodded. She didn't have to say anything. Jake knew she was prepared. Pamela leaned over the sacrifice. She opened her mouth.

The sack pulsed red. Its veins pulsed blue. The orifices squelched within the lining. The uterine cords quivered.

Jake laughed.

He began the ritual. "Sacrifice, bought and paid—are you ready to give The Innocent your gift?"

The female moaned. The sound resonated within Pamela's chest.

"Sacrifice, trauma endured—are you ready to share Your Story of survival?"

The female groaned. Pamela felt their souls intertwine.

"Sacrifice, hollow shell—are you ready to speak The Words that will protect this child's future?"

The female screamed. Pamela felt her mind rip open, ready to receive her thoughts.

Jake smiled. "Sacrifice. It's time."

Pamela's insides pulsed. She was one with the female, one with the sack, one with Jake, and one with the universe. Her mind sweltered in the heat emanating from the sacrifice's tormented thoughts. Pamela's soul burned within her chest.

Jake intoned. "How did you get those scars, Sacrifice?"

Words rose from the female's mouth and floated into Pamela's. "I hurt the Different One."

Memory crystalized in Pamela's mind.

She stood with a group of students, all dressed in grey frocks. They circled around a young boy. His eyes were slack. His shoulders slumped.

Pamela chanted with the students as she punched and hit the Different One. "You don't belong. Go away. You're not wanted."

Pamela began to cry. She didn't want to hurt the Different One, but if she stopped kicking him the grey students would turn on her next. She punched, and hit, and watched the boy's slack-eyed face purple and bleed.

Pamela screamed. The sacrifice screamed. A scar lifted off the female's body, then floated over to Pamela. It landed on her skin. Pamela shrieked as the scar burned—then she stopped as it turned cold. Instantly the female's feelings of self-loathing and fear disappeared. Pamela held the memory of beating the Different One, but none of the pain of the sacrifice's remorse.

Pamela smiled. She leaned over the female's face and opened her mouth.

Jake hummed. "Where did you get those scars, Sacrifice?"

Words rose from the female's mouth. Pamela ate them all. "I lied to protect My Friend."

The memory came.

Pamela sat on a stool, in front of a large imposing desk. A sharp-faced male sat behind the table, surveying her from under his white-flecked eyebrows. Pamela's hand rested on a girl's leg—Her Friend's, sitting beside her. Her Friend's face was bruised. Her Friend's lip was cut. Her Friend's uniform was torn.

Pamela turned to the male, then spoke. "I saw who did this. I saw what happened. They grabbed her after class and hurt her. You have to expel them."

Pamela said a name. The sharp-faced male connected with the Informers, who transferred the call to the Autocracy. Officers arrived, spoke with the male and the girls, then dragged a teenager out of a classroom. The teenager's eyes burned holes into Pamela's face. Shame and regret burned in her belly.

Her Friend whispered in Pamela's ear, "But—that wasn't him."

Pamela whispered back. "It had to be. Your abuser is too powerful. But if we start with the small, the mighty will fall."

Her Friend whispered, "I feel bad."

Pamela swallowed her shame as she stared at Her Friend's bruised face. "Don't."

The sacrifice screamed. A scar lifted off her body, floated over to Pamela, then landed on Pamela's skin. The scar burned, then cooled. Pamela lost her guilt—but kept the memory of the lesson.

Jake continued.

There were many scars. There were many memories. The sacrifice had protected herself—and others—in many desperate ways. She'd abandoned a child that wasn't wanted. She'd traded secrets in exchange for safety. She'd lied to herself, again and again, about behaviors and choices that blurred the line between what was harmful and what was necessary. She'd made so many excuses—attained so many scars—that the ritual took hours to complete.

When it was over, the female's soul was gone. All that remained was a frail, transparent body; a corpse with no definition, no substance. The sacrifice was nothing without her scars.

An orifice opened beneath the corpse. With a *slurp!* it sucked the body into its lining and began digesting the female's remains: the sack's payment for its service.

Jake fell onto the membrane, depleted.

Pamela rose to her feet, strong.

Covered in someone else's scars from head to toe, Pamela planted her feet on the heaving lining. She grabbed Jake's wounded palm and hoisted him to his feet. It was easy. She was powerful. Pamela was protected, imbued with the earned defenses—the mighty strength—of another's wisdom, without any of the traumatic side effects of lived experience.

Jake rubbed his sweating palms on his trousers. "Well?"

Pamela smirked. "You were right."

Jake hooted. The sack recoiled, then swayed once more. Jake clutched Pamela's arm. "I told you! We can do anything now. We can leave the country, put all this behind us—"

"No." Pamela's voice dropped to a whisper. "We're staying in Canuckia."

"What?" Jake squeezed her arm; he shook his ragged head. "No, Pammy. We have to go. I told you. I made this choice for you so we could—"

"I don't want to go." Pamela shook off her brothers hand. She crossed her arms. "I want to work with the government; for Prime Billadeau. Now that I know what power feels like, I want to stay." Pamela pulled her ponytail over her scarred shoulder. "I want more."

Jake winced. "That's not the plan, Pammy."

"I'm strong, Jake. I can handle anything." Pamela looked down at the puckered hole where the sacrifice had lain. "I'm going to take care of us, now."

"Pammy—"

Pamela strode over to the sack's entryway—confident on the slippery floor—dragging Jake behind her. She pressed her hand against the orifice. It spiraled open.

Pamela grinned at the orifice, then sneered at her brother. "You were wrong. We can't survive in the outside world—we can control it. *I* can control it." Her steely gaze absorbed the pathetic, scarred boy who hovered by her side. Pamela grabbed Jake's elbow, then shoved him through the orifice, headfirst. "I choose pain."

YOU DIDN'T HAVE TO

11

A girl with hair in piglet tails
    sat on a weathered seat.
Her eyes ran up, then down along
    a windy, rainy street.
Her heart was open, ready for
    the boy she'd come to greet—

                But the road stayed empty.

The girl was anxious, waiting for
    the hero from her dreams.
He was a movie starlet on
    the biggest brightest screens.
A DM sent and he'd replied,
    "I'll meet you—by all means."

                But the road stayed empty.

Just as the girl stood up to go
    the starlet showed his face.

He seemed a bit remorseful 'bout
    his disrespectful pace

But when the girl expressed her sorrow
    for his lack of grace

He said:
    "You didn't have to come.

    "You didn't have to show.

    "You didn't have to listen to

    "Someone you do not know.

    "You didn't have to trust.

    "You didn't have to stay—"

And then the starlet gave a smirk and quickly walked away.

                        The road stayed empty.

The public waited for the verdict
    of the civic race.

The leader that they wanted was
    an economic ace.

Their stress was high because the current
    Prime was a disgrace,

                 And the influential stayed silent.

The town grew quiet, holding tight
    to hopes and frantic wants.

They'd had enough of turmoil and

debate with hate and taunts.

Exhausted and unwell the people

    prayed for a détente

           As the influential stayed silent.

A crackle from the podium,

    then Red and Green appeared.

Green seemed a bit disheveled,

    and her speech a tad dog-eared.

The public held their breath and hoped

    it wasn't as they feared.

Green said:

    "You didn't have to vote.

    "You didn't have to try.

    "Despite your valiant efforts

    "Force has passed to the Red guy.

    "You didn't have to speak,

    "You could have saved your words—"

And then the Red stepped up and Green gal went away, unheard.

           The influential stayed silent.

The nurse behind her desk waved in

    the person who'd arrived

To hear the diagnosis for

    the strain they'd just survived.

The patient waited patiently—

    their fear rudely revived—

                                                    But time stayed still.

The doctor knocked, then entered in
    the patient's waiting room.
Her face was drawn and sullen
    and she held an air of gloom.
The patient held their breath as they
    foresaw impending doom,

                                                 And time stayed still.

The patient nodded, fast, then softly
    asked what they had caught.
The doctor shook her head and said,
    "It wasn't what we thought.
"Your illness is more serious,
    but—please—don't be distraught."

She said:
    "You don't have to go on.
    "You don't have to make do.
    "It might be best to stop—at least,
    "That is my point of view.
    "You don't have to endure
    "The hell that's going to come."
And then the doctor exited. The patient sat there, numb—

                                               And time stayed still.

A boy with eyes of hazel brown
    hid in his room, alone.

He huddled in the corner of
    the space he'd always known.
His fingers twisted 'round and 'round
    a shattered, broken phone,

             And no one could see him.

The yelling from the study caused
    the boy to jump with fright.
He scuttled underneath his bed—
    he planned to stay all night.
The phone within his fingers shook.
    His face fell winter white,

             But no one could see him.

A crash of glass. An angry yell.
    The boy curled tighter still.
The sweat that trickled down his spine
    unleashed a frigid chill.
He hoped the noise that fled his face
    was soft and not too shrill—

             And that no one would see him.

A holy *bang!* then up the stairs
    the villain edged and spurred.
The boy allowed his mind to wander
    as the worst occurred.
He clutched his phone. The beast withdrew;
    his fury briefly cured.

Only a woman heard them.

The woman tiptoed up the stairs:

    the villain was asleep.

She crept into her son's safe place.

    The boy began to weep.

The mother held her crying child

    and whispered him to sleep.

She said:

    "You don't have to be scared.

    "I need you to be strong.

    "Your father is a tortured man

    "Who can't tell good from wrong.

    "You didn't have to freeze.

    "You could have fought him back—"

But Mother knew that wasn't true. There'd be a new attack—

    —because we don't see them.

He didn't have to snub.

They don't have to look away.

She didn't have to watch him cry, then simply sniff and pray.

They could've raised their voices louder every single day—

But time moves quickly down the empty road of silent grey.

We could've shared the painful lessons that we had to learn:

That life is gained from reaching out, instead of self-concern.

We need to speak, we still can grow, we have to overturn

the "foolish" dream

the "useless" cause

the assumed end

the deflected blame.

If we want to see—and don't try to deny—

If we choose to lift our chins and hold our faces high,

If we shout and yell and scream and look truth in the eye,

We could build a reality we all can justify,

Because we have to.

You have to.

TECH SUPPORT

12

INTRODUCTIONS, ICE-BREAKER,
& REVIEWING THE BASICS
1:00pm EST
Saturday, October 26, 2024
Chamber of Commons—West Block
The Chateau—2 Pouvoir Avenue
Oakland, UN—Canuckia

"Good morning, everyone." Jim Geffers pushed his wire-framed glasses up onto his forehead. He flipped his glasses back over his eyes, then smiled at the parliamentary members sitting in his sharing circle. He glanced around the empty Chamber of Commons, then counted the MPs in the group—taking rapid, informal attendance. "Wonderful. We're all here."

Jim smiled again, trying to break the tension coursing through the government room. Support sessions like this one always started rough, but his calm demeanor and likeable authenticity were usually enough to open up even the most reluctant of officials.

Sure enough, as he smiled and nodded at the ministry members surrounding his high-backed chair, Jim could sense their anxiety easing. The jiggling feet slowed, the darting eyes stilled, and the tapping fingertips settled peacefully in the attendees' laps.

Jim nodded. "Before we begin today's session, I'd like to do a meet-and-greet. Let's go around the circle. Please share your first names and roles within parliament, and maybe a fun fact. Something to lighten the mood. Or, as my son would say, 'let's get turnt.'" Jim chuckled. "Kids. They're so creative."

A curly-haired brunette in a navy blazer tentatively raised her fingers.

Jim looked down at his tablet, raised his glasses to his forehead, squinted at the screen, then looked up at the woman. "Yes? Mrs. Chaise?"

The woman swallowed. Her finger tapping started up again. "It's Ms."

"My apologies. Thank you for correcting me." Jim smiled.

Chaise's fingers stilled.

Jim nodded. "It's important we show each other respect during our time together. Now, Ms. Chaise. You had a question?"

"Yes." The brunette rubbed behind her ear. "Shouldn't we say— I mean, would you like us to say why we're here?"

"Great question, Ms. Chaise." Jim dropped his glasses back over his eyes. "After introductions and basic training, we'll deal with each of your specific cases. That's the beauty of these group sessions. There's plenty of time for your individual needs to be addressed."

"Okay," Chaise said. "Thank you, Mr—"

"Jim. Call me Jim." Jim chuckled. "I guess that takes care of my introduction." He waved at the assembly. "Hello, friends! I'm the federal government's special liaison for minister conduct and behaviour. I'm here to teach, guide, assess, and listen." Jim's smile broadened. "Mostly listen. Now, if we can start with the official to my right?" He turned to the minister sitting next to him—a brown man in a rumpled suit.

The brown man jumped, then gave a weak laugh. He sucked on the side of his mouth as he shrugged his thin shoulders. "You all know me—well, a specific part of me."

A ripple of laughter travelled around the circle. The man seemed to take heart from the reaction. He sat up a little straighter. "I'm Spencer."

"Hi, Spencer."

He waved. "Hey, guys." The man frowned. "I mean, team. I mean, friends. I mean—oh, boy-o."

Jim tilted his head towards Spencer as he addressed the group. "This is the informal part of our meeting. Please feel free to address us how you'd like."

"Okay." Spencer shifted on his chair. "I don't want to offend anyone, though."

"You're safe here." Jim gestured around the Chamber of Commons: the West Block interim room where the support group was situated. "This is a safe space."

Spencer looked at the rows of lime green velvet seats, solid oak benches, and tiered white and golden archways. He gulped. "Why are we meeting in this Block again?"

Jim pushed his glasses up on his forehead. "I thought it might remind you of the majesty and magnificence of your responsibilities. Which will help you. Going forward."

"Right." Spencer adjusted his rumpled shirt. "So long as it helps."

"Please, Spencer," Jim said. "Continue."

"Okay, well—I'm Spencer."

"Hi, Spencer."

"Hey, guys. I'm the Minister of Environment and Climate Change—but, you know that. And, a fun fact? About me?" Spencer gulped. "I like to go jogging, but—you know that, too."

"Thank you, Spencer. That was a wonderful introduction." Jim turned to the navy-blazered woman sitting on Spencer's right. "Ms. Chaise?"

Chaise rubbed behind her ear. "I'm Ms. Chaise—"

"Hi, Ms. Chaise."

Chaise blinked. "I'm the Minister of Foreign Affairs and…" She shrugged. "I'm about to celebrate my thirty-year citizenship anniversary."

Jim clapped his hands together. "Congratulations!"

"Thank you." Chaise frowned. "I'm very happy about it."

"As you should be." Jim nodded, then beamed at the next MP—a sour-looking woman with deep shadows under her eyes.

The sour MP crossed her arms over her chest, then scowled at the lime green carpet running under the circle's feet. "I'm the Honourable Mrs. Reta—"

"Hi, the Honourable Mrs—"

"Stop it." Reta's tired eyes flared as she scowled around the circle. "I'm the Minister of Families, Children, and Social Development, and I haven't had a decent night's sleep in eight years." She growled at the carpet. "Ninety-six months, one week and three days, to be precise."

"Thank you for sharing," Jim said. "I'm sorry you've been struggling. I assume it's because of..." He nodded at the baby seat that rocked beside Reta's chair.

"Him?" Reta scowled down at the three-month-old, asleep in his carrier. "Yes, of course that's why. Jesus."

"I can only imagine how difficult managing an infant—and a role in parliament—must be for you." Jim's glasses slid down his nose. "It's a real treat to have your child here."

"If you say so." Reta hugged her arms tighter.

"My turn?" An older woman with a string of beads around her neck leaned forward. "I can be quick. My name is Pearl—"

"Hi, Pe—"

"—and I'm the Minister of Health. I like to weed my garden when the Chamber is dismissed every summer." She yanked on her beads. "That's what I do for fun."

Jim smiled. "That sounds like an enjoyable activity."

Pearl flipped her grey hair over her shoulder, then jerked her head at the official to her right.

"Thank you for your efficiency, Pearl," Jim said. "Who's up next?"

"Me." A fellow with twinkling eyes and a paunch that extended over his belt planted his feet widely on the floor. He leaned over his knees, nodding at the group. "My name is Bill, and you don't have to do that AA manure with me. We all know who we are. We've been working together for a long while now."

"Very well," Jim said. "Let's drop the auto-responses for the rest of the introductions. Is that okay with everyone else?"

The group nodded. They were definitely relaxing. The paunchy man, Bill, had a charming personality that was well-known in government circles. Jim had been counting on his energy to help the day's session, so he waved for Bill to continue.

"Well, ah. So, I'm Bill, I manage Agriculture and—ah, I like to knit toques in my spare time." His eyes twinkled as the circle broke out in congenial laughter. "I knew that'd surprise you. Big Bill: a wool weaver. If you stay on my good side, I'll send you a hat for the holidays."

"Thank you, Bill." The group's titters subsided as Jim nodded at the official sitting to Bill's right. "Mx. LeTout?"

"*Oui. Bonjour.*" The official sitting beside Bill nodded smartly at the group, then leapt into rapid-fire speech—a combination of French and English. "*D'accord*, so, you can call me LeTout, *s'il vous plaît, mon pronom est iel*, or they/them, *si vous préférez*, I am *le ministre des* Finances and a fun fact about me *est que* I enjoy talking with the supernatural world *autant que je peux donc je peux aider à combler le fossé entre les vivants et les morts et le bien et le mal*, hopefully, and with the intent to make society a more equitable place."

Jim pushed his glasses up on his forehead, then frowned at LeTout. "Sorry, I didn't catch all that. My Frahn-cez isn't the best."

The final official in the circle smirked at Jim. "Trust me. You didn't want to." He tucked one long leg under his seat, then smiled at the assembly. "I'm Edwin. I'm the Minister of Veteran Affairs. You want a fun fact?" He cocked his head towards LeTout. "Or should I say, *une fait amusant*?"

Smirking, Edwin crossed, then uncrossed his legs as he leaned back in his folding chair. "Here's a few for ya. Every morning I have a bran muffin for breakfast, every afternoon I walk the promenade to stretch my legs—" Which he crossed, then uncrossed, "—and every evening I watch Jeopardy—which, let's be honest, really lost its edge after that quirky girl had her historic streak. Then, every weekend, I visit my uncle at his cabin in Werth. We do some fishing, hike a bit—mostly drink beer. Pretty standard stuff. And now that we've spent thirty minutes hashing out what everybody already knows and nobody cares about, can we talk about the reason we've been forced to gather on a weekend to act out this charade in the Chateau?"

The playful energy that permeated the West Block during the first introductions dissipated. The original tension returned.

Jim dropped his glasses in front of his eyes. "Thank you, everyone, for your valuable sharing—but I agree with Edwin. We'll cover the basics of this course, then dive right into your individual cases. Can you please pull out your tablets?"

With a rustle, the ministers leaned over, behind, and around their seats as they grabbed their government iTabs from their briefcases, purses, and—in Reta's case—the bottom of her baby carrier. After a few seconds of swiping and connecting with the Wifi, Jim launched into the educational portion of the session.

"Wonderful," Jim said. "So, we're going to go around the circle—left to right, this time—and each read a paragraph from the learning module."

Jim hated schlogging through this part but, sadly, it was mandated for this particular group. He knew the one-to-one section would be far more helpful, but also hoped this read-a-loud time would give everyone a chance to transition into 'serious mode'—especially the arrogant ruffian, Edwin, who was still smirking at LeTout and not his screen.

Jim frowned. "Edwin? Can you tackle the title? Right there, at the top of the digidoc?"

"Can I tackle the title?"

Jim snapped his smile back on his face. "At the top."

"Yeah, I think I can handle one sentence." Edwin cleared his throat—loudly expiring phlegm. "The Basics of Navigating Virtual Meetings: Entering the Call, Turning On/Off Your Video, Muting Your Audio, Leaving the Call." He looked up, his sneer in place. "How'd I do?"

"Wonderful. Let's keep going." Jim nodded at LeTout. "One at a time, each take a paragraph—no need to pause."

LeTout looked up, puzzled.

Jim smiled more generously. "Voo poovehiz ahler ehn-sweet. Voolliz leer lay paragraph sweevant."

LeTout's buggy eyes blinked. "*Oui, merci. Uh—anglais ou français?*"

"In ahn-glayis see voo play."

"*Oui, merci.*" LeTout's buggy eyes shifted to their tablet. "Ah… Entering the Call. Ah… to enter the call for a virtual online session of parliament, simply open your laptop, open the schedule for the day's session, then click on the link that takes you to the Chamber of Commons' feed. *C'est ça. C'est tout ce qu'il dit.*"

"Wonderful," Jim said. "Next paragraph?"

"Turning On Your Video," Bill said. "Click the camera image on the bottom left of your session screen. This will connect your live image to the parliamentary session."

"Thank you. Next?"

"Turning Off Your Video," Pearl said. "If you don't wish to be seen by the Chamber's live stream—"

The ministers shifted on their seats.

"—you can click on the camera image again and your camera will go dark. You will still be able to see the session, but—" Pearl articulated each word with deliberate vitriol. "No. One. Will. See. You."

"Very good. Reta?"

Reta rocked her baby carrier, then mumbled out her paragraph. "Muting and unmuting your audio; if you don't want to be heard you can click on the microphone image which is next to the camera image on the bottom left of the session screen and your sound will be muted and you won't be broadcast to the entire Chamber." She looked up. "Good?"

"Very, very good." Jim turned to Chaise. Her fingers tapped her armrests. Jim nodded, supportively. "Two to go. Ms. Chaise?"

"Yes. My turn," Chaise said. "Leaving the Call: To leave the call for a virtual online session of parliament, simply click on the 'X' in the upper right corner of your screen. You will exit the sitting."

"Thank you. And last, but not least?"

Spencer shrugged. "Basic Etiquette: Before you engage in any behaviour that does not align with in-person parliamentary sessions, please ensure you have mastered these technical skills."

The ministers shifted again, then shut their tablets.

Jim beamed. "Wonderful. Does anyone have any questions?"

A cricket chirping behind the gilded Throne sitting at the apex of the Block could've been heard in the silence that followed.

"Wonderful," Jim said. "Let's take a quick fifteen-minute break—there are snacks for you in the atrium—then resume our session. Next up, we'll delve into the specific reasons you're here. So, re-group, and we'll get you those training certificates." He stood, then closed his tablet with a satisfying *smack!* "You'll be allowed back in parliament in no time. Easy peasy, tech is breezy."

MINISTER OF ENVIRONMENT AND CLIMATE CHANGE
(The Honourable Mr. Spencer)
1:45pm EST

"Wonderful. We're back." Jim smiled as the MPs took their seats—some carrying in food from the atrium, some empty handed—but all seeming more relaxed than they were before the break.

Jim patted a modest stack of papers resting on top of a wide oak table that ran the length of the Block—behind his seat. "Time to dive into our real work for the day; addressing the infraction you each committed that had you thrown out of the Chamber of

Commons. First? A few etiquette rules. We'll go around the circle, one at a time, and I will guide the sharing. You will take in what's offered—use your learning ears and your growing hearts—and at the end of your time (I'll keep you to a tight twenty minutes), there will be a brief moment for comments, questions, and reflections from the group. Remember, leave your judgement at the door and respect the sanctity of this process. You are all safe here. This is a safe place. It's safe."

The cricket behind the Throne chirped in the resounding silence.

Jim pushed his glasses onto his forehead. "Spencer? You're up, my friend."

Spencer buried his face in his hands, then spoke into his palms. "I'm always first at these things." He shrugged his shoulders, face firmly ensconced in his fingers. "You know why I'm here. But, I guess, if I have to say it out loud… I got thrown out of the CoC because I changed out of my jogging shorts and into my suit pants in front of my computer and my video screen was on so the whole thing was shared with everyone in the sitting. Live." He peeked through his hands. "You all saw my ding-a-ling."

"Twice." Reta held up her fingers. "We saw your penis twice."

"*You* saw it twice, the rest of us saw it four times." Pearl shook her grey head. "You missed the other sessions, Reta. Spencer has a real penchant for pornography."

"Oh!" Jim waggled his finger. "Etiquette! Only Spencer and I have the floor at the moment. Or, as my son says, 'ATM.'" He chuckled. "I love a good colloquialism. Anyway, back to Spencer." Jim dropped his glasses on his nose. "Why did you change four times during active parliament sessions?"

"He flashed us at least a dozen times, Jim," Edwin said. "I'm a diehard—I attend every session. Spencer performed his little peep show twelve times. Didn't you, Spence?"

Spencer disappeared behind his hands. "I go jogging a lot."

"Now we're getting to the heart of the issue." Jim faced the MP head on. "You love to exercise, don't you?"

Spencer peeked through his fingers. "I do."

"You take pride in your physical fitness."

"I do." Spencer dropped his hands. "I really do."

"And it's an unfortunate coincidence that sessions coincide with your daily calisthenics routine."

"It is!" Spencer glared around the circle. "I had no idea what the commitment would be like when I ran for office. I mean, we have all these meetings, and we have to talk to people, and file reports. How is that sustainable if we also want to be healthy? Being able to eat well is difficult. Finding the time to cultivate a thriving personal life is impossible. Keeping in shape is really hard—but I want to have it all. A good job, a great dating life, a—"

"Burgeoning softcore porn career?" Edwin smirked as the circle descended into silence. "What?" His eyes widened with fake innocence. "Come on. You can't expect us to sit here and accept his excuses—"

"You don't have to accept anything," Jim said. "You have to listen. Just listen." Jim turned back to Spencer, who had burrowed into his hands. "Spencer? Do you regret what you did?"

Spencer peeked through his fingers. "I do."

"Can you remember to turn off your video the next time you change your clothes in your office after a run?"

"I can." Spencer sat up. "I really, really can."

"Then I'm satisfied." Jim reached behind his chair and grabbed a document from the oak table. He signed the form, then passed it to Spencer—who took it gingerly.

"Wonderful," Jim said. "One down, six to go. Ms. Chaise? You're up."

MINISTER OF FOREIGN AFFAIRS
(The Honourable Ms. Chaise)
2:02pm EST

Chaise tugged on the sleeve of her navy blazer, then her cheeks flushed under her curls. "I'm absolutely mortified to be here. See, well—oh, this is absolutely mortifying." She squeaked. "So, last month, when we were called to decide on Bill 195-A—you know, the motion to allow the Opinion Biased Augmented Reality to pass?—I had an episode of food poisoning and—"

"You know what?" Jim waved his hand. "You don't have to be specific, Ms. Chaise. Why not just describe the indiscretion itself that lead to your ejection, not the circumstances that preceded it."

"Yes." Chaise's cheeks darkened. "I can do that. See, I wasn't feeling well, so I had to leave the sitting—just for a bit—and I brought my phone with me. I'd installed the CoC app which, as you know, allows the sittings to be portable. So, during the sitting, I left the video on—and the audio on—and, see, my phone screen is different from my iTab screen. I didn't know where the mute button was. So, uh, while I was in the, uh—" She whispered, "—in the lavatory—" Chaise swallowed, then raised her voice so it rang out in the West Block. "You all heard me take a dump."

The group broke into loud barks of laughter. Chaise's lip quivered but she kept her head high. Only the two spots of colour on her cheeks gave a clue to her discomfort.

Jim waved the circle into silence, then leaned towards Chaise. He used his most comforting tone of voice. "Ms. Chaise. You know what you did was wrong."

"One hundred percent. I am mortified."

"Well." Jim grabbed a form from the top of his document stack and, with a flourish, signed Chaise's approval.

Her cheeks returned to their normal colour as Chaise snatched the paper from Jim's hands.

He smiled. "That wasn't so hard."

"Actually, it *was* hard," Edwin said. "She had high-fat dairy for lunch."

"Oh, you would know. Very mature." Chaise lifted her nose to sniff at the Minister of Veteran Affairs. "Just wait until it's your turn. What you did was way worse than my stomach issues."

"Hey." Edwin waggled his finger in a passable imitation of Jim, who watched the interchange with dismay as he pushed his glasses up on his forehead. Edwin cooed, "You're not supposed to judge. This is a safe place."

"Oh, go kill a cow." Chaise busied herself by putting her approval form in her purse.

"Awww, don't spoil Bill's fun—"

"The Honourable Mrs. Reta?" Jim turned to the scowling mother. "You can begin, if you'd like?"

"Sure. Let's get this over with." Reta reached into her baby carrier, then dragged her son out of his seat and onto her lap.

MINISTER OF FAMILIES, CHILDREN &
SOCIAL DEVELOPMENT
(The Honourable Mrs. Reta)
2:14pm EST

"I don't see what the fuss is about." Reta perched her son on her hip, then jiggled her thigh. The baby gurgled happily as his mother jostled him up and down.

Reta ignored the cheerful sounds coming from her infant as she glared around the circle. "If I'm being honest, this whole situation comes down to gender inequality. No, scratch that—gender inequity. If a man did what I did, he would never have been ejected from the Chamber of Commons. But, no. A woman dedicates her life to public service—and bends to the pressures of society by popping out a bunch of kids—and what does she get for it? Nothing but criticism. You should hear my partner. I'm never at home, my children don't see me enough, I missed Cecilia's violin concert. You should hear the Prime! I'm never in session, I forgot to vote in the last sitting, I have spit-up in my hair. It's not fair. *You* try raising a family while keeping your spouse happy and adequately representing your constituents. This whole virtual thing was supposed to make life easier. So, I used the technology. For a little while, I was able to attend every meeting—then the next thing you know I'm ejected from the Chamber, I have to attend this stupid session to get back in, and you jackasses are judging me. I'm only one woman! With multiple mouths to feed! You can't punish—"

"Mrs. Reta?" Jim lowered his glasses. "I'm sorry to cut you off, but could you please expand upon the nature of your indiscretion?"

"Isn't it obvious?" Bill winked at Reta, who soothed her baby as he started to sniffle. Bill stroked his paunch. "This legislative lassie breastfed in public."

"I did not. I *have* breastfed in session, but breastfeeding isn't a problem." Reta glared at Bill, indignant. "That's such a typical, straight, cis-male thing to assume—that my breasts are the issue."

"You weren't expelled for breast feeding?" Pearl tugged on her beads as she narrowed her eyes at Reta. "That's what I heard."

"Look, Pearl, I know that in *your* day, taking care of your family came second to your job—"

"My family always came first."

"—but you need to wake up." Reta patted her son's back. He burped and a yellow glob of spittle fell onto Reta's shoulder. She wiped up the spittle with the child's nursing cloth and raised her voice. "Haven't you seen the booth?"

Pearl blinked. "The booth?"

"Yeah, the booth," Spencer said. "Over there." He pointed to a wall where a panel of dark glass stretched behind the seats. "The moms go there to feed."

"We aren't Bill's cattle, Spencer," Reta said. "We use the booth to take care of our kids so we don't inconvenience the older cur-mudgeons, like Bill, who raise a stink every time our babies do."

Bill winked. "She's not wrong."

"So—wait." Ms. Chaise frowned. "If you didn't get ejected for breast feeding, what did you do?"

"Hey, now." Jim waggled his finger. "Etiquette. It should only be me and Reta engaged in a dialogue at the moment. ATM. Please, everybody. Focus on listening and let Mrs. Reta speak."

The circle leaned towards the Honourable mother; ears perked.

Reta jiggled her knee. "I attended a session from the hospital. I brought my laptop into the delivery room and accidentally reversed the camera. The Chamber of Commons watched me give birth." She patted her baby's back. "To this little munchkin."

The circle collectively widened their eyes.

Pearl worried her beads between her fingers. "How did I miss *that* session?"

"It was in February." Reta rocked her son. "Not much happens in Canuckia except snowplow accidents and the cast of *Ferè Grand* getting announced."

Jim cleared his throat. "Are you planning on expanding your family?"

"Are you kidding?" Reta shook her head as she rocked her child. "Never. Five is plenty. I won't display my hoo-hah to the Chamber again."

"That's good enough for me." Jim signed Reta's form, then handed it to the ministerial mother.

MINISTER OF HEALTH
(The Honourable Ms. Pearl)
2:31pm EST

Pearl adjusted her beads, then raised her voice to the rafters running between the West Block's archways. "Aright, listen up—or grow, or whatever. My indiscretion is straightforward. After a particularly exciting session of parliament, to which I attended virtually, my spouse came home early and caught me in a particularly randy mood. The Speaker was wearing a new suit that day, and I do love a woman with a good tailor. So, my wife and I engaged in our own late-night session, if you get my drift. We knocked the backbench, if you understand my meaning. She rewrote my constitution, if you appreciate my metaphor. I stood on her order, if you follow my allegory. I raised her member on the question of privilege to bring my procedural issue to the attention of her Chair, and she called upon my Throne to interpret how her rule should apply, and my Board of Internal Economy took steps to resolve her issue—if you see where I'm—"

"Cumming from?" Edwin smirked. The group shifted uncomfortably. "You had sex with your wife in front of the CoC?"

Pearl tugged on her beads. "You do get my drift."

"Yes, we do." Jim removed his glasses from his head and wiped sweat off his brow. He placed his frames on his nose, then blinked at the pearled minister, who was staring around the room serenely. Jim attached his smile, though it wavered a bit. "Thank you for so succinctly describing the circumstances of your expulsion."

"I'd like to hear more about her wife's expulsion, if you get *my*—"

"Enough, Edwin." Jim's smile slid off his face. "If you speak out of turn one more time, you'll fail this class." He handed over Pearl's signed approval form, then wiped his brow.

"Good thing it's Bill's turn, then," Edwin said. "I won't make a sound. Can't wait to listen. And grow."

MINISTER OF AGRICULTURE
(The Honourable Mr. Bill)
2:40pm EST

Bill's eyes twinkled affably. His belly undulated as he shifted on his folding chair, but his good humour stayed intact. Bill lifted his brows with childlike charm, then sent his warm voice out to the heights of the Block. "You know, I feel awful bad about what I did. I'm not someone who does well with newfangled technology, even though I'm a modern master when it comes to farming. Have you seen the eco equipment the Prime's rolling out? It'll save my constituents, not to mention my own acreage, a lot of hassle in the decades to come. Cheaper, safer, more efficient—I'm a fan of Agri tech. But computer tech?" He sighed, stroking his belly sadly. "That's another story."

"What happened, Bill?"

"Well, I was showing my cousin how the virtual sessions work. Have you met my cousin? Cousin Jaimie? She loves the city, but she never leaves the farm—especially during the cull. So, I was showing her our session; let her watch the proceedings while we were out in the barn. I thought I turned off my audio. I thought I turned off my video. But—it turned out—I hadn't. So, I'm showing Jaimie the feed while parliament's in session when one of our ranch hands runs in, wanting to show us the animal-friendly depopulation system. You know, the Prime's 'ventilation shutdown' method."

Jim whipped his glasses off his face. "Oh, god."

"Well, God don't come into this much. Humans do—we're the ones that eat the beasties. Anyway, my ranch hand grabs Jaimie to take her to the shutdown stable—"

"No."

"—then Jaimie grabs me, because she's real, *real* eager—"

"Holy mother."

"—and I grab my laptop so I can keep participating in the session—"

"Son of a weasel."

"—and next thing you know, the entire Chamber of Commons is watching hundreds of cows suffocate to death—humanely—in real time." Bill grabbed his belt buckle. "I tell you, depopulation's a real heartstopper. The cattle screams are enough to turn you off steak the rest of your life. Why do you think Jaimie and me are veggie-tarians?"

This time, the cricket stayed silent behind the Throne.

Jim desperately tried to figure out how to salvage this session—fortunately, the ministers had all witnessed Bill's live-stream and were now staring into the heavens of the Block, trying not to remember the look on the sweet little cows' faces as they met their sweet little maker—hopefully in a sweet little bovine heaven.

Jim wiped his glasses on his shirt. "Well." He placed the frames on his forehead. "So, um. Bill." He slid the glasses down on his nose. "What did you learn from this? Or, as my son would say, 'What's the plan, Bill?'"

"The plan?" Bill grinned. "Next time Jaimie wants to visit parliament, she'll get her butt in her truck and drive here."

Jim handed over the signed form. "Wonderful."

MINISTER OF FINANCE
(The Honourable Mx. LeTout)
2:50pm EST

"Alright. Mx. LeTout." Jim cleared his throat and the circle shifted to face the bug-eyed francophone. "We are ahead of schedule—very ahead of schedule—which allows us to honour your French preference by having someone translate for you. You can speak freely and authentically." Jim glanced at his tablet, frowned, then looked over at Ms. Chaise. "You're bi?"

"Yes, I am." Chaise smiled. "But I don't see why that's relevant."

Jim cleared his throat. "Bilingual."

"Oh!" The dots on Chaise's cheeks reappeared.

"I can translate," Edwin said. "I'm bi, too. Lingual, not—"

"No, no," Chaise said. "I'm happy to speak for Mx. LeTout—*si ça vous va?*"

"*Oui, merci.*" Mx. LeTout nodded, then gesticulated as they articulated. "*La raison pour laquelle j'ai été expulsé de la Chambre des communes, c'est parce—*"

"Hold on." Chaise dragged her chair across the circle until she sat directly in front of LeTout. "Slow down, and I'll translate one sentence at a time. *Ralentissez pour qu'ils vous comprennent.*"

"*Oui, merci,*" LeTout said. "*Donc, la raison pour laquelle le Trône—*"

"Um, the reason the Throne…"

"*—m'a expulsé de la Chambre des communes—*"

"Uh, expelled me—oh, um, them. Expelled them from the Chamber of Commons…"

"—*c'est parce que*—"

"Is because…" Chaise waved her hands. "You can go faster than that, if you want. *Dis-en plus, c'est bon.*"

LeTout rolled their buggy eyes at the golden ceiling. "*Vous voyez, je suis un fervent partisan de l'au-delà. Le surnaturel, les fantômes, l'éternel.*"

"They—Mx. LeTout—believes in supernatural things," Chaise said. "Ghosts, and stuff like that. Oh, they said 'the eternal,' but I don't really know what that—"

"*Depuis que je suis enfant, ma mère et ses sœurs m'ont appris à parler avec les morts.*"

"Whoops! When LeTout was a kid, their *maman* and her sisters showed them how to talk to dead people." Chaise paused. "What?"

"*Nous avions l'habitude d'avoir des séances hebdomadaires. Je suis devenu très bon dans ce domaine et j'ai acquis la réputation dans mon village d'être capable d'aider les gens. Ils me parleraient, je parlerais à leurs proches décédés, et nous trouverions un moyen de faire la paix.*"

"Whoa, that was a lot," Chaise said. "So, LeTout said they used to help people. In their village. They'd talk to their dead family members, or something, and then the dead person would find peace." Chaise glanced over her shoulder at Jim. "Is this a joke? I think I missed the session about being deceased in parliament."

"We all saw this one," Pearl said. "Keep translating."

Chaise turned back to LeTout, who hadn't stopped speaking. "Oh, shoot. Sorry. Uh, they're saying that one time, they were talking with a ghost and there was an interference. A dark interference." She rubbed behind her ear. "I'm not sure if I want to do this anymore."

"Oh, calm down." Reta scowled. "LeTout's incident was nothing. Get it done."

LeTout—who had paused during this interchange—nodded, then resumed their French patter. "*Je me suis connecté avec le côté obscur de l'éternel. Celui où les fantômes ne cherchent pas le repos, mais la rétribution.*" They stopped, staring at the navy-clad woman through their bugged-out eyes.

Chaise took a breath. "Okay, I'll translate exactly what they say, hereon out. Remember, this is what LeTout is saying, not me." Chaise's fingers tapped her lap. "'I connected with the darker side of the eternal. The one where the ghosts do not seek rest, but retribution.'"

"*J'ai réalisé le potentiel de créer des relations avec ces es prits violents.*"

"'I realized the potential in creating relationships with these violent spirits.'"

"*Non seulement je pouvais apporter la paix aux personnes dans le besoin, mais je pouvais aussi apporter le pouvoir.*"

"'Not only could I bring peace to people in need, but I could also bring power.'"

"*J'ai développé mon village et nous avons commencé à invoquer une spiritualité plus profonde, une magie plus sombre.*"

"'I grew my influence in my village and we began invoking a deeper spirituality, a darker magic and'—uhhh, fudge."

Jim leaned forward. "Keep going, Ms. Chaise."

Chaise turned back to LeTout, who picked up their speech the second her eyes locked on theirs. "Okay, LeTout is saying that as their connections with the dark eternal grew, so did their influence over their village. Their city. Their province. Their—"

The globe lights on the walls flickered in their wall brackets.

Chaise clenched her armrests. "Did those just dim?"

"Focus on LeTout, Ms. Chaise!"

"*C'est bon. Donc mon pouvoir grandissait avec mon influence. Après quelques années—*"

"Their power was growing along with their influence. After a few years, LeTout noticed that they had an unprecedented amount of control over election outcomes—"

"*—utilisant le pouvoir que j'invoquais par ma connexion avec l'éternel obscur—*"

"Using the power they invoked through their connection with the dark eternal, LeTout rose rapidly in the ranks of the municipal, then provincial, then the federal government—"

"*—mais il y avait un prix—*"

"But there was a price—ahhh, shite, shite, shite—"

"Chaise!"

"*—si vous voulez le pouvoir dans ce monde, si vous voulez partager ce pouvoir avec les autres—*"

"'If you want power, and if you want to share that power with others, sacrifices must be made—'"

"*—je savais ce qu'était le sacrifice. Je savais—*"

"LeTout knew what the sacrifice was. They knew what they had to do. All that was required of them was the sacrifice itself, and—

okay, I can't do this. I'm pretty sure LeTout is about to tell us they murdered someone."

"Calm down, woman," Pearl snarled. "Keep going."

"Yeah, keep going," Bill said. "We're getting to the fireworks."

"*Souhaitez-vous entendre la fin? Voulez-vous savoir pourquoi je suis ici?*"

Chaise sighed. "Yes."

LeTout nodded. "*Alors. Une nuit, lors d'une séance—*"

"One night, during a midnight sitting, the dark eternal called down to them and requested his sacrifice. LeTout had no choice. They had to do the dark eternal's bidding, no matter when he needed it. So LeTout went to—Jiiiiiiiiim!"

"*—et j'ai laissé sa lumière briller de l'intérieur. J'invoquai le saint nom de* Satan, *et—*"

"You know what?" Jim walked across the circle and thrust the signed form into LeTout's hands. "You seem remorseful to me. I say we drop this, never speak of it again, and move on. As my son says, 'what happens during invocations of Satan, stays during invocations of Satan.'"

Jim grabbed Chaise's arm, pulled her and her chair back to their places in the circle, then turned his attention to Edwin—after raising and dropping his glasses several times.

MINISTER OF VETERAN AFFAIRS
(The Honourable Mr. Edwin)
3:26pm EST

"I hate to follow an eleven o'clock number like that one," Edwin said, "but losers can't be choosers."

"Everyone here wants to support you." Jim stretched his lips, knowing his smile wasn't as helpful as it had been at the beginning of the day. "Or, as my son says—never mind. Just tell us why you're here."

Edwin shrugged. "Two nights ago—during our annual MP photo shoot—I yelled, 'cheese!' before the photographer took the picture."

That damned cricket: Jim could hear it mocking him from behind the Throne. He cleared his throat. "You said, 'cheese'?"

"Stop." Pearl shut her eyes as she clutched her necklace. "I can't go through this again."

Jim blinked. "Excuse me?"

"Once was bad enough." Pearl shook her greying head. "I can't relive the nightmare."

"Sorry?" Jim blinked again. "Nightmare?"

Chaise sobbed.

Jim turned to the brunette, who was bent over in her chair, weeping. Chaise's hands griped her armrests. "You weren't there. You don't know!"

"What don't I know?" Jim looked around the circle: the other MPs were frozen in paroxysms of grief. He cleaned his glasses on his shirt. "What's going on?"

"I said 'cheese.'" Edwin struck a peppy pose on the edge of his seat. "Cheeeeeeese!"

"Stop it, Edwin! Look what you're doing to him!" Reta's son started crying, screaming louder than Chaise's sobs. "Haven't you had your fun? Haven't you done enough?"

Jim placed his glasses on his head, undoing the lens cleaning as they passed across his face. "Am I missing something?"

"Here, buddy—let me lay it out for you." Bill leaned over his knees, wincing as his chest pinched his stomach. "The kid— Edwin—thought he'd have a laugh. So, like a first-class wiseass, he called out—" He looked at Throne, fighting back tears. "When I think of everything the dairy farmers have done for this country."

"Excuse me?" Jim stared around the circle. "The dairy farmers?"

"They didn't need to be insulted that way." Bill wiped his eyes with his beefy hand. "In the Block, too. A place of majesty and magnificence. Like you said."

"Well, hold on. When we're talking about inappropriate behaviour, I don't know if saying 'cheese' before taking a photo exactly lines up with every other instance of misconduct—"

"Not just the dairy farmers." Spencer's shoulders shook. "How do you think lactose intolerant people felt when he said that? Or those who have a lactase deficiency? Or are hypolactasiac, or alactasiac, or lactose challenged? The photo shoot was broadcast across the country." He buried his face in his hands. "Children were watching."

Jim slipped his glasses onto his nose. "Let me get this clear. You think that Edwin saying chee—"

"*Non!*" LeTout leapt to their feet, flinging aside their chair. "*Avoir se moquer d'une occasion aussi propice, dire 'fromage', c'est comme cracher sur le visage de nos ancêtres. Je ne l'aurai pas. Non. Non!*" They stormed out of the West Block, yelling '*merde.*'

Jim blushed. He lifted his glasses. He dropped his glasses.

"Edwin? Do you apologize for your... misconduct?"

"What can I say?" Edwin smirked. "I've always been an *au lait* asshole."

REVIEW, TAKEAWAYS, & CLOSING STATEMENTS
3:49pm EST
Saturday, October 26, 2024
Chamber of Commons—West Block
The Chateau—2 Pouvoir Avenue
Oakland, UN—Canuckia

Jim smiled—a pinched, shaky smile—as he handed over Edwin's signed form. "Well. It seems you all have... learned your lesson. Does anyone have any questions? Or final comments?"

The cricket danced a jig of glee behind, under, on, and over the Throne.

"Then that's that," Jim said. "You can return to your ministerial duties. You've been educated, you've shown appropriate—if varying—degrees of understanding and regret, and I don't believe you will break the Commons code of conduct again."

He peered at the officials, who were beaming at him like they had halos attached to their craniums.

Jim grabbed his briefcase, then stood. As he strode out of the majestic and magnificent West Block, he looked up at the ceiling that had covered parliamentary proceedings for well over a century. Though the officials sitting alongside the ancient oak table struggled to grasp its significance, Jim knew that the Throne, the Block, and the Chamber of Commons deserved respect.

He looked over his shoulder as he passed under the golden archways—at the ministers grinning at him on their folding chairs—

and knew that whatever support was required in the future, he would be there with a smile and a nod to provide whatever education became necessary.

So long as technology advanced slower than—as his son would say—'the simps' who prolonged progress.

USE THE GIFT

13

Aya sits on Oscar's chair in his—well, no, not his chair. His *guest* chair. His employee chair. The chair employees sit on at the International Foundation for Robotics—or IFR—when they visit Oscar's Human Resources office. The chair where the staff in her department—the lawyers, and clerks, and barristers—settle when they have a request, or need assistance, or require support, or want to file a complaint.

Aya takes a breath.

She sits on Oscar's guest chair in his office at IFR, peering through her blunt, cheekbone-length bangs. She glances at RoboCloc—the shiny, white, Artificially Intelligent timepiece placed on the staff representative's desk—then Aya compares the hour to the numbers blinking on her ArmCom. Oscar is thirty minutes late.

Again.

Aya blows her bangs out of her eyes as she stares at her wrist device, watching the seconds on her screen pass by, blinking and ticking, blinking and ticking; two minutes, six minutes, nine minutes, eleven minutes, eleven-and-a-half minutes—

Oscar's glass door slides open as he strides into the room. "Mindi's a beast." He claps Aya's shoulder as he walks around her chair—no, *his* chair. Oscar walks around his guest chair to get to his desk, flashing his feral teeth in a vicious grin. "Sometimes I wonder why she sends us agendas for the divisional meetings. All she does is talk about her cottage in the woods."

"Isn't Mindi in the middle of renos?" Aya flutters her hands weakly. "Her hot stones arrive this week."

"Hot stones, sauna benches, steam vents, exercise swings. None of it is work related." Oscar leans back in his chair—*his* chair, not his guest chair—and winks. "Unless the rumours are true, and she hired a DaLE Bot to 'subcontract.'"

Aya flutters again. "She wouldn't be the first boss to take advantage of IFR's relaxation perks."

"Careful," Oscar says. "You shouldn't say the things we're all thinking." He pats the back of his sleek, oiled hair, then rifles through his desk drawers. "You're meeting with Mindi later?"

"At three." Aya glances at RoboCloc. "Soon."

"Is that why you wanted to meet with me?" Oscar disappears behind the desk. "Your complaint has to do with Mindi?"

"Oh. No." Aya blows her bangs. RoboCloc's blue, dome-shaped eyes whir softly. "That's a separate matter. I wanted to speak with you because—"

"Aha!" Oscar reappears, a tablet clutched in his hand. "Found it." He places the portable computer on his desk, squinting at the type on its screen. "We have to transition to EyeSpy. Remind me to talk to CepI the receptionist about talking to Mindi about cutting off our tangible tech supplier."

"I'm a lawyer, not a note taker," Aya says. "RoboCloc can ask CepI—"

Oscar shakes his slick head. "I'll never figure out why IFR—the most successful company in the country—continues to rely on ancient equipment."

"My aunties are the same." Aya shrugs. "Stuck in their materialistic ways."

"Mine too," Oscar says. "I still get a greeting card from my parents every holiday, even though the Bots at their retirement complex write songs for the residents. Have you ever heard a Bot sing?"

"Not personally." Aya tries a tentative smile. "Sue me."

"Careful. That's not an empty threat, here." Oscar bends over the tablet, his nose an inch from the surface. "Harassment? Again?" He looks up. "This is the third time you've filed this complaint."

Aya flushes. She straightens the cuffs of her charcoal uniform. "You said you would take care of it. The first two times."

Oscar holds her gaze a second longer, then flashes his teeth. "Yeah, about that—I can explain. See, I spoke with Po and TiNS, and their version of the incident is different than yours." He shakes his head sadly, like he's upset Aya called out her bullies—no, her coworkers. She filed a complaint against her coworkers.

Aya swallows. "Shouldn't it be? I mean, I accused them of professional misconduct. Did you expect the Bots to admit to it?"

"Of course not," Oscar says. "But I wasn't expecting their statements to be *so* different. A few discrepancies here and there, maybe. But their version of what happened is totally unique. It makes it hard to do my job, you know?"

"What did they say?"

"Aya," Oscar says. "You know I can't speak about colleagues without their permission. Especially the Bots. That would be unprofessional. And immoral." He wipes a drop of oil off his neck. "You're a lawyer. You know about Bot rights—they're not like us. They can't help gossiping a bit."

"Right." Aya knows about Bot rights; she minored in Ethical Bot/Human Interactions at law school. "So—what should I do?"

"Have you talked to them?"

"To Po and TiNS?"

"No, to President RoboReiwa." Oscar chuckles. "Yes, I mean Po and TiNS. Aya? Where is your head?"

"So—" Aya looks at her hands. "No. I didn't bring it up. I didn't feel comfortable. Given the circumstances."

"Aya!" Oscar's laugh fills the tiny office. "That's the problem! Before I can do anything, you have to talk to them. Po and TiNS are good Bots, even if they are a little indiscreet. They want this issue resolved just as much as you do."

"Right." Aya blows on her bangs—they keep falling in front of her eyes. "Sure. So—"

Oscar leans back in his chair. "You have to work on that confidence, Aya. Professionals respond much better to confidence. Just buy the Bots a battery and put the incident behind you: behind us. No need to turn this into a big thing, you know?"

"Yes." Aya looks up. "It's just that I—"

RoboCloc's blue eyes buzz.

Aya's ArmCom beeps. She shakily stands. "Sorry, Oscar. I have my Mindi meeting."

Oscar's chuckle follows her out the sliding door and into the glass-lined hallway. "Don't let her go on too long about her bubbly tub from Eurasia." He winks. "Confidence, Aya. Confidence."

Aya sits behind her boss' desk calmly, mumbling under her breath, "—and I log more hours than anyone on my team, including the filing Bots—" Her ArmCom blinks and ticks, blinks and ticks, "—and I've brought more clients to the firm than anyone else in their first year, ever, and three of those clients tipped our quarterly profits into unprecedented margins—" Aya brushes her bangs off her face.

Cubic AmbiAir and plastic BoBoChair purr as they automatically adjust their soothing settings. Aya's heart slows as the fans begin to whir in their vents and her chair warms to a comforting ninety-eight degrees. No, not her chair. Mindi's chair. The chair employees sit in when they meet with Mindi.

Aya's ArmCom beeps: it's a News Alert. She glances at her screen. The update could be important. No. The train tracks on

Route 89 have twisted. The Sky Trains are shut down. Vines again. Pernicious creepers often halt transportation.

Aya clears the Alert from her ArmCom, then clears her throat. "And with my decade of experience at Avatar Technologies prior to starting my contract here, I think—"

The glass door slides open and Mindi lopes into the room, unbuttoning her charcoal-coloured blazer. "That's the last time I order a triple with lunch. Whisky sours make me piss."

Aya leaps to her feet. She adjusts her shirt cuffs, then tries a tentative laugh. She is light. She is funny. She's a team player. "I get it. Lots of, um... piss."

"So much piss." Mindi strokes ULa—her shiny, white, Bot assistant—on her oblong head. ULa hums as Mindi twirls on her charcoal heels to lean against the edge of her floating table. "What can I do for you, Aya?"

"See, so—" Aya casually leans against the table, too. "See, so I—"

"Careful!"

Aya jumps back, raising her hands over her head.

Mindi bends over the table, rearranging the stack of digifiles Aya's hand has brushed.

Casually brushed. It was an accident—she doesn't want to hurt anybody. No, anything. Files aren't people or robots. Well, not *real* robots. Files aren't anything.

Aya swallows. "I'm sorry. I didn't think those were important."

"Why would you?" Mindi taps the uppermost file with her razor-sharp fingertip—she must've had a fresh fill before her whisky sours. "This is my research for the reno. I'm obsessed with luxury. Fabrics, tile, patterns, texture. So many choices." She glances at her digistack lovingly. "I like choice."

"Me three!"

Mindi stares at Aya quizzically.

"I mean—me, too," Aya says. "I like choice, too. Lots of... choice."

"Who doesn't?" Mindi passes the stack of files over to ULa, who zips over to a floating processor to scan the digis into her database. "She's so efficient." Mindi stares at the Bot fondly. "Are you and Sam doing any apartment upgrades this year?"

"We'd like to, but it's not in the budget," Aya says, fluttering her hands. "At least, not yet. We're saving for a vacation to Orcinus. See, so—my budget is what I wanted to talk to you about. See—"

"Orcinus?" Mindi tilts her head; the charcoal streaks in her bot-made wig shine. "Why would you take a trip to that old rock? Especially when the cottage properties are so hot right now. I could get you a deal on a cute cabin like mine."

"That's so generous of you," Aya says. Generous, generous, soooooo generous. "But a cottage might be out of our price range. Isn't your cabin large? 1000 square feet?"

"Oh, pish." Mindi waves her razors. "I know people. I'll get you a good deal."

"See, so—" Aya swallows. "I've always wanted to visit Orcinus. My great-grandmother lived there. But maybe Sam and I could do both—take a trip *and* look at cottage properties. See, I wanted to talk to you about my salary?"

Mindi grins. "Are you sure? I'm only asking since you seem to be asking."

Aya licks her lips, then launches into her practiced speech; using statements, not questions. "I was supposed to get a raise this year. It's in my contract. But—"

"I can explain." Mindi walks around her floating table, then pushes a button that changes the tint of the office's light.

The polluted air shifts from its typical sludge to a brilliant aquamarine. The blue tone floods the glass-lined room, and Aya widens her eyes to adjust to the abrupt filter change.

"You are a valuable employee at this firm," Mindi says, unaffected by the moody light. "Very valuable. An important asset. Very important. I don't know what we'd do without you."

The fans spin faster. ULa murmurs a stream of gargle babble— *ooomaaa, ooomaaa*. Aya falls onto her chair, then bites the side of her mouth to keep from yelping; the seat is burning hot.

"But you know how this works." Mindi's charcoal heels *snap!* together. "The stock market is hell, trade has gone in the toilet with the geothermal cesspools mugging up the eastern seaboard, and fiscal uncertainty across the globe is something we all have to factor into our plans."

Aya blows on her bangs. "Times are tricky."

"Very tricky," Mindi says. "But you are very valuable. Let's chat next quarter. Right now, I need to pee. Triple whisky sours make me piss."

Aya walks up fourteen flights of stairs, dragging her body to her Living Complex's floor. Her feet lag in her charcoal sidewalk sneakers, and her purse pulls her arm towards the ground. Her ArmCom beeps. She squints at the screen as she reaches her floor. Sam is supposed to direct contact her, but the only flashing message on her device is from her aunties—they left a voicemail on her cellphone.

Aya leans her forehead on her condo door's glass exterior and curses the inconvenience of having to find her cell. It might be in her bedroom. Or her Bot staff might've moved it to the Complex's underground storage locker during the bi-annual purge—and if they did, she's going to cry. The last thing she needs is to have to trudge underground for her phone: to hear a voicemail from her aunties.

Aya places her palm on her door's scan-panel. It buzzes as it reads her prints, then the door slides open. She drags her sidewalk shoes into her condo. Why do her aunties still leave voicemails? She's told them not to, countless times.

Aya drags herself into her living room and throws her purse on the couch. Her work heels fall out of her bag, tumbling to her living room rug. SofWi—the shiny, white, keeper of her Bot staff—zooms across the condo to straighten up; tucking Aya's heels into a shoe rack and whisking her charcoal jacket off her shoulders to shove in the auto-clean closet.

Aya falls onto her couch. Why are her aunties the only people in the world who still rely on outdated tech? They still ship her physical objects, too, whenever it's a holiday. Two years ago, for Peace Day, they sent Aya a pillow—like she and Sam need more than one pillow. And last year, for their anniversary, her aunties airmailed over a book. A book! Nobody reads books. Her aunties' gifts are antiquated relics.

Aya never uses them.

Aya rubs her temple as SofWi directs the Bot staff in their evening chores: prepping dinner, giving Aya's aching feet a massage, changing the window settings so the light in the apartment looks aquamarine instead of smoky sludge.

Aya sighs. Do her aunties want to spite her with the cellphone message? Make contacting them harder? Do they like the idea of Aya having to scramble every time they call? Or does it give the aunties a sense of familiarity—of comfort—in this bot-made 'verse where everything is digitized and audio is rapidly fading into the past—

A grunt in her bedroom startles Aya. She stares at the door. The bedroom light flickers on. Aya frowns. Who's in there?

"SofWi?" Aya lowers her voice as her Bot-keeper zooms to her side. "Is Sam home?"

SofWi's bulging blue eyes whir, affirmatively answering Aya's question. Aya strokes her Bot-keeper's plastic cheek and the Bot calms. Aya slides into her sneakers, creeps across her rug, then presses her ear against the bedroom door. The grunting gets louder; and she can hear a breathless giggle. Aya presses her ear harder into the door. The grunts turn into a growl and the giggle into a squeal.

Aya swallows. "Sam?" She slowly places her fluttering hand on the doorknob. "Sam are you home?"

The growling silences, like a tune Bot hitting its mute button. A dull *thud!* sounds in her bedroom, followed by a whispered swear word. Aya backs away from the door—as it's flung open. Sam lumbers into the living room, shirtless and in his baggiest boxers. His mass of chest hair is soaked with sweat.

Sam closes the bedroom door behind him, then grins. "Did I scare you?"

Aya takes another step back. She trips over the disc-like Bot vac—it buzzes as it dashes across the rug and into the recharge cupboard. Aya flutters her hands. "Sorry, CleanBi."

Her husband chortles.

"What were you—" Aya swallows. "What was going on in there?"

"Napping." Sam lumbers to her side and plants a wet kiss on her cheek. "Big day at work. I left early and conked out. You get it."

"Sure." Aya reaches for Sam's hand but he lumbers away, heading for the kitchen. "What kind of day?"

"Oh, wow." Sam rummages around in a kitchen cabinet. "That's a loaded question."

FiChef—their meal Bot equipped with choppers, slicers, and whiskers—zooms out of the Bot cupboard and around Sam's feet as her husband shifts from one cabinet to another. One shelf to another. One drawer to another: always turning around empty handed.

Sam calls over his hairy shoulder. "Same as always. The power grid sucks and the city can't handle the heat; boring maintenance stuff. Oh, you'll think this is funny." He pulls out a glass, then hands it to FiChef. "The AI Mowers 'managed' another family again," Sam says as FiChef fills the glass with water from his hydro tank.

240

"Those suburban idiots keep refusing to wear their uniforms." He nods at Aya's charcoal jumper. "Talk about stubborn. My crew's going in next week to clean up. The neighbourhood wants to sue. I should give my boss your direct contact code—"

"Bebe?" A tiny voice calls from the bedroom. "Samuel? Don't forget my ice."

Sam's chest turns a dull, dark red. "I can explain."

"Bebe?" The bedroom door is flung open. A tall, fit, sheet-wrapped Bot stands in the doorway.

Aya's sidewalk sneakers melt. "Sam?"

"Bebe?" The Bot cocks his shiny, white, plastic hip to the side and hitches his bedsheet—no, her bedsheet! Hers!—higher around his streamlined waist. "Who's this?"

Sam lumbers over to Aya and grabs her hand. "I know this doesn't look great, but I can explain."

Aya tries to pull her hand out of her husband's grip, but he won't let go. "Sam—"

"Oh!" The Bot's bulging blue eyes widen. "Oh, no. Oh, dear. Oh, oops."

"I can explain. You see, Aya, um—this is DaLE." Sam nods manically at the Bot. "DaLE from work."

DaLE. DaLE from work. DaLE, the sex Bot businesses have secretly started stocking to include in their employees benefit plans. So they can relax. As a perk.

Sam squeezes Aya's hand. "DaLE and I worked the same shift, but DaLE lives uptown, and the Sky Train was down again—"

"The tracks twisted on Route 89." The Bot nods vehemently.

DaLE nods vehemently. DaLE the sex Bot hitches her sheet higher. Vehemently. "Vines again."

"Right, the vines. Yes!" Sam crushes Aya's fingers. "You got the News Alert about the vines, didn't you? Didn't you, Aya?"

Aya swallows. "I did."

"Good! That's good." Sam places his glass of water on the counter and pulls Aya under his hairy arm. "See, DaLE and me both had the same shift, and we were both really tired—"

"An AI Mower managed a neighborhood again." DaLE winds Aya's bedsheet around his trim machinery like a toga. The sheet juts forward—because he's a sex Bot, and his sex appliance was erect. Because he was doing sex things. With her husband. The sex Bot laughs, oblivious to his tented toga. "Suburbanites don't wear their uniforms."

"Good one, DaLE." Sam nods at the relaxation companion. "Don't you think DaLE's funny, Aya? He's like a real male. We call him DaLE the male at work. Isn't that funny? Hilarious?"

Aya yanks her hand out of Sam's grip and falls backwards, over her couch. She lays on her side—bangs in her eyes—and blinks at her aquamarine ceiling. "You were both really tired?"

"Yes. So tired." Sam laughs—low and booming.

DaLE laughs—loud and high. "*So* so tired."

"So, we both took a nap." Sam peers over the back of the couch and at Aya's prostrate body. "Isn't that funny?"

Aya rolls onto her stomach, then fumbles around the couch until she finds her purse. She pulls the bag onto her lap. "Are you done?"

Sam's grin wavers. "Done?"

"Your nap." Aya's knuckles turn tan as her hands crush the life out of her purse's handle. "Are you done your nap?"

Sam's baggy shorts slip down on one side, exposing his hairy hipbone. He doesn't hitch them up. "Obviously we're done. We're definitely, definitely done."

Aya paces the café, glaring at her ArmCom's screen. The streetlight Bots twinkle on the path outside the matcha shop. People slide in and out of their light as they manoeuver along the city's streets. Aya's sidewalk sneakers squeak as she paces the length of the café. Her ArmCom blinks as it ticks the time.

Twinkle, squeak, blink, tick. Twinkle, squeak, blink, tick. Squeak, blink, ti—

A burst of air flows into the café. A person wrapped in a filmy scarf sweeps in on the wind's blustery heels. The scarf unwinds, revealing a long, snake-like braid that coils around a female's head. The braid spills over the female's shoulder and onto the café floor. The female winds her braid around her hand several times, then throws her arms around Aya. She hugs her close, squeezing the breath out of Aya's lungs.

The female hisses in her ear. "What a little scamp."

"I'm glad you're the one who said it." Aya holds onto her friend, burying her face in the female's braid. "What am I supposed to do?"

"Well. First—" The female grabs Aya's elbow and leads her to a felt-covered booth. "You need to jolt up. Then we can talk this whole thing out."

Aya nods. She feels better about her day now that she can safely vent her frustrations to her friend. No, not vent. Scream. Scream her frustrations. Very, very loudly.

Aya climbs into the booth, then strokes the velvety fabric. "I'm glad you were free, Isobel."

"For you? Always." The female—Isobel—snaps her fingers around her fist of braid and the shiny, white, wheeled Bot server zooms over to the booth.

Two pronged rods extend from its ordering panel and connect with the humans' ArmComs. The Bot server buzzes as it registers the females' desires. It zooms towards the back of the café. Soon, steam rises from the bean-shaped Bot barista as nutmilk heats and green tea shots fill the café's signature organo cups.

Isobel taps her wrist. Her ArmCom beeps. "Alright, Aya. Tell me everything. Tell your best friend about Sam the Sex Scamp."

"And Oscar."

"Yuppers. Oscar the Egomaniac."

"See, so—right. And Mindi. I'm upset about Mindi, too."

"Mindi the—"

"And my aunties. My aunties are being—" Aya sighs. "My aunties are being themselves."

Isobel removes a tiny box in the shape of a seashell from her charcoal jacket pocket and flips open the lid. "Your aunties are at it again?"

"See—" Aya watches her friend lift the shell to her nose and inhale.

Isobel's eyes roll back into her head.

Aya bites her mouth; it's best to ignore her friend's powder addiction. "My aunties are up to their usual stuff. Literally. Actual stuff. They left me a voicemail."

"Your vent list is a big one. I get it." Isobel leans over the booth's table, staring at Aya: her pupils shrink to tiny pinpricks. "Start with the worst. Start with Sam. We have plenty of time to get through everyone tonight."

"See, so—" Aya stares at her hands. "So, I went home."

"Uh huh."

"Because I'd had a bad day."

"Uh huh."

"Because Mindi didn't give me the raise."

"Uh huh."

"And because Oscar said I have to talk to Po and TiNS."

"Back to Sam, beauty. Back to Sam."

"Well, so—" Aya swallows. "So, I went home."

"Uh huh."

"And I heard weird sounds coming from the bedroom."

"Noooooooooo."

"Yeah, and Sam came out and said he was napping."

"But, really, he was being serviced by a DaLE." Isobel smirks. "Who knew Sammy had it in him?"

"And then Sam lied to me, right to my face, like—"

"Wait." Isobel sniffs her shell. She slowly strokes her braid. "What about Orcinus? Your trip?"

Aya shrugs.

Isobel leans closer. Her pupils spin diagonally until they look like vertical slits within her irises. "I already booked my copter so I can meet you out there to do my next round of vids. My agent set it up. You remember CraiND, right?" She holds her flattened palm over her head. "Big Bot? Silver? Looks like she'll kill you if you disagree with her?" Isobel giggles. "She's the best agent ever."

"I'm not sure if I should visit Orcinus anymore." Aya covers her face—she doesn't want Isobel to see water welling in her eyes. "If Sam and I break up, I'll have a lot to take care of over here."

"You want to break up?" Isobel unwinds her braid. "What about your life? Your plans? Our vacation?"

"Orcinus will always be there. We can visit any time."

"Nah. Didn't you see today's News Alert? The country lost another mile of coast. There are only a few beachfront resorts left. We need to go soon, beauty."

"Oh." Aya pushes her bangs off her face. "I thought we were taking a historical trip. To see museums, and—"

"We can figure that out later," Isobel says. "Anyway, back to your story. Tell me about Sam."

"I already told you everything."

"Then tell me about the others." Isobel hisses. "Spill it all."

The sound of steam rising from the matcha machines fills Aya's mind. Before she can stop them, her feelings tumble out her mouth. "You don't understand what it's like—being me."

"What?" Isobel smirks. "A powerful lawyer in the best city on the planet?"

"No," Aya says. "A passive child who everybody steps on. In

246

their charcoal heels."

Isobel squints her dilated eyes. "What are you talking about?"

"It never seems to end," Aya says. "Everyone in my life tells me what to do. How to feel. Who to be. It's like everyone thinks I'm a baby—like I'm incompetent, or I don't have brains. They expect me to do what they want, but when I need help, or have a problem…" Aya sighs. "If I say what *I* want, it's this huge inconvenience: my role is to be nice, and accommodating, and flexible, not… real." She stares at her hands, then clenches them in her lap. "I don't understand why people think they're better than me."

Isobel snorts. "Beauty."

Aya looks up. "What?"

"Nobody thinks they're better than you," Isobel says. "They think you're… you know, cool. They think you like them, and you want to help them out. Don't take it personally if they boss you around. People never know when they're being hypocritical." She sniffs her shell. "Everyone thinks the world revolves them."

Aya swallows. "I don't."

"Well, you're different," Isobel says. "You're a lamb. A law-yer lamb. You need to stand up for yourself and go after what you want."

"That's not—" Aya stares at her hands. "That's not my only problem. I told you Sam lied to me tonight: he didn't even try very hard. I think other people are lying to me, too."

"People?" Isobel giggles. "Not Bots?"

"You know who I mean," Aya says. "Mindi. And Oscar. And who knows who else. I'm pretty sure—" She stops.

Isobel's ArmCom isn't blinking. The comm light is a solid, unwavering orange.

Aya nods at her friend's device. "Are you recording this?"

Isobel lets go of her braid—it spirals to the café floor. "Recording what?"

"This." Aya looks around the café. "Us. Talking."

"No."

"Why is your ArmCom on?"

"That?" Isobel looks at her wrist. "Oh. I can explain. See, on the way here my iLeg ran over a delivery Bot, and it fell. I hit my arm on the ground when we tipped over." She waggles her hand. "My ArmCom has been glitching ever since. You get it."

Aya swallows. "Weren't you supposed to do a live-share this evening?"

"Nah." Isobel raises the shell to her nostril. She sniffs. "That's tomorrow." She giggles, then stares at Aya.

"Are you sure?" Aya squints at her friend's wrist. "I got a News Alert on my way over—it said you were going to do a live-share. Tonight."

Isobel grins. "Nah."

Aya climbs out of the booth—and knocks over the server Bot. The Bot's tray of hot drinks goes flying. Aya doesn't notice. "Are your 60mil followers watching this?"

"That would be insane." Isobel laughs—high and thin. "Only 59mil are watching. Most of them have lives, beauty."

Aya digs through the plastic storage cubes in her Living Complex's underground storage locker. They're covered with a thick layer of dirt, even though the airtight seals on the underground doors are supposed to prevent dust from gathering.

On her ArmCom a second message from her aunties beeps its warning beep. Aya bites the side of her mouth as she rifles through a cube marked 2070, then sneezes as dust flits into her nose. Grumbling, she pushes aside years of gifts—garbage—from her aunties: the book, the pillow, several photo albums, a tray of watercolour paints—

"Found you." Aya pulls out her cellphone triumphantly. As she holds the phone to her ArmCom, it sparks to life. The back of her phone reads her handprint, then it *hmmms!* as it siphons through her thoughts.

Before Aya can make her playback request, Auntie's voice spills from her phone, echoing in the dusty locker. "Aya. This is me and your Auntie. Say 'hi,' Auntie."

"Hi, sweetpea!"

"Aya. We are calling to wish you Happy Birthday."

"Happy Birthday, petunia!"

"We know we missed the actual day of your birth—"

"We were on vacation!"

"Quiet, or Aya will get annoyed and keep pretending we do not exist. Aya—Happy Birthday."

"Last week!"

"Last week. We mailed you a birthday gift, so make sure you get it from your security Bot."

"We mailed it through the airmail! The actual airmail!"

"It is special. We sent it before we left so it should have arrived."

"Through the sky! By an airmail drone and everything!"

"Auntie is very excited about this gift. We think you could use a gift like this. Make sure you call us after you open it. We love you, we miss you—call us back. We are looking forward to seeing you on Peace Day."

"I thought she was going to Orcinus on Peace Day?"

"She can't afford that."

"Samuel can afford to take them. He works for the city—he can cover the cost."

"Aya has too much pride to let her partner do that."

"It's not about being a partner, honey, it's about being able to contribute. That what all the Gen Cers say, isn't it?"

"I have no idea was the Cers say. I do not talk to them."

"Trust me. We chat when they iWheel in front of our apartment."

"Aya? Ignore your Auntie. We love you, we miss you—but your life is a mess. Open this gift. You will thank us. Call us back."

Aya's message stops. Blinking back tears—her aunties think she's a mess?—she lifts her hand to throw her cell into the corner of the storage locker so she never has to hear someone insult her again—then she pauses, arm in the air. Her aunties may be rude, but they tell the truth. Her life *is* a mess. Aya drops her arm, and the second message starts playing.

"Aya. We heard what you said about Sam. And your boss. And that administration male. We are disappointed."

"Oh, you poor girl! Our poor petunia!"

"I know you like Isobel. It was kind of you to retain the friendship for as long as you have—"

"But she's not worth it, sweetpea! The friendship isn't worth keeping, not after what she did to you!"

"All our friends heard the live-share. They all follow Isobel. Your life is an embarrassment—across the globe. You have to open the gift we sent you. Tonight. Before it is too late."

"You don't have to be so harsh with her. She can't force her husband to love her."

"She should not have to force him. We showed her how to handle a partner."

"But she's just a girl. Girls get hurt all the time. You can't honestly—"

"Aya? Open your gift. Tonight. It is very important to both of us. You have to open it."

"You'll love it, peaches. Trust us!"

"And after you open it, call us back."

"You really need to open the gift, flutterbug!"

"And you need to *use* the gift—not hide it in your storage room with the rest of the presents we give you."

"Don't be mean to the girl. It's not her fault her generation rejects kindness."

"Aya? Your life is a mess. *You* are a mess. But you are also better than the awful people in your life. No matter what the rest of the world thinks of you—"

"They're laughing at you, sweetpea."

"We think you are perfect. Messy, but perfect. And too good for those awful people."

"Our sweet, darling child!"

"Aya? Open the gift. *Use* the gift. We love you, we miss you— call us back. Oh. Happy Birthday."

"We already said Happy Birthday. This morning."

"We did? I don't remember calling."

"Yes, we left a message. We told her about the gift. You remember. You were complaining because the last time the three of us had a conversation was six months ago and—"

The second message stops. Aya stares at her darkened screen, then—with a furious burst of energy—throws the cell into the plastic cube. She kicks the cube, just to make sure it knows what a terrible cube it is. Aya strides across the storage locker, then kicks open the door that connects to the Complex's underground foyer. The shiny, white, plastic security Bot—UgO—murmurs soothing sounds as it detects her distress: *ooopaaa, ooop—*

"UgO!" Aya marches over to the giant Bot. "My aunties sent me a package in the—" She shudders. "In the mail. Did you receive anything?"

UgO *ooopaaas*, then reaches behind the foyer's floating desk. The Bot pulls out a cardboard box and gently hands it over to Aya. She snatches the box out of UgO's pronged rods, then marches into the storage locker. She throws the cardboard gift to the ground: the flaps burst open and a head-sized globe rolls out; onto the concrete floor. Aya stares at the silver sphere.

The sphere stares back.

"You're different." Aya nudges the cardboard box aside with her sidewalk-sneakered toe. She rolls the sphere until it stands on its attached base. The sphere's silver surface ripples under her palm, and a baleful face framed by painted hair stares up at her.

"What are you?" Aya sits on the floor, then pulls the sphere into her lap. She traces the face's design with her finger: crude calligraphy'd eyebrows overtop two empty eyes above a twirly black moustache.

Not eyebrows. Not a moustache. The sphere's facial design reminds her of something else—something older.

Something ancient.

Aya blows away her bangs as she tries to remember where she's seen those carvings before. As she reaches to thumb her ArmCom so she can search for the answer, it bursts into her mind unaided: the eyebrows are robins! The red-breasted birds that went extinct decades ago! And the moustache is a beaver—no, not a beaver. A beaver *tail*. A beaver tail on its side: inverted and upside down. The moustache is an inverted, upside down, scrawled image of a beaver tail.

Satisfied, Aya smiles at the strange little face. She runs her fingers across its robin brows, then sees a slip of paper resting on the ground beside the cardboard box. Aya slides the paper off the floor, still holding her strange, silver friend in her lap. She blows her bangs out of her eyes so she can read the note:

'Aya—

'You have received our message and opened our gift. Inside you have found your gift: a Volonté marionette. Paint in the left eye and make a wish. Use the watercolours we gave you last Peace Day. When your wish comes true, paint in the right eye. This will guarantee your personal and professional transformation. We love you, we miss you—call us back.

—your Aunties'

Her ArmCom blinks. Ticks. Blinks. Ticks. Blinks.

Aya crumples up the paper. She bends over to hide the gift in her plastic cube with the rest of her aunties' junk. Then she stops.

Nestled in her arms, the Volonté stares up at her. Aya swallows, caught in its empty gaze. She rifles through her cubes until she finds her watercolours. Placing Volonté on his base, Aya snaps open the watercolour palette, spits on the bristles of the attached brush, then whirls the moist brush head around in the purple pigment. The bristles turn a deep indigo.

Cradling Volonté with one arm, Aya deftly paints in the left eye. The empty orb flushes with colour, drying instantly in the cold underground air. Aya places the one-eyed marionette on his base, then stares at her silver, spherical friend as she considers her wish.

Her ArmCom beeps—a message, but this time it's a proper one though the regular channel, the normal way. Aya doesn't read it. It might be Sam, direct contacting to apologize. Or Isobel, reaching out to say she was wrong. Or Mindi, re-evaluating Aya's raise. Or Oscar, deciding to do his job for once. Or—

Or—maybe—they contacted her to tell the truth. *Their* truth, instead of their lies. Frowning, Aya thumbs her screen. Her wrist vibrates and buzzes. A sound pops in her ears.

A whispered voice—

    the shadow of a whispered voice—

        the echo of a shadow of a whispered voice—

            vibrates, buzzes, pops—

                then floats into Aya's mind.

your heart's wish is seen

painting the scroll of your soul

to grant your desire

Aya swallows.

The glass office door slides open and Oscar strides into the room. "Mindi's a bitch." He claps Aya's shoulder as he walks around her chair, flashing his feral teeth. "I hate her so much. All she does is brag about her S&M cottage."

"What?" Aya looks around Oscar's office, eyes wide behind her bangs. "Huh?"

"None of it is work related," Oscar says. "Unless the rumours are true and—"

"Where am I—" Aya clears her throat. "What are you—sorry,

do we have a meeting?"

"Stay focused, Aya." Oscar rifles through his desk drawers. "You've been bothering me all week about this appointment. 'Oscar, don't forget we're talking on Thursday. Oscar, we have that meeting tomorrow. Oscar, don't be late, I'll see you at two.'"

"Sorry?"

Oscar disappears behind the desk. "Aya."

"Uh—" Aya stares at the date on RoboCloc as its blue eyes whir softly: it was morning. *That* morning. She was repeating that morning.

Impossible.

RoboCloc blinks one of its bulging eyes. The other flashes—a deep purple.

Aya swallows. "Okay, so—"

"Aha!" Oscar reappears, a tablet clutched in his hand.

Aya watches RoboCloc—its eye turns back to blue. "Oscar?"

"Harassment?" Oscar leans over the tablet. "Again? This is the third time you've filed this report."

Aya straightens her shoulders. "Why haven't you dealt with it?"

Oscar sits back, smirking. "Yeah, about that—I can explain. I spoke with Po and TiNS, and if I'm being honest…" His smile melts away. "I'm not going to take your complaint any further."

"What?" Aya's eyes dart to RoboCloc, then back to Oscar. "Wait—what?"

"Yeah." Oscar's sneer locks on his sharp face. "This harassment claim is a waste of time. Po and TiNS are the most popular Bots at this firm. Their afterwork parties are legendary—and they know all the office gossip. You couldn't pay me to reset their rumour-spreading program." Oscar slides the tablet into his desk drawer. "I'm never going to speak with them about this."

"What?"

"Aya." Oscar chuckles. "You know how things work around here. Be professional. Get it?"

"Right." Aya swallows. "You want this to go away."

"You get it."

"Should I talk to Po and TiNS?"

"Not if you want to have working relationships with them," Oscar says. "They've been slamming you behind your back for weeks. You need to play nice. Tell them a secret—something sinfully naughty, like you caught Mindi in the copy room with a DaLE Bot—" he winks, "—and they'll love you."

"See, so—" Aya stares at RoboCloc. Its eye flashes indigo, then blazes blue. "Yes. Thank you for being honest."

Oscar leans back in his chair. "You have to work on that confidence, Aya. You wouldn't get picked on so much if you were more confident. It's your uptight, repressed personality that turns these little issues into big problems."

"Of course." Aya stands. "I have to go. Mindi."

Oscar's chuckle follows her into the hallway. "Don't let her gab on too long about her S&M cottage. Confidence, lady."

The glass door slides open and Mindi strides into the room. "That's the last time I order a laxative after lunch. Being in poly-amorous relationships wreaks havoc on my poop pipes."

Aya follows Mindi into her office—she'd been waiting outside, standing guard. "I want to talk to you about my raise."

"Hold up, girl. We just got here." Mindi pats ULa on the head. "Give the boss a second to catch her breath."

"Right." Aya takes her own breath. "I know how busy you are. I'm trying to be respectful of your—"

"Careful!"

Aya jumps back. "I didn't touch anything."

"You were about to." Mindi taps her stack of digifiles with her fingertip. "This is my research for my cottage reno. I'm obsessed with sex toys right now. Sex swings, sex straps, high-end sex whips and chains. So many choices." She glances at her stack lovingly. "I love choice. That's why I'm outfitting my cottage. It's the perfect location to have secret affairs—I picked up a DaLE last night on the company dime, and he's charged and ready to go." She flexes her nails. "All night long."

"Mindi, I'd like to discuss my raise."

"Who doesn't?"

"Mindi, I'm a top performer at this company. I've been here for two years, and I'm overdue for my—"

"I can explain," Mindi says. "If I'm being honest, you aren't an employee we give raises to."

The fans pick up speed. ULa's left eye flashes violet as she murmurs gargle babble—*ooomaaa, ooomaaa.*

Mindi runs her long, sharp fingernail along her desktop. "You're a pushover, Aya. A pushover who works their ass off, which is the perfect combination at this firm. We dump everything on you, and you churn out high-quality results without saying a word. And if you do complain, we feed you some bullshit about an upcoming promotion, or a staffing shuffle, or 'when you hit your five-year mark we'll reconsider your placement'—shit like that. And you eat it up. Every time. You eat shit, Aya. You eat shit."

Aya nods. "Yes."

"I know, it's great," Mindi says. "So we'll proceed as usual. I'll give you shit, and you'll love it like it was platinum plated. I don't want to see you in here again, unless I'm foisting off more work employees with high self-esteem won't touch. Right now, I need to shit. For real. You get it."

Aya flings open her bedroom door. Sam lumbers into the living room, shirtless and in his baggiest boxers.

He grins. "What are you doing here?"

Aya steps forward. "What's going on, Sam?"

"I was having sex with a robot."

Aya marches past her husband and into the bedroom.

DaLE gasps, then covers his plastic body with her sheet. The sex Bot's blue eyes widen, then flash purple. "You're home early."

Sam lumbers into the bedroom. "I can ex—"

Aya points at her condo's glass sliding door. "Get out."

"Wait."

"Get out!"

"This is DaLE."

"Get out, Sam."

"Listen, Aya. I bought DaLE this morning. If I'm being honest, I'm not attracted to you anymore."

"I never get tired," DaLE says. "Or get headaches. Or nag him to manage the chore Bots."

"Exactly," Sam says. "You've really let yourself go since you started your job. And look at DaLE. Look at him! Have you ever seen an appendage that big? And straight? Plus, it vibrates, and—"

Aya hits Sam's arm. "What the hell!"

"It's called self-respect, Aya." DaLE winds her bedsheet around his shining body. "How do you expect someone to love you if you don't love yourself?"

Aya storms out of the bedroom. She grabs her purse. "If you won't leave, I will."

Sam follows her into the living room. His baggy shorts slip down on one side, exposing his hairy hipbone. "Obviously I'm not going anywhere. You should definitely, definitely leave."

A burst of cold air rushes into the café with a scarf-wrapped person on its heels. The scarf unwinds and Isobel throws her arms around Aya. "Sam's a shithead."

"Turn off your ArmCom." Aya slaps Isobel's wrist. "I see the light. You're live-sharing."

"Huh?" Isobel winds her braid around her head, covering her ears. "I can't hear you."

Aya points at Isobel's device. "Turn it off, or I'm leaving. My embarrassing life is not some story to get more likes from your followers."

Isobel flips her braid over her shoulder. "You're paranoid."

The server Bot buzzes at Aya from behind the café counter. The barista Bot stops its matcha steaming. The two Bots' eyes flash purple—laser-bright, and penetrating—before the Bots turn back to their tasks.

Aya breathes in the steamy air. "I'm not paranoid, Isobel. Your ArmCom is on."

"That?" Isobel looks at her wrist. "I can explain. I am supposed to share a vid tonight. If I miss another scheduled fan event, my agent—CraiND—said she'll delete 59mil followers. So, I figured I'd multi-task. Use you, please my followers, and make CraiND not want to destroy my life. You get it."

"I get it," Aya says. "You think fame is more important than me."

Isobel takes her shell out of her pocket. "Talk louder—my ArmCom's mic has been weird lately. Solar flares, ammi right?"

Pinning her cellphone to her ear with her shoulder, Aya kicks open the door to the underground storage locker and storms over to her plastic cubes. "Yes, Auntie, I got your gift. It's great. No, really great. Thank Other Auntie for—yes, I used it. I did, I promise. That's why I called. I need your help."

As Aya speaks, Volonté stares—one-eyed—from where she'd left him the day before. No, the *evening* from the day before. Or the evening that day. In the past. The past that strangely didn't happen for anyone else, but seemed to have happened for her.

Aya ends the call with her aunties. She opens the watercolour palette, spits on the bristles of the attached paintbrush, then whirls the moist head around the purple pigment. The bristles turn a deep indigo.

Cradling Volonté in one arm, Aya paints the right eye. The empty orb flushes with colour, then dries instantly. Aya places

Volonté on his attached base, and pats her silver spherical friend on his head. She walks out of the room.

The glass door slides open. Oscar strides into his office. "Mindi's a monster." He walks around Aya's chair. "This is our second meeting in two days, Aya. I thought you'd agreed to drop the—"

"Oscar." Aya thrusts a tablet at her HR rep. "This is for you."

"What is it?" Oscar smirks. "An invitation to an afterwork party, I hope."

"Read it."

Oscar squints at the tablet. "Is this... your resignation?"

"Yes." Aya strides to the glass door. She pauses on the threshold—and smiles. "My aunties gave me an awesome gift for my birthday this year—well, two gifts. But the second one arrived this morning. It's a plane ticket. I'm moving to Orcinus. Effective immediately. If you make me come in for my final two weeks, I'll sue IFR for gross misconduct. And negligence. And they'll fire you for engaging in relationships that are a conflict of interest. I spoke with Po and TiNS this morning. You were right. They're very nice Bots who'll happily share office gossip. All of it. Under oath. Especially the gossip about you, Mindi, her DaLE bot—and the weekends the three of you spend at her S&M cottage."

RoboCloc's eyes flash purple as Aya strides into the hall, calling to Oscar, "You were also right about me needing more confidence. You get it."

YOU DIDN'T HAVE TO

acknowledgements

Thank you to Alex Lyall, who proofread this collection. Much thanks to Marisa Roggeveen for modelling for the book cover; and to Matthew Barnfather for being an objective and critical voice throughout my writing process. Thank you to the ARC readers who read and reviewed this collection—and special thanks to Fred Kraziese: his never-ceasing support helped this book make it to publication.

notes

Many different sources inspired the tales this book, including some of the characters and worlds in my other stories. However, I felt it was important to specifically mention the source of *Story Thirteen: Use The Gift*, because it was inspired by Japanese Daruma Dolls. I love writing about the futuristic possibilities of technology; especially about artificial intelligence in robotics. So far, I've focused my research primarily on the work being done in Japan—and while I was learning about the astounding innovations that are slowly trickling across the globe, I stumbled upon the legend of the daruma. The daruma is a rounded luck talisman, modelled after the Bodhidharma. In recent years, daruma dolls have been commercialized and sold to inspire users to reach their goals. Because I try to integrate Canadian culture into my work, I used the concept of daruma dolls to craft the Volénte; which means "willing." If you'd like to learn more about the cultural origins of Aya's gift, I highly recommend reading relevant articles.

biography

STEFANIE BARNFATHER is a Canadian author. Previously, she taught high school arts and inclusive education. Stefanie graduated with honours from Sheridan College's Music Theatre—Performance program, and has a BFA and BED in secondary fine arts from the University of Calgary. Her debut book of short stories, *You Know What I Think?* ranked first on the Calgary Herald's bestselling fiction list in 2023. When Stefanie isn't writing she enjoys painting, hiking, and spending time with her husband and pug.

If you want to read more stories by Stefanie Barnfather, feel free to show your support by following @barnfatherbooks on Instagram and TikTok. You can leave a review or rating on Amazon, Kobo, and Goodreads.

Visit www.barnfatherbooks.com to join Barnfather Books' mailing list and receive the monthly newsletter.

Other Books by Stefanie Barnfather
available on Amazon, Kobo, and Audible
in eBook, paperback, and audiobook

Novels
WE CALL HER ROSE (2023)

Short Story Collections
YOU KNOW WHAT I THINK? (2022)

coming in 2024
WHY'D YOU STOP?
A SOLITARY STORY

Manufactured by Amazon.ca
Acheson, AB

11453509R00159